TARGET FOR TERROR

LAURA SCOTT

READSCAPE PUBLISHING, LLC

Copyright © 2020 by Laura Scott

All rights reserved.

No part of this book may be reproduced in any form or by any electronic or mechanical means, including information storage and retrieval systems, without written permission from the author, except for the use of brief quotations in a book review.

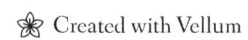

❀ Created with Vellum

CHAPTER ONE

June 30 – 7:06 p.m. – Washington, DC

"I SAW the man who shot me."

Natalia Sokolova heard the words in rapid Russian, the language of her birth, and glanced in surprise at her patient. Her fingers faltered in the process of hanging the second unit of blood on his IV pump.

"Are you sure?" she responded in Russian.

Josef Korolev nodded, his gaze boring into hers. "The FBI agent in the front row of the crowd shot me."

What? An FBI agent shot him? "That can't be. You must be mistaken."

"*Eto ne oshibk.* There was no mistake." The deputy prime minister of Russia's voice was hoarse, scratchy because of the breathing tube that had been removed just a short while ago. "I saw him."

She finished connecting the unit of blood, then placed a reassuring hand on his arm. The deputy prime minister had come to Washington, DC, to deliver a speech regarding the importance of the Middle East Peace Summit to take place at the International Conference scheduled in Moscow. During the speech he'd been shot, which had caused quite the international incident. The entire country was in an uproar over the event.

Josef Korolev grabbed her hand as if willing her to believe him. "Listen to me. I saw him. The bullet came from close range. They didn't think I'd live long enough to tell."

He spoke with such heartfelt conviction the ugly shadow of doubt was difficult to ignore. Especially given the tenuous relationship between the US and Russia. Could her patient be confused? Thinking back over the few hours since Josef had returned from the OR, she counted the amount of narcotics she'd given him. A total of ten milligrams of morphine wasn't too much for such a large man over a three-hour period. Obviously, Josef Korolev had been shot, the Secret Service agents standing guard outside his room substantiated that. But by an FBI agent? She seriously doubted it.

The rumor zipping through the hospital grapevine claimed some sort of disgruntled assassin from the Russian mob was the prime suspect in the shooting because the Russian government was losing its battle against the Mafia underworld. The hospital had cops stationed at each entrance and several more in the ICU.

Yet all the police in the world couldn't keep Korolev safe if the suspect was really an FBI agent.

No, she couldn't believe it. Likely, the morphine was too much for him.

"You're safe here," she assured him. "This is the surgical intensive care unit at Washington University Hospital, and I'm your nurse, Natalia. There are two men from your country here with you, but they've stepped out to discuss arrangements for your transfer home. They'll be back soon."

"I am not safe. Will never be safe, not until I get back to Russia. You must help me." He was old enough to be her father, but his grip was strong as he clung desperately to her hand. "Do not leave me alone with anyone from the American government."

"I won't." She leaned over to pull his blanket up over his chest, knowing the blood transfusion would give him a chill.

"Where did you get this?" His gaze zeroed in on the two pendants dangling from around her neck. His heart rate jumped up, causing his monitor to alarm overhead, but she ignored the noise when he touched the crescent-shaped moon with the three amethyst stars pendant that hung above her Christian cross. "Who gave this to you?"

"My mother." The treasured pendant was the only item she possessed from her Russian birth mother. She would have explained more, but Josef had grown agitated, muttering something she couldn't quite make out, so she tucked the pendants underneath the collar of her scrubs. "Shh. Relax now."

Before Josef could say anything more, she noticed a trio of official-looking American men walking toward her patient's room. Natalia straightened, watching through the glass window as they paused to speak with the Secret Service agent and the Russian countrymen before entering. Instinctively, she took a step closer as if her mere presence would save Josef from harm.

"The deputy prime minister is awake?" The shortest of the three, a man whose FBI name tag identified him as T. Saunders, pinned her with a sharp gaze. "The breathing tube is out? He's able to answer questions?"

"Yes." She winced as Josef's hand grabbed hers and

squeezed tightly to the point of bringing pain. She tried to smile. "Well, not really," she amended. "He's confused, speaking gibberish. The medication has strongly affected him."

The iron hold on her hand didn't ease at her words because Josef did not understand English. She bent close to her patient, speaking in Russian, "Shh, relax. I explained how you are too confused from the narcotics to discuss anything about the shooting right now."

Josef's grip on her hand subsided, and he closed his eyes, feigning sleep.

"You speak Russian too?" Saunders was clearly the leader of the three. The sneer on his face suggested he accused her of something vile.

"Yes, but only a little." Natalia forced a smile. "My adopted mother had dual citizenship in both Russia and here in the US. She taught me some basics of the language. But I'm afraid I have grown very rusty over the years since she passed away." After her adopted mother died, she continued to practice her Russian with her friend Ivan. Yet she couldn't explain the deep-seated certainty that she needed to downplay the extent of her knowledge of the Russian language.

"What exactly did he say to you?" Saunders persisted.

"I don't know, the words didn't make sense. I told you, he's confused. I've given him about ten milligrams of morphine."

"Maybe we need one of our own interpreters in here to tell us just how confused he is." Saunders's gaze challenged her opinion.

She schooled her features not to show her annoyance. "Please do. There is a Russian interpreter, Ivan Rasacovich, available through the hospital social service department if you are interested. As I mentioned, I am not an expert."

"It's a miracle he's survived the shooting," the tallest of the three commented as if to change the direction of the conversation and ease the tension in the room. He was the only one without an FBI name tag, his badge simply read visitor.

"Yeah, no thanks to you, Dreyer," Saunders said in a snide tone.

Dreyer's mouth tightened. "Or to any of us assigned to protect him. The whole event was a debacle, and we can't even get a clear view of the shootings from the cameras." His gaze swept back to the patient. "He's lucky the bullet missed his heart and only grazed his lung."

Natalia doubted Josef Korolev felt very lucky considering the lengthy surgical incision extending around the side of his chest, but she held her tongue. As the FBI agents argued about who might have wanted to silence the deputy prime minister, the man named Dreyer stared at her to the point he made her uncomfortable. He was younger than the others and not dressed in the traditional FBI garb consisting of black suit and matching tie. The simple black T-shirt, stretched across his taut chest, dark jacket, and slacks looked far too casual for an official visit. He might be described as handsome if you liked tall, dark-haired American men with square jaws and brilliant blue eyes.

Good thing she didn't. A broken heart had cured her of such foolishness. She preferred peace and quiet in her life compared to the never-ending drama of a so-called relationship.

"Please, I must ask you all to leave. It's time to change his dressing." Another blatant lie, but she didn't care. She didn't know who these men were or which person she could trust. There was no reason on earth for the FBI to shoot a Russian diplomat, especially while he happened to be ensconced in their protection, but she couldn't totally discount her patient's accusation either. Something wasn't quite right with this picture, and she wanted these men to go away because she didn't have time to waste figuring it out.

Her job was to provide nursing care to her patients. When the men simply stood there, she scowled. "The chest dressing needs to be changed. Would you rather I risk infection?"

"No, of course not." Dreyer nodded as if he completely understood. "We'll give you the privacy you need. Gentlemen?" He gestured toward the door.

The other two sent her hostile looks but, eventually, turned and left the room. Dreyer lingered. She tried not to squirm under his intense gaze.

"Natalia, do you also understand Ukrainian?" His attempt at the language was stilted at best, and his tone was low as if he didn't want anyone to overhear.

At first she was suspicious when he used her name, then she realized she was wearing her hospital ID badge. She sniffed. Someone should tell the man his accent was terrible. "Not fluently, but enough to understand the basics," she answered in Ukrainian. Russian was very different from Ukrainian, a fact he should know. "Why do you ask?"

"No reason in particular. Good night, Natalia." The man turned and followed the others out of the room, leaving her to wonder what test she'd just taken.

And if she'd passed—or failed?

JUNE 30 – 9:18 p.m. – Washington, DC

. . .

SHE DIDN'T GET much time alone with Josef from that point on, mostly because she was running back and forth helping one of her co-workers whose patient took a sudden turn for the worse. She had wanted to ask Josef about her pendant though, since he acted as if it were familiar. Had he seen one just like it? Did he perhaps know who designed the dainty Russian jewelry? The idea her pendant might hold a clue to the true identity of her birth parents filled her with excitement. She couldn't wait to ask him more.

Natalia sat down at the workstation outside her patient's room to make a quick notation in Josef's chart when a shrill triple-beeping sound grabbed her attention. Her gaze snapped from the computer to the blinking red alarm on the central bank of monitors.

Josef's heart rate had gone into a life-threatening arrhythmia.

"Call a code blue." Natalia jumped from her seat and dashed into the room, knocking aside the wide-eyed guard in her haste to reach her patient. V-tach without a pulse. She crawled up to kneel on the side of his bed to perform chest compressions.

The room flooded with medical staff who shoved the hovering Russian countrymen out of the way. Someone took over CPR while another began to give breaths with an Ambu bag.

"Shock him," the surgeon snapped.

Natalia was already slapping the defib patches onto his chest. She connected them to the defibrillator and twisted the knob to 200 joules. "All clear?" she asked before she administered a shock.

"Shock him again," Dr. Ventura ordered. She did as she was told, knowing the algorithm.

"Give him a third shock." All eyes in the room were on the monitor, hoping and praying for a conversion into a normal heart rhythm. But that didn't happen. "Continue CPR and give a bolus of amiodarone," the surgeon ordered. "Then start a drip."

Natalia injected the medication. She grabbed the drip prepared by the pharmacist on duty and hung it on the IV tubing. The surgeon continued to shout orders for labs, for more medication, and to place a breathing tube. They shocked the patient again, then one last time after another round of CPR. As a team, they labored over the patient for a good forty minutes, but despite their best efforts, his heart went into asystole.

Dr. Ventura, the surgeon who'd operated on Josef Korolev, finally shook his head and raised a hand. "Stop CPR. There's nothing more to do."

No! How had this happened? Her pulse raced from the adrenaline coursing through her system, yet she could only stare at the still, peaceful features of Josef Korolev. Less than three hours ago he'd spoken to her.

Now he was dead.

She put a hand to her chest as if to ease the pressure there. Dear Lord, she couldn't believe he was *dead*. Loud vocal protests from the Russian countrymen in the room ricocheted off the walls. Words of comfort failed her.

What could she say to them? She didn't know what had happened. Why had a stable patient suddenly gone into V-tach? Was there something she'd missed? She had several years of nursing experience, but no one was perfect. Yet, in retracing her actions during her shift, she could not think of a single thing she would have done differently. The only oddity, other than all the political hoopla of taking care of a VIP, had been the strange visit from the three Americans.

And Josef's wild accusations.

FBI and Secret Service agents swarmed the room. She stayed close, listening as they grilled the poor guard who'd been left on duty. When they'd finished with the guard, they turned their attention to her.

"Who else has access to this room, besides you?" the FBI agent named Wilcox asked in a harsh tone. "Was he left alone at all?"

"Most of the time he wasn't alone, the Russian countrymen were with him." Natalia glanced nervously between the two men. Why were they asking these questions? Did they honestly suspect something had been done to Josef intentionally?

Should she tell them what Josef had claimed? Yet, if his off-the-wall accusations were true, would telling the FBI help? Saunders and Bentley, the two men who'd come in with Dreyer, hadn't seemed at all sympathetic. She could easily imagine them protecting their own, especially given the political ramifications.

"Yeah, but they spent most of their time in the corner talking in low tones," the guard who'd been on duty said with disgust. "As if I could understand what they babbled about."

"Any member of the hospital staff would have access to his room," Natalia added. "But none of them would have come in unless it was to troubleshoot an alarm or respond to a call light. This isn't the first VIP we've taken care of."

"She wasn't in the room for the past forty minutes," the guard bailed her out. "The only person to come into the room was the housekeeping guy who cleaned the room." When twin sets of cold eyes stared at him, the guard shrugged. "Hey, I took his name—Ray Johnson—it's on the list. Johnson left the room about five minutes before the monitor alarmed."

The FBI agent turned back to her. "Do you know this housekeeper named Ray Johnson?"

"Of course I do." She frantically searched her memory, but she couldn't honestly remember seeing him at any time during her shift. A chill slid down her spine. "I don't remember seeing him around, but I was busy."

The two men exchanged a long glance. "What does he look like?"

"Tall, close to six feet, and very thin. Black hair, usually uncombed." She shrugged. It wasn't as if she knew the man on a personal basis, just enough to say hello.

"Caucasian?"

She nodded.

The guard frowned. "Sounds right, although I didn't think he was that tall, closer to five-ten or eleven. And his hair was more brown than black."

Wilcox, the FBI agent, turned toward the hospital security guard. "Pull up Ray Johnson's picture."

"I tried, but there's something wrong with the computer program." The security guard hunched his shoulders at their incredulous look. "They're working on it."

Wilcox muttered a curse.

Tiny hairs along her nape lifted in warning. *Stop it.* She gave her head a hard shake. Too many crime novels had gone straight to her head. There was no reason to let Josef's outrageous suspicions make her see something sinister in what had caused the code blue. Josef was in his late fifties, and he obviously had a bad heart. She'd noticed minor changes in his EKG after surgery, indicating a possible mild myocardial infarction. The surgeon had ordered serial cardiac enzyme tests to see how much damage his heart had sustained.

Obviously more than they'd realized.

The ruckus didn't settle down for a long while. After she'd given her story to what seemed like dozens of agents, they allowed her to leave. As she gathered her scattered paperwork into some semblance of order, she listened to the ongoing debate.

Some of the problems were simple, like who should talk to the media at the press conference. But others were more difficult, such as who would oversee Josef Korolev's autopsy—someone from the US government or Russian medical examiners? After a heated argument, it was decided both sides would be present during the procedure.

But by the time she was able to leave, a couple of hours after the code blue, she had not seen any of the three men who'd stopped in to visit Josef's room earlier that evening. She'd mentioned it to the agents, and their names were on the guard's infamous list.

Their glaring absence, in the face of Josef's death, gnawed at her on the way home.

Natalia fingered her moon pendant and cross as she rode the red Metro train, grateful for its calming effect. Had she imagined Josef Korolev's odd reaction to her pendant? Had he recognized it, or was it similar to something he'd seen before? Maybe the design, the symbol of a crescent moon with three stars on one end, was specifically Russian in nature. She could easily picture a little shop in Moscow where dozens of pendants just like hers were sold.

She'd concentrated on finding her birth mother through deciphering her adopted mother's journal. She'd never considered the necklace design in itself to be important.

Josef's reaction convinced her that the moon-shaped

pendant was a clue. Her chest swelled with anticipation at the thought. She knew her birth mother was Russian, as her adopted mother was. Other than the first name of Anya, she didn't know anything else about her birth mother. Since her adopted mother had passed away three years ago, she'd intensified her search for her roots. Had become obsessed with knowing who she was and who the woman was who'd given her away. Natalia had collected as much information as she could about Kazan, the city of her birth.

As soon as she got home, she'd add this new puzzle piece to the other bits of information she'd gathered about her birth mother. Maybe researching the pendant on the internet would reveal something she'd missed.

A young man shuffled past her, pressing purposefully against her. She dodged him, slipped a hand into her canvas bag, and closed her fingers around the can of pepper spray hidden in there. The crime rate was notorious in DC, and she was jittery enough after the strange events during her shift.

The guy took a seat across from her on the other side of the train. She took a deep breath, then let it out slowly, but she didn't relax her grip on the pepper spray. Illegal or not, she intended to use the weapon if needed.

Ignoring the man staring at her, she trained her gaze on a spider web in the corner of the car. A fly caught in the silken strands fought to get free.

A shiver rippled along her nerves, and she glanced away. Anxious, she waited for her stop to come up. She wanted nothing more than to get home.

Stepping off the train at her Brookland stop, she hurried up the stairs to the main level, staring straight ahead but screening the people around her from the corner of her eye. The events at the hospital had put her on edge. For a moment, she thought the man coming up on her left side looked familiar, but then he turned and headed off in the opposite direction.

Ridiculous to be so paranoid. She gave herself a mental shake. She was a critical care nurse. It wasn't as if she were the one in danger.

Not like Josef Korolev had been. Someone hated him or what he represented enough to shoot him. To ultimately cause his death. Although the Cold War had been declared over decades ago, the animosity between Russia and the US hadn't changed much. If a member of the Russian Mafia was the killer, why wait until Josef was on US soil to finish him off?

Nothing made sense.

She used her rideshare app to get a ride. It didn't take long for a guy in a black sedan to drive up next to her. "Are you Natalia?"

"Yes, thanks." Her house was only a dozen blocks from the Metro station, but she didn't care. She'd pay him extra for his time. "My address is eleven forty-one Girard Street."

The driver grunted, shrugged, and pulled into traffic. Natalia dropped her head against the back of the seat. Thankfully, she was almost home. She considered having a dish of ice cream to relax after her wretched day. At least tomorrow was Friday and she had the weekend off.

"Here ya go, lady."

She opened her eyes, realizing the rideshare had pulled over to the curb. He'd stopped in front of the house next to hers, but she wasn't in the mood to argue.

"Thank you." She added a tip to the rideshare fare via the app on her phone, then opened the door, swung her legs out, gathered her canvas bag, and stood.

Ka-boom! The blast rocked the stillness of the night.

The ground trembled beneath her feet. She stumbled and fell backward into the sedan.

The windows burst outward in a hailstorm of glass. Shards rained down against the car like bullets from a machine gun as a second explosion shattered the night.

It took her a moment to realize it was her house, the precious home she had once shared with her mother, engulfed in roaring flames.

CHAPTER TWO

June 30 – 11:25 p.m. – Washington, DC

"WHAT THE—GET OUT!" the rideshare driver she'd gone to such pains to overtip screamed at her from the front seat of his car. "I'm outta here!"

Numb from shock, she clamored out of the vehicle, barely clearing the door before he stomped on the gas and sped away. The back passenger door slammed shut when he screeched around a tight curve, then disappeared from view.

She stared at the debris littering the area around her feet. Icy fingers of fear danced along her nape. Her previous paranoia returned in full force. She looked toward her flame-engulfed house and noticed a man standing on the street. He lit a cigarette, and she sucked in a breath when his profile reminded her of the creepy guy from the train. Then he looked straight at her, taking a determined step toward her.

Run. Belgi. Run!

Natalia didn't question her instincts. She sprinted down the street in the opposite direction from the man and her burning house. People poured from nearby houses and wailing sirens filled the air, but still she ran. Bitter regret swelled, choking her. She imagined the guy was behind her, chasing her. She dodged through neighborhood shortcuts hoping to lose whoever might be following.

To keep moving, she wove through the small space between several houses to another street. Then she took another, putting as much distance as possible between herself and the man who had stood outside the charred remnants of her home.

The image of the explosion ran through her mind over and over, like a video stuck in a loop. Her elderly, half-blind tabby, Peety, had been in the house. He was old, his arthritis preventing him from moving very fast, but he had been her companion since she'd saved him from being put down at the animal rescue center. Silent tears escaped as her breath heaved from her lungs, and she brushed them impatiently. Silly to mourn the loss of her ailing pet when she'd come so close to losing much more.

A few minutes earlier and she'd have been in the house when it exploded.

Her near miss made her stumble, and she fell hard on her knees. The enormity of her loss was too much to bear. All her precious keepsakes, memories of her mother, were gone. Vanished as if they'd never been. Everything she had was lost forever. She pounded her fist on the pavement, inwardly wailing at the unfairness of it all.

Something, a voice in her head maybe, or the gut instincts she normally trusted, urged her to keep going. She pulled herself together and rose to her feet, glancing behind her. She couldn't see the man from the train, but she continued to run. Her thoughts whirled as she zigzagged through the streets.

Her house had burst into flames. What had happened? A freak accident such as a gas leak? Or something much worse? A bomb? Who would have done such a terrible thing? The man outside who'd followed her from the train? She didn't have known enemies, yet fear and suspicion wouldn't leave her alone. Too much had happened for one day. First losing her high-profile patient so unexpectedly, and now this explosion.

The streets were dark and unfamiliar. Where should she go? What should she do? She'd have to talk to the police, she knew, but not now. Not until she'd pulled herself together. Natalia pushed onward, running until her legs felt like cement-filled stumps. Finally, she stopped and bent over, gasping for breath and bracing her hands on her scraped knees.

She needed a plan. A place to go. Gallivanting through the streets of DC was not a good idea. But where? A friend's house? Who would be willing to take her in for what remained of the night?

Ivan Rasacovich. She wanted to see Ivan. He was her closest friend. Her confidant. She met the Russian interpreter at the hospital four years ago. He was her source of information for all things Russian and had helped tremendously in the search for her birth mother. And right now, with her world falling apart around her, she craved the comfort of hearing Ivan's thick Russian accent telling her everything was going to be all right.

He'd accompany her to the police station. The idea of not being alone filled her with hope and a measure of relief.

A firm destination in mind, she experienced a renewed spurt of energy. She straightened and slung her canvas bag over her shoulder before turning to head back in the direction of the Metro station. She picked a different location than the stop where she'd gotten off to come home. As she fled through the night, she kept a careful eye out for any possible source of danger. The trains stopped running at midnight, but she could try another rideshare if needed.

She bit back a sob. *Don't dwell on the loss.* There wasn't time to fall apart now. She needed to find Ivan. He would wrap her in his bearlike arms and offer immense comfort. Somehow, she was certain Ivan's cool, Russian logic would help make sense of this devastation.

JUNE 30 – 11:38 p.m. – Washington, DC

ALEK NEVSKY STARED at the dull gray walls of the room, apprehension dark, growing. He'd been here for hours, first for questioning, and now, waiting.

"Alek Nevsky?" They'd both held out their FBI badges as identification. Puzzled, he'd nodded. The shorter man continued, "I'm Special Agent Gerald Harper, and this is my partner, Special Agent Ethan Wilcox. We have a few questions to ask you."

"Questions?" He hadn't understood. Up until now, his only contact had been with Special Agent Michael Cummings.

"Where were you this afternoon?" Harper seemed to be the one in charge.

"I, uh, at The Washington Center. To hear the speech by Deputy Prime Minister Josef Korolev." He frowned when the two agents exchanged a knowing look. "Why?"

"Did you shoot the deputy prime minister?" Harper's question rocked him back on his heels.

"Of course not!" Shocked, he stared at the FBI agent. "I don't even own a gun."

"You don't?" Special Agent Harper quirked one brow, his gaze raking him from head to toe. "Interesting, since a witness described the shooter, a man about five feet eleven inches tall, in his middle forties, roughly one hundred and eighty pounds with graying hair at his temples."

The description of himself was less than flattering. Had it been the real reason Lara left him? Oh, she'd claimed not, but what did he really know for sure? "Ridiculous. Why would I do such a thing? I don't own a gun. And I have no reason to want the deputy prime minister dead. I think he is attempting to do good things for the country and the nation."

"If you have something to tell us, it's better to come clean right now." Special Agent Harper leaned close. "Because we're in the process of obtaining a search warrant to go through your house. If you're hiding anything, we'll find it."

"I'm not hiding anything," Alek had responded, although it wasn't entirely the truth. Several things in his past would be better off to stay hidden. Still, he had to try. "I'd like to speak to Special Agent Michael Cummings."

The two exchanged a knowing smirk. "We don't know anyone by the name of Michael Cummings. See, the way this works, we ask the questions and you answer them. Understand?"

The barrage of questions had gone on and on. Finally, they'd left him alone, here in this room, presumably to search his home.

He didn't like the idea of FBI agents Harper and Wilcox pawing through his things, through the bedroom he'd once shared with his wife, Lara. Since she'd left him, he'd slept on the sofa in the living room, unwilling to use the bedroom until he convinced her to come back. He closed his eyes and pinched the bridge of his nose. What if they broke one of Lara's sculptures during their search? Should he call her?

No. Lara would only get upset. He'd get in touch with her after they'd released him.

If they let him go.

His head ached, and he could feel tendrils of panic struggling to break loose.

How long would they leave him here?

He closed his eyes again and prayed for God to watch over him and Lara.

Especially Lara.

The door to the interrogation room flew open. Agents Wilcox and Harper walked in; Wilcox held a plastic bag containing a gun.

"Look what we found under your bed." Wilcox smirked. "Not a very original hiding place, Nevsky."

The tendrils of panic wrapped tighter around his throat. He struggled to speak. "That isn't mine. I don't own a gun. Someone must have put it there."

"Oh really?" Agent Harper arched a brow. "Then why did we find one of your fingerprints on the barrel? And isn't it amazing how this gun uses the same ammo pulled from the wound in Korolev's chest? It's only a matter of time before we match the ballistics."

A cold chill seeped through his pores. If his fingerprints were on the gun, it was because someone else put them there. He was being framed. Where was Michael Cummings? He didn't want to believe his FBI contact had anything to do with this.

Lara. What would Lara think?

"Alek Nevsky, you are under arrest for the murder of Josef Korolev. You have the right to remain silent. Anything you say can and will be used against you in a court of law. You have a right to an attorney. If you cannot afford an attorney, one will be appointed to you. Do you understand these rights as I've described them?"

"Yes." Feeling helplessness, he stood stoic as Harper roughly dragged his hands behind his back, then slapped handcuffs around his wrists.

Humiliation burned as they marched him from the room. For the first time in the year since his wife of twenty-five years had left him, he was glad Lara wasn't here to see him like this.

JUNE 30 – 11:45 p.m. – Washington, DC

SLOAN DREYER SLOUCHED in his chair, sipping a ginger ale while staring blankly at the television screen across the room. The rotten taste of failure still lingered in his mouth, and he took another sip of his soft drink, desperate to swipe the bitterness away. Hadn't he tried to convince Jordan he wasn't the right man for the job? The fact that he knew how to speak Ukrainian didn't mean anything, and he'd sure proved it during the fiasco this afternoon.

He'd failed in his job. Again. Security Specialists, Inc. wasn't going to survive its first year in business if they continued losing the people they were supposed to protect.

The deputy prime minister of Russia was dead. Had been shot right under his nose. Sloan had stuck as close to Josef Korolev as the bodyguards Korolev had brought with him from Russia, but still, when the screaming had started, he hadn't even realized Korolev had been hit.

The Russian bodyguards had known, though, and they'd gone berserk, creating massive chaos that had taken hours to sort out. They'd managed to get Korolev to the closest hospital, and the guy had actually survived surgery long enough to make it to the ICU.

Only to die of complications a few hours later.

Sloan swallowed hard. He had no business protecting a toad, much less a Russian VIP. Jordan should have known better than to drop the assignment in his lap at the last minute. The fact that he spoke Ukrainian shouldn't have even entered the picture. Ukrainian was a softer language, nothing like pronouncing the hard consonants of Russian. But had Jordan listened? No. Instead, Jordan had demanded he practice Russian for hours as if cramming for a final exam, yet he'd still only caught a fourth of what the Russians had talked about.

The nurse, Natalia, had spoken in a slow, calm manner to Korolev, but all Sloan could figure out for sure was that she'd said something along the lines of the patient not needing to talk to the three of them.

In his mind's eye, he remembered the beautiful nurse. The baggy scrubs didn't detract from her appearance. Her long blonde hair had been clipped back at the nape of her neck, but her high cheekbones, clear green eyes, and husky voice had been more than enough to capture his interest.

And the attention of every other guy standing within fifteen feet of her. After months of not feeling anything for anybody, this sudden awareness disturbed him.

What exactly had Josef told Natalia? Had her patient confided any secrets to her? Or had Korolev babbled nonsense from the pain meds as she'd claimed? The blatant distrust in her eyes when he'd walked in with the two FBI agents, including the assistant director himself, hadn't been reassuring. But the sound of her voice answering him in Ukrainian sent shivers of awareness darting down his spine. He discovered he had a weakness for a woman who could speak Ukrainian.

Late breaking news on the television diverted his attention from Natalia.

"Firefighters are still battling the five-alarm blaze in the northeast area of DC. One house has been declared as the original source of the fire, and so far the cause of the blaze is unknown. Police are searching for the homeowner, Natalia Sokolova."

The name had him straightening in his seat, his gaze arrested on the TV.

"At this time, they don't believe she was in the house during the explosion since she was working the evening shift at a local hospital. But the police have not yet confirmed her whereabouts at this time."

What? No way could this be a coincidence. He leapt from his seat, snagged his cell phone, and punched in a single number to speed-dial his partner.

"Yeah?" Jordan's groggy, sleep-filled voice came from the other end of the line.

"We have a problem." Sloan shoved his shoes back onto his feet and reached for his car keys. He headed for the door at a run. "I need every piece of intel you have on Natalia Sokolova, and I need it now. Someone just tried to kill her."

CHAPTER THREE

July 1 – 12:02 a.m. – Moscow, Russia

"IS THE JOB COMPLETE?"

"Yes."

"And the rest of the plan has been put into place?"

"Don't worry. Everything is on track."

"Do you know the woman's location?"

A long pause. "No. But all bureau resources are working on it. We'll find her."

"You'd better. There's a bonus if you find her and eliminate her within the next three days."

"A bonus?"

"Double your usual fee."

"Consider it done."

Satisfaction surged as the line was disconnected. Another loose end had been successfully snipped. Soon, nothing would stand in the way of the grand plan. A plan so perfect even the Russian allies buried deep in the US were unaware of it.

Russia would once again become a powerful force to be reckoned with.

Beware all those who would take the country lightly.

JULY 1 – 12:19 a.m. – Washington, DC

NATALIA WAS NEVER SO thankful to see the innocuous sign indicating the location of the Metro station. The trains didn't run after midnight, but it was a good neutral location. She rummaged through her canvas bag for her phone, to get another rideshare. As before, the driver pulled up a few minutes later. She peered through the window. Not the same driver, thankfully, or he might have refused to take her.

"Where to?"

"Twelve thirty-one Domingo Street."

"Sure thing."

Natalia leaned back against the seat of the car. Calm. She needed to remain calm. The muscles in her legs quivered from exertion, and her scrubs clung to her sweat-dampened skin. Several controlled, deep breaths helped to slow her racing heart.

She placed a hand over the two pendants she wore around her neck, searching for strength. God was watching over her tonight, that was for certain. And she knew Josef had recognized the crescent-shaped moon pendant too. She'd been adopted when she was only four years old and didn't have any memories at all of her birth mother. Nothing except the necklace she wore along with her crucifix. If she hadn't been wearing it, the necklace would have been gone too, along with everything else she owned.

She spared another wistful thought for her precious things belonging to her mother. And all her research notes. Not that she'd been very close to finding her birth mother, but the clues she'd gathered in relation to her past had been blown to bits.

Her eyes filled with tears, and she blinked them back determinedly. Enough. Crying was useless and wouldn't change anything. She needed to count her blessings. Peety was out of his arthritis-filled misery, and she could recreate her notes. Her memories of her dear adopted mother would remain alive in her heart. Her home could be replaced. Ivan would help her. He'd gladly allow her to stay with them until she could find something else.

Her life would go on. This was just a small setback in her otherwise peaceful existence.

The rideshare driver pulled up to Ivan's house. Gratefully, she climbed from the vehicle. Using her phone, she once again added a tip, before closing the door behind her.

Ivan's townhouse was dark. Natalia hesitated outside the doorway, debating what to do. Now that she'd calmed down a bit, knocking on the door at well past midnight didn't seem prudent, so she raised up on her tiptoes and helped herself to the spare key Ivan kept hidden along the inside edge of his fancy light fixture. Ivan was like a big brother to her; she knew he wouldn't mind.

She quietly unlocked and opened the door, flipping on the hallway light as she stepped inside. Blinking, she gave her eyes a few minutes to adjust to the brightness. She headed down the short hallway.

Stopped.

Dark crimson smears stained lily-white walls and impeccable hardwood floors. The awful metallic stench grabbed her about the throat, pressing against her trachea. Blood? She stepped closer, unable to believe her senses.

Oh no. Please, God, no!

Ivan!

She fisted a hand in her mouth to keep from screaming. She knew she should run in case the attacker was still there, but she couldn't leave. She had to find Ivan. She took one step, then another, until she reached the kitchen.

And found him.

Lying facedown on the kitchen floor, bathed in blood.

Ivan! No! This couldn't be real. This couldn't be happening. Deep, gasping sobs rose from her chest. Five years of ingrained critical care nursing broke through the panic enough to force her to approach, leaning over his body to check for a pulse, even though in some corner of her brain she knew the action was useless. Her fingers confirmed her brain's suspicions.

His pale skin was cold, lifeless. Ivan was dead.

Her stomach heaved, rising into her throat in a bilious wave. *Run. Belgi. Run!* She spun from the horrific sight and ran. Out of the townhouse and down the steps. Tears blurred her vision, and she ran face-first into a wall of solid male muscle.

The killer!

She fought against the arms that came round her, kicking and punching as her momentum carried them down onto the grassy embankment, landing hard enough to make her teeth rattle. He was too strong for her. His arms held hers easily in spite of her wild, thrashing attempts to get free. She opened her mouth to scream, but a hard hand closed over her mouth as an even harder body pinned hers against the unyielding earth.

"Natalia, stop fighting. I'm here to help you."

The words, spoken in bad Ukrainian, snaked through the waves of hysteria, making sense when nothing else would have. She stopped her fierce struggle and peered through the darkness at the man who held her firmly in his grasp.

Her heart thudded against her chest when she recognized him as the tall, dark-haired man from the hospital. The knowledge he was one of the three government men who'd come to pry information from Josef Korolev was not reassuring.

"You promise not to scream?" he whispered in Ukrainian. She nodded and then tried to turn her head away to free her mouth. He moved his hand but kept her body pinned beneath him.

"What are you doing here?" she asked in a vicious whisper. *"Da poshel ti!* Did you hurt Ivan? Are you going to kill me too?"

Natalia didn't know what to expect but braced herself for the worst. Instead, he rose to his feet in a quick movement, dragging her upright too.

"No, I don't want to kill you. But someone else sure does. If you want to stay alive, you'd better come with me." He tugged on her hand.

She dug in her heels and wrenched out of his grip. No way on this green earth was she going with him. Not when there had already been too much death and destruction for her shell-shocked mind to handle. "I don't think so. I'm going to the police." Where she should have gone right away. Stupid. She'd been so stupid.

"If you leave on your own, you'll be dead by morning."

The hard, flat words stopped her. She didn't know this tall man, didn't know who to trust, but Ivan had been brutally murdered. Her house was gone. What was going on? She couldn't even begin to fathom the horrific nightmare she'd stumbled into.

"I'll keep you safe." His low voice didn't exactly ring with confidence, but he stood, tall and capable, waiting for her response.

She hesitated, even though logic told her if this man in front of her had killed Ivan, he could have already done away with her by now as well.

"We don't have a lot of time," he warned in Ukrainian. "These guys are playing for keeps. If they have already killed your friends, then there is truly nothing to stop them from killing you."

She didn't know who *they* were, and right now she couldn't even fathom a guess. But for some ridiculous reason, his bad Ukrainian accent reassured her. She gave in and nodded. "Okay, I'll go with you. But we need to report this to the police."

"Safety first, then police." He headed down to the sidewalk toward the car he'd parked a few houses down the road from Ivan's townhouse. She trailed behind him, wondering if she'd been jettisoned into a scene from the set of the latest thriller. Would she wake up in the morning to discover this was all nothing more than a horrible dream? She could only hope so.

Dear Lord, help me. Show me the way. Help me understand who I can trust.

"Get in." He opened the passenger door and nudged her inside, then slammed the door behind her. In moments, they were racing away from the crime scene.

She glanced at his hard, chiseled profile and clutched her canvas bag to her chest because it was the only thing left on this earth she possessed. "Who are you?" she finally asked. "What's your name?"

"Sloan Dreyer. I used to be with the FBI, but now I work for Security Specialists, Incorporated."

She digested this information, but the facts spinning through her brain didn't make sense. At least his being a former agent made her feel a little better. Dreyer, she remembered the name now from the visit at the hospital. How on earth had he found her at Ivan's house? What did Ivan have to do with Josef Korolev? "So if you're not with the FBI anymore, then why were you in Josef's hospital room with those other men?"

The slight hesitation made her frown, before he admitted, "Security Specialists, Incorporated was hired to help keep Korolev safe."

Safe? He must be kidding. One glance at his clenched jaw convinced her he wasn't joking. Her heart sank. "But he's dead."

"I know." Sloan's voice was devoid of all emotion as he navigated the streets of DC. "I messed up."

"How reassuring." She didn't bother to hide her snide tone.

He slanted another hard glance in her direction, although he didn't seem angry with her. "Yeah, well unless you have a better plan, you're stuck with me until I can hand you over to my partner, Jordan Rashid."

JULY 1 – 1:01 a.m. – Washington, DC

SLOAN NAVIGATED THE DARK STREETS, avoiding all major highways while trying to ignore the woman sitting beside him. She was alive, which was all that mattered. His luck had held out long enough for him to stumble across her bolting from Rasacovich's house, the first place he'd gone to look for her based on Jordan's intel and his own gut instinct.

The entire situation had gone downhill fast, but his only concern right now was Natalia's safety. Once he turned her over to Jordan, he'd feel better. He didn't mind being in the line of fire; he welcomed it. But he couldn't stomach the thought of Natalia being anywhere near the center of the target.

"Now that you mention it, I do have a better plan." Natalia's gaze challenged his in the darkness. "Stop the car, I'm getting out."

He scowled in a way that normally made smart men back off, but oh, no, not Natalia. He swallowed a sigh. The woman just would not give up. What was her problem anyway? He needed this like he needed a swift kick upside the head.

"No."

Her eyes rounded. "No? What do you mean, no?" She smacked him in the shoulder with her canvas bag, and he swerved yet managed to stay on the road. "I'm not going anywhere with you, you pig. *Svinya*. Stop the car."

She'd lapsed into Russian, but he'd caught the gist of what she'd said. Of course, the way she kept swatting at him with her bag helped get the message across.

Irritated, he ripped the bag from her grasp. "I thought you didn't understand much Russian? I thought you were rusty?"

"Give me the bag." She lunged across him, and he let her wrestle the bag from his grip. She'd surprised him, and frankly her Russian accent was making him crazy. He ignored her burst of temper. "What else did you lie about, Natalia?"

"Nothing." With the bag safely in her grasp, she edged

as far from him as the seat would allow, hugging the door. "I didn't lie about anything."

He should have seen it coming, but man, it was just past one o'clock in the morning and he wasn't thinking clearly. When he slowed to take a right-handed turn, she opened her passenger door. He tried to grab her, but she curled away from him and rolled out of the car, hitting the pavement with a soft thud.

"No! Stop!" He punched the brake and threw the car into park, then leaped out after her. She was up and running, seeming to fly through the streets on those ridiculously long legs of hers. She had a good head start, but no way was he going to let her slip away. He cranked up the speed, closing the gap between them.

Surprisingly, she grew tired before he expected her to, slowing her pace, her breath heaving in and out of her lungs as if she'd run a marathon. He lengthened his stride, reached out, and grabbed a fistful of her scrub top, yanking hard. She stumbled, and he used the momentary weakness to haul her back against him.

"What is wrong with you?" He bit out the words in a low tone as he spun her around and held her shoulders tight. He wanted to shake some sense into her. "Do you have a death wish? Is that it? The police can't keep you safe. Don't you realize you've stumbled into something big?"

"No. This isn't about me. I'm innocent. Let me go." She gasped for breath as she struggled against him, but her efforts were halfhearted at best. He let her work the frustration out of her system until she finally sagged against him, resting her forehead on his shoulder. "I want to go home."

Her voice, thick with tears, pelted him between the eyes. She was so strong, but she had obviously reached her limit. Against his will, he held her close, smoothed a hand down the gentle curve of her back.

"You can't go home, Natalia." Her home was nothing but a pitiful pile of ashes. "Let me keep you safe." Man, what was he thinking to make such a rash promise? Given his miserable track record, his ability to keep her safe had the same probability as little green men beaming down from Mars. No way was he good enough to keep her safe, but Jordan was. Sloan had the utmost confidence in his partner, his only friend. He forced himself to soften his tone. "Come back to the car. Let me take you to my partner, Jordan."

"No." She pushed away from him, her brief moment of weakness disappearing in a puff of smoke. She tossed her head back and glared at him. "I don't know Jordan, and I don't know you. I'll be safer on my own. With a little cash, I can find a hotel to stay the night."

He strove to remain calm, although she'd tempt Gandhi into a display of violence. "Look, we're sitting ducks out here. Come back to the car. We'll find a hotel and talk." At this point he'd do anything to get her off the street.

"Promise you will take me to a hotel," she said in Ukrainian. "A hotel, not to Jordan, whoever he is."

He dragged in a harsh breath. "I promise."

Sloan stayed close behind her, keeping a wary eye out for any threat as he hustled her toward his car. At least it hadn't disappeared in the short time they were gone. Once they were safely inside, he drove like a madman toward the opposite side of the city, to a small, non-chain hotel.

No way was he giving her another chance to run.

"Come on." He pulled up to the small place that catered to the less picky clientele. The motel was decrepit, no doubt about it. There were only a half dozen rooms, all overlooking the parking lot. "I'll book us a room."

Sloan braced himself for the worst, but she took the news better than he expected. He urged her inside, then spoke to the night shift clerk, a pimple-faced kid barely out of his teens, who agreed to give them a room for cash without asking for an ID.

The hovel carried the rank scent of mold and wasn't much bigger than a walk-in closet. He closed and locked the door behind them, feeling marginally better.

Without saying a word, Natalia disappeared into the bathroom. The lock clicked loudly in the silence. He collapsed in the chair beside the bed, scrubbed his hands over his face, and tried not to remember all the ways he'd failed in the past.

Failure was not an option. Not tonight. He'd keep his promise—he wouldn't turn her over to Jordan until the morning.

Okay, technically it was morning, but he'd at least wait until a decent hour. A little rest would do Natalia a world of good. Once she'd gotten some sleep, and maybe something to eat, he was sure he could convince her to listen to reason. And besides, Jordan shouldn't have to suffer, getting yanked out of bed at such an early hour.

With the heavy responsibility of keeping Natalia alive, he was sure he'd suffer enough for both of them.

JULY 1 – 2:23 a.m. – Washington, DC

NATALIA STAYED under the hot shower until every one of her fingers and toes turned wrinkly. Then she turned off the water and stood, wrapped in a towel, staring in distaste at her stained scrubs lying in a pool on the floor.

The bloody smears could have been from her shift at the hospital, or from when she'd hit the pavement escaping from Sloan's car, or from Ivan's house. Dear Ivan. Her friend. One of the few who loved her without condition. And she'd loved him too. He was the older brother she'd never had. She closed her eyes against a wave of fresh tears. She couldn't bring Ivan back no matter how much she wanted to. Sniffling hard, she pushed away the painful thoughts and rummaged through her canvas bag for something, anything, other than her soiled, ripped scrubs to wear.

No such luck.

Her gaze landed on her cell phone. Pulling it out, she set it on the sink in front of her.

Since going out into the hotel room she happened to be sharing with a strange man wearing nothing but her underwear was not an option, she bent down and pulled on her discarded clothes.

She sat on the closed lid of the commode, finger-combing her damp hair and staring at her phone. There was just a little over half her battery life left. She didn't have her charger. In her panicky marathon run after her house explosion, she hadn't thought of using her phone to make a simple call to the police. But now, her thoughts were clear. Concise.

No reason to feel trapped here with Sloan Dreyer. What did she really know about the man? Just because he was full of muscles and easy on the eyes didn't mean he was one of the good guys. It was creepy how he'd found her at Ivan's townhouse. Even creepier that he'd been in with the Feds wanting to talk to Josef before he died.

Could she really trust him?

Why not call her adopted father and ask him to come and pick her up? Surely he'd come get her, give her a ride to the police. Granted, she hadn't seen him in the three years since her mother's funeral. Her parents had divorced when she was only ten, and she'd lived with her mother. Her father had moved on, married again, creating a whole new family of his own.

Early on, she'd enjoyed spending time with her new half siblings. The twins, Daryl and Daniel, had been cute babies. But soon she realized her father didn't really want to spend time with her. His new wife, Darlene, didn't care for the reminder of his first marriage either, especially the child they had adopted together. After hitting her awkward teenage years, Natalia had stopped calling, and her father seemed content enough with his new family.

She'd pretended not to be hurt and concentrated on spending time with her mother. Their Russian bond certainly helped. Her father had often gotten annoyed when she and her mother would speak together in the same language, one he didn't understand.

Natalia momentarily closed her eyes, wishing her mother were here now. She'd give anything not to feel so alone.

With grim determination, she dialed her father's home number, despite the hour. She flushed the toilet for background noise and braced herself for her father's wife to answer. Instead, the answering machine clicked on. Her hopes deflated. Maybe her father had taken his perfect little family on vacation.

"Dad, it's me, Natalia." She kept her voice low, even with the whirling noise of the toilet to prevent it from carrying to the man waiting in the other room. "I need you. My house exploded. I think I'm in danger. Please help me. Call my cell phone as soon as you get this message. Hurry."

She hung up and debated turning the phone off to

preserve the battery. Then she changed the settings to vibrate and slid it back into the recesses of her bag. She'd keep her phone on for now and check it often. Although the chances her father would actually return her message anytime soon were slim, no way did she want to miss his call, whenever he made it.

Drawing a deep breath, Natalia stood and slung her bag over her shoulder. Opening the door, she entered the cramped motel room, half expecting—or at least hoping—to find her self-imposed bodyguard asleep.

He wasn't.

Sloan straightened in his chair when he saw her, his dark gaze so penetrating she wondered if he had X-ray vision to see through her bag to zero in on her phone. With his black T-shirt and black jeans, he blended with the night. He looked more dangerous than anyone else she'd met so far since being assigned to take care of Josef Korolev. She swallowed hard and self-consciously ran her fingers through her damp hair. "I don't have a comb."

"Neither do I." He remained seated in his chair positioned between the bed and the door. No doubt he'd chosen the spot on purpose, both to keep intruders out and to keep her in. The thought should have annoyed her. "Why don't you try to get a few hours of sleep?"

Was he kidding? Sleep would be impossible. Yet, the bed was the only comfy spot in the whole room, other than the chair he'd commandeered for himself. Keeping her bag close, she crawled in beneath the sheets and propped the pillow behind her back. The only light in the room was a small lamp next to his chair. "I can't sleep. Tell me what's going on."

She caught a flicker of annoyance in his eyes before he averted his gaze. "I don't know. If I did, I'd get the cops involved right now and you'd be safe in their care rather than sitting here in a dive hotel room with me."

Twice now he'd mentioned keeping her safe. She didn't know him, shouldn't be comfortable with him, but she felt herself beginning to relax.

"Give me one good reason we shouldn't call the police right now."

He stared at her. "Because I'm not willing to risk your life by trusting the wrong person. Security Specialists can protect you better than the police can."

She shivered. Maybe he was right. She didn't want to risk her life either. "Why do you think someone is trying to harm me? I haven't done anything wrong."

"Do you think your house blew up by accident?" His harsh tone grated on her nerves. "Do you think a string of strange coincidences caused the death of your friend Ivan? Come on, Natalia, you can't possibly be that naïve."

She didn't appreciate his patronizing tone. Her fingers gripped the sheets. "But why? I haven't done anything wrong. I pay my taxes. I don't lie or cheat or steal. I've lived in DC for over twenty years and have been working at Washington University Hospital as a critical care nurse since I graduated from college. My life is boring. Stable. Predictable. Why would someone try to hurt me?"

Sloan stared at her for a long minute, then gave a self-deprecating bark of laughter and scrubbed a hand over his face. "How should I know? I was hoping you'd be able to tell me."

CHAPTER FOUR

July 1 – 2:49 a.m. – Washington, DC

SLOAN WISHED Natalia would lie down, close her eyes, and go to sleep. But in the short time he'd known her, when had the stubborn woman ever done what he wanted? She drove him crazy, the way she glared at him from her seemingly regal perch on the bed.

If he hadn't seen her working in the hospital as a nurse, he'd suspect she was some sort of Russian princess with that pert nose of hers constantly in the air. Her haughty tone only reinforced the image.

"Why was your company hired to protect Josef Korolev?" she asked. Her husky tone sent shivers of awareness flickering through his veins. There was something genetically wrong with him if he could be attracted to a woman who'd called him a pig. "Isn't that the job of the FBI or the Secret Service?"

He rubbed a hand over his gritty eyes. "Yeah. And for

the Department of Homeland Security. But in this particular case, their resources were overstretched, and they happened to need someone who could speak and understand Russian. Everyone else was tied up on other, more important projects." Discussing his failure in detail wasn't making him feel any better. Jordan had tried to convince him the threat to the deputy prime minister was negligible. A simple speech. An easy job.

Yeah, right.

She arched an elegant brow. "Ukrainian isn't Russian."

No kidding. He strove for patience. "The FBI has been putting all their resources into the Arabic dialects, so they can't keep up with the number of language specialists they need. I was a last-minute addition." *And a lousy one at that.*

"A last-minute addition," she repeated and narrowed her gaze. "Maybe you wormed your way next to Josef Korolev for the sole purpose of shooting him?"

For Pete's sake, what next? He suppressed a sigh. "Princess, I have no reason on earth to want Josef Korolev dead. His death isn't exactly doing great things for my company's reputation." In fact, he wouldn't blame Jordan for cutting him loose after this. They were partners in the business, but at the moment, his side of the deal was turning out to be more of a liability than either of them had planned. "Nor do I want anyone else dead." Except maybe the terrorists who'd murdered his sister.

He'd been trying to track them down. Something he'd much rather do if given a choice between that and sitting here playing nanny to a princess.

"I suppose you found me by accident, then?" she challenged.

"No. I tracked you down after I saw your house burning

on the news. Jordan's info on you gave me Rasacovich's name, and I remembered you mentioning him in the hospital, when Saunders and Bentley both were trying to get Korolev to talk. I'm amazed I found you before they did. I don't believe in coincidences, and it's obvious someone wants you dead."

"So you say." She still didn't look convinced.

"Get some rest." He didn't have the energy to argue with her anymore. "I promise I'm not going to do anything except sit here and make sure nothing happens to you."

To his surprise, she didn't push any further but finally snuggled down into the sheets and curled onto her side with her hand tucked beneath the pillow. He reached over and turned off the lamp, plunging the room into darkness.

Edgy exhaustion tugged at him. He tried to keep his mind on more important matters.

Despite his annoyance with her, Natalia had asked perceptively relevant questions. Why blow up her house? To scare her? Or had some trigger mechanism gone off prematurely? Given the murder of her friends, his gut leaned toward the latter.

The threat on Natalia's life had to be somehow linked to Josef's death. Retaliation maybe? Did someone blame his death on her lack of nursing care? If so, it had to be someone with impressive access to information as the FBI and Secret Service hadn't exactly broadcasted her identity to the press. Other hospital employees knew, though, so it wasn't as if a determined person couldn't have gotten the information somehow. Still, whoever had rigged her house had to have moved fast. She hadn't even finished a complete eight-hour shift.

The area in the center of his back itched in warning.

The whole thing just didn't fit together. There was something he was missing.

But what?

He listened for the sound of her breathing, trying to gauge if she'd fallen asleep. She certainly needed to rest.

A muffled thud from outside made him tense. A car door? Made sense. It wasn't as if they had the whole hotel to themselves. He waited a few moments, then relaxed back in his seat.

How much longer? A few hours, maybe less, and he'd call Jordan. He peered at his watch but couldn't read the dial in the dark. Rising to his feet, he stretched life into his stiff muscles, then meandered toward the window overlooking the parking lot of the hotel.

After pushing aside one corner of the heavily lined curtain, he glanced outside. Bright lights illuminated the parking lot. There couldn't be more than a half dozen cars scattered about.

The barest hint of a shadow in the form of a silhouette grew on the concrete surface in front of his window. With a frown, Sloan eased back and reached down for the mini-Glock he carried in his ankle holster. He was still annoyed at how his regular firearm, along with dozens of other agent's weapons, had been confiscated by the FBI after Korolev had been shot to verify they hadn't been fired.

He strained to listen but couldn't hear the normal sounds of someone entering their key into a door.

His pulse kicked up a notch. He couldn't believe anyone had tailed them here, not without him noticing. Unless he was seriously losing his touch. Which, given his current track record, was definitely possible. Moving the curtain just a hair, he peered out.

The shadow was gone.

A chill seeped through his gut. He slid over to the far side of the bed, placed a hand on Natalia's shoulder, and bent low to whisper in her ear.

"Get up. Someone's outside."

For once he didn't have to convince her to listen. She bolted upright, her eyes wide, and when he put a finger over his lips, she didn't utter a sound. She crawled from the bed, then shoved her feet into her nursing shoes. She grabbed her bag, slinging it over her shoulder. He led the way across the room, keeping her tucked safely behind him, making sure he gave the window a wide berth as he crept up alongside the hotel room door.

They had barely gotten situated when the door burst open. Soft poofing sounds, along with the harsh scent of cordite, filled the air as the gunman pounded a round of bullets into the lumpy covers on the bed.

What in the world? Sloan held his breath and waited a heartbeat for the intruder to advance past the door. His patience paid off. The minute his target was in view, he lifted his gun and brought it down hard on the base of the guy's skull with all the force he possessed.

The intruder went down like a rock and didn't move.

The guy had a fancy cross tattoo on the back of his neck and a strange-looking gun. Instantly curious, he stepped closer to see them. A low anguished sound escaped from Natalia.

Sloan turned toward her, abandoning the dead gunman. Her safety was his first priority. Keeping a firm hand on her arm, he hesitated. One man was down, but how many others waited outside? With the well-lit parking lot, they'd be in plain view if they tried to leave.

He imagined the layout of the vehicles in the parking lot. The closest car was about five yards away. He'd chance it himself, but with Natalia? The thought of risking her life made his stomach roll.

The seconds stretched into a minute, making him feel like a rat caught in a trap. He couldn't wait forever. There was no other way out of the hotel room. It was time to make their move.

"We're going to run toward the blue truck parked in the first row. Keep your head down and stay behind me."

He could hear her breathing now, shallow quick breaths that were going to make her pass out if she didn't get a grip. She gave a jerky nod. He took a deep breath.

"Now."

In a low crouch, they came out from behind the hotel room door and ran across the sidewalk to the brightly lit parking lot. Sloan positioned himself behind her, expecting to feel the blazing pain of a bullet hitting its mark, but somehow they managed to reach the side of the blue truck without an ounce of bloodshed.

He sat with his back against the truck's passenger door, planning their next move. His car wasn't far, but if they'd been followed, using his car again was just plain stupid. Yet he wanted to get as far as possible from the dead guy. Stealing a car here, with potential assassins nearby, was just as idiotic and would take far too much time.

"Our car is just down a few cars to the left." He spoke in a low voice, his mouth near her ear. "Can you make it?"

"Yes."

Sloan nodded. She was holding up far better than he had a right to expect. "Follow me." Using the cars as cover, he made his way to the nondescript Chevy he drove.

There wasn't time to do more than a cursory search for

hidden bombs. After making sure Natalia had gotten safely in, he slid into the driver's seat. Slouching, he gingerly started the car. The engine turned over easily. Nothing happened. A gazillion men armed with automatic weapons didn't rush at them like crazed warriors. The car didn't explode in a burst of fire.

So far, so good. He floored the accelerator, peeling out of the parking lot, sacrificing silence for speed.

No one followed.

He couldn't relax his guard. The silent yet deadly attack had the taste and smell of a professional hit. He wished he'd gotten a closer look at the tattoo. And the gun the guy used was not your average weapon. As a former agent, he'd seen the whole gamut of usual Saturday night specials. Was the gunman working on his own? If the guy was a pro, and Sloan suspected he was, it was unusual that he'd underestimated his quarry.

Unless he'd expected to find Natalia in the room alone. Hadn't they known he was with her? Where on earth were they getting their information? Granted, he hadn't used a credit card, not even his business one. And the only one who knew he was with Natalia was Jordan. Thankfully, he could trust Jordan.

He straightened in his seat. Maybe they hadn't followed him from Rasacovich's house at all. Maybe they'd only tagged Natalia. He slid a glance toward her.

She sat like a shell-shocked war victim in the seat beside him, clutching her bag to her chest, her green eyes bruised and dark in her face. He felt a momentary loss for the way her innocence had been stripped by the nearly successful attempt on her life.

Frankly, on both of their lives.

His gaze zeroed in on the canvas bag half tucked under

her arm between them. His brief flash of kindness vanished. He snatched the bag from her grip.

"What in the world do you have in there?"

JULY 1 – 5:16 a.m. – Washington, DC

SHE GRABBED INSTINCTIVELY for her bag, irritated with him. "What's wrong with you?"

"What did you do, Princess?" He drove one-handed, rummaging through the bag with the other. "Did you call someone? Tell them where we were staying?"

"No!" But her denial fell flat when he triumphantly picked up her phone. He scrolled through looking for the most recent outgoing number. With a sense of dread, she tried to explain. "I didn't speak to anyone. I left a message for my father, asking him to call me back, but I never said where I was staying."

Sloan's expression turned grim. He opened his window and tossed the phone out. It shattered into millions of pieces on the side of the road.

She gasped. "*Durachok.* Are you crazy? Why did you do that?"

"Phones have built-in GPS tracking devices." His hard voice betrayed his anger. "Turning your phone on to call your father almost got us killed."

"I don't believe this." Her hands began to shake, and she linked them together in an effort to gain control.

"You'd better believe someone is trying to kill you." He continued poking through her things. He pulled out her canister of pepper spray and frowned. "Don't you know this stuff is illegal?"

"Yes." And it wouldn't have done any good against a man with a silent gun. A shiver rippled along her arms, and she rubbed her hands over them. The horror replayed over and over in her mind. Sloan knocked a man out cold. That alone was bad enough. But he had done it for her. To keep her safe. If not for Sloan, she'd be dead.

The knowledge slammed against the center of her forehead like a brick. Her empty stomach heaved, and she swallowed hard to prevent herself from throwing up.

He'd saved her life. It galled her to admit he was right. Someone actually wanted her dead. If the gunman had found them behind the door, she didn't doubt he would have killed them.

God was looking out for her. For them.

Sloan grunted and stuck the can back inside, then tossed the bag at her. "Anything else I need to know about?"

Numb and shaking, she shook her head. "No."

Sloan pulled out his cell phone, put the battery back in one-handed, and then pushed a button.

"You're using your phone," she accused.

"Because I'm not the target, Princess. You are." His dark brows pulled into a frown as he listened, then spoke tersely, "Jordan, call me as soon as you get this message." He snapped his phone shut.

"How do I know that man wasn't after you? Maybe he recognized your car in the parking lot." Natalia knew she was being ridiculously stubborn, but she was tired and hungry and wanted to go home. Except she didn't have a home, not anymore. Better to be mad and stubborn than depressed. "Maybe he traced the GPS on your cell phone. This could all be related to your stupid security business. My life didn't turn upside down until after I met you." Actually, that wasn't exactly true. Her life had spiraled out of control when she'd been assigned to take care of Josef Korolev.

"I didn't have my phone on in the hotel room. I take the battery out just to avoid being tracked the way you were." He scowled and clipped the phone back on his belt.

She wished very much she didn't believe him. But she did. "So you claim some man just went online into a computer program, pushed a button, and traced us to the hotel from the single call I made to my father?"

He slid a glance at her. "Yeah, pretty much, although usually they'd need to know the serial number." He paused, then frowned. "Was that a new phone? Or did you get it from someone?"

"No. I've had that phone for more than two years."

Sloan relaxed. "Then I would say only a person with the technical resources to get your phone's serial number could have pulled this off."

She shivered and swallowed hard. The deliberate way the man dressed totally in black had burst through the hotel room door and pierced the mattress with gunfire was seared into her brain. Whoever had opened the door had intended to kill her. She slammed a door on the image and tried to think rationally. "Strong technical resources. Like the FBI?"

His brows rose. "The Feds have the resources, but sending a hired gun to blow a suspect away isn't quite their style. They tend to operate on the right side of the law."

Once she would have agreed, but Natalia didn't know what to think anymore. Nothing made sense. Not her house blowing up. Not Ivan's brutal murder. Not the stealthy attempt to kill her in the hotel room. Chilled, she rubbed her hands over her arms. "No? Then why did Josef Korolev tell me someone in the FBI shot him?"

. . .

JULY 1 – 5:38 *a.m.* – *Washington, DC*

SLOAN STARED at her for several long seconds. She managed to surprise him. Again. And he hated surprises. He pinned her with a narrow gaze. "He told you that?"

Natalia massaged her scalp with one hand and nodded. "Yes. I'd been speaking to him in Russian since he came back from surgery. I took his breathing tube out and gave him an ice chip for his throat. Then, as I was about to hang another unit of blood, he told me he saw who shot him." She swallowed hard. "Then he went on to say it was an FBI agent."

So Korolev had talked to her after all. He didn't feel a surge of satisfaction at the knowledge. Instead, his stomach knotted. This mess was far worse than what he'd originally thought. The deputy prime minister's speech had contained the usual drivel about Middle East peace, but nothing worth getting shot over, even if the US didn't appreciate Russia's interference. Still, he'd heard the rumors just like everyone else had, about sanctioned assassinations by the CIA. But never here, on US soil. A stunt like that would take more guts than anyone in the CIA possessed. "Who did you report the information to?"

Her eyes widened. "No one. I didn't think it would help to tell the FBI."

"Someone must have overheard him talking to you." Sloan hit the brakes as early morning DC traffic was already clogging the city streets. Jordan still hadn't returned his call. What was he supposed to do with the princess in the meantime if the guy didn't return his phone calls?

"No one overheard." She sounded certain. "I was alone in the room, and he spoke in Russian. Even if the agent outside the room had heard, he wouldn't have understood what Josef said. Besides, a few minutes after Josef told me the FBI shot him, you and your two FBI friends came into the room."

Saunders, his former boss, and Bentley, the guy who'd hired them to protect Korolev, weren't exactly his friends, but he didn't argue. "What about Korolev's countrymen?" The two solemn-faced guys he'd dubbed Tweedledee and Tweedledum had been Korolev's shadow throughout the early afternoon speech at The Washington Center. "They must have been in the room."

But she shook her head. "No. They were out in the hallway as well, arranging transportation home once Josef was stable enough."

Sloan frowned. Actually, now that she mentioned it, he didn't remember seeing them in the room. Hard to believe they'd actually left her alone with their precious deputy prime minister, but they must have. Then a little over an hour later, the guy ends up dead. Was he overreacting here? This couldn't possibly be a sanctioned assassination. Besides, he couldn't imagine anyone in the CIA planning to kill Natalia, even if they believed she knew more than she should. If the CIA or the FBI had been involved, they wouldn't have sent only one hit man after her in the motel room. They would have sent a team to take her out.

No, he didn't buy it. No point in making this fiasco more complicated than it needed to be. Did the Russians blame Natalia for Korolev's demise? Did they have the technical and personnel resources here in DC to pull this off? He didn't know.

He rubbed a hand over his gritty eyes. He needed food. Coffee. A safe place to pass the princess off to Jordan. He drove past a pancake house and slowed down. "Are you hungry?"

"Not really."

Yeah, she looked a little pale and green, not that he could blame her. But driving in this parking lot that passed as a road was giving him heartburn. He cranked the wheel on a hard right, keeping an eye on his charge to make sure she didn't try another Houdini escape stunt.

There were dark circles beneath her eyes, marring her porcelain skin. Natalia stared straight ahead, her gaze blank, as if she didn't have an ounce of fight left inside her. He wrestled against the stupid urge to draw her into his arms.

He pulled his phone off his belt and glared at the screen. Nope, he hadn't somehow missed Jordan's call. With a groan, he slid the phone back onto his belt and made his way around the block to the pancake house.

"Come on." He threw the car into park and turned off the engine. "Let's get something to eat."

She walked inside, a carefully blank expression on her face, looking like something out of *The Stepford Wives*. He followed close behind, guarding her back. He sent a wary glance around the room, expecting the worst, but the area was filled with ordinary people eating breakfast on a Thursday morning.

He felt as if he was losing it. The close call in the hotel room had rattled him, badly. He'd nearly failed again. The bitter knowledge had him grinding his teeth in frustration. A hostess came to seat them, and he directed her to a corner booth, as far from the rest of the restaurant patrons as possible.

Natalia sat like a lump of Play-Doh while the waitress brought water and menus. Once the woman left them alone, he reached over and waved his hand past her face.

"Hey, Princess. What do you want to eat?"

His attempt to rile her up worked. Her green eyes flashed and then narrowed. "Don't call me that."

He couldn't help but grin. Having her snap at him was better than having her look so lost and forlorn. "What? Princess? Why not?"

"Idiot." She shook her head and glanced at the menu. "Coffee. Toast. No eggs. I hate eggs."

"Duly noted. Her highness doesn't like eggs."

She scowled as he signaled for the waitress.

"So now what?" Natalia asked as she sipped her coffee and stared at him over the rim. "Where do we go from here?"

Good question. Sloan wished he had just as good of an answer. He didn't. "As soon as I get in touch with Jordan, we'll get you someplace safe," he hedged.

"Why do you keep trying to pawn me off on this Jordan?" Natalia carefully set her coffee down and leaned her forearms on the cheap Formica table. "I have the distinct impression you resent the job of protecting me."

Bingo. Give the princess a prize. "Jordan is my partner. He's former FBI too. He's very good at what he does. You'll be safe in his hands."

She arched one slim eyebrow. "Really? And what's wrong with your hands?"

He glanced at his hands, seeing old blood stains from his past failures. He gave himself a mental shake. "Nothing. Playing bodyguard isn't my area of expertise." And wasn't that the understatement of the year?

"What is your area of expertise? Other than speaking Ukrainian, that is?" The smirk that tugged at the corner of her mouth gave her a regal air. He itched to kiss it away.

"Investigations." He didn't owe this woman an explanation. Especially not his not-so-secret obsession with the group responsible for killing his sister, Shari, as a way to get to him. Their food arrived and he dug in, suddenly starving.

"So, you'll investigate Josef's shooting?" She played with her toast.

Her question forced him to meet her gaze. "His death, your house, your friend's death, and the attempt on your life. Yeah, I think they're all connected, and I'm going to investigate each and every one of them." Not that he had any official, legal grounds to do any such thing, but he couldn't walk away. There was something rotten beneath the carnage trailing in Natalia's wake. And despite everything he'd lost in the past year, he still possessed a strong sense of justice.

Innocent people had died.

Someone had to pay.

"Good." Her smile was grim. "Then there's no need to call Jordan. I'll investigate with you."

No way. Uh-uh. Over his stone-cold, dead body. Sloan refrained from speaking his thoughts out loud. A newspaper lying on a nearby table caught his eye, and he reached out to snag it. Not surprising to discover the shooting of the Russian deputy prime minister had made the headline news.

"What does it say?" Natalia leaned forward as if she could read the text upside down.

Ignoring her, he scanned the article. There wasn't much he didn't already know, having been on the scene when Korolev went down, but a reference to a man named Alek Nevsky had him sitting straighter in his chair.

"Tell me." She was doing it again, using that snooty tone of hers. "What does it say?"

"They have a suspect in custody." Sloan felt a measure

of relief at the news. He folded the newspaper and handed it to her across the table so she could read the story for herself. "And it's not the FBI. They believe the shooter has ties to a well-known faction of the Russian mob. Some guy by the name of Alek Nevsky."

CHAPTER FIVE

July 1 – 7:52 a.m. – Washington, DC

NATALIA FROZE. Alek Nevsky? No, it couldn't be. Toast slipped from her fingers and dropped unheeded to her plate.

"Let me see that." Dread unfurled in her stomach as Natalia snatched the paper to read the article for herself. Impossible for Alek Nevsky to be involved in something so horrible. Yet there was his name printed clearly in small, black letters.

Alek Nevsky. Her uncle. Unless there were two men with the same name living in DC? No, she couldn't make herself believe it.

"What's the matter?" Sloan's gaze raked her face. "You look sick."

"Nothing." She did feel as if she might throw up, but she schooled her features not to show a hint of emotion as she lowered the newspaper to the table. "I think this answer is too pat. Too easy."

"Really." Sloan arched a sardonic brow. "What, you don't believe the Russian Mafia is as evil as they claim? Trust me when I tell you they are." His expression turned dark. "I should know."

Nausea surged, and she swallowed hard. Beneath the cover of the table, she pressed a hand over her stomach as if to keep everything inside by will alone. "Of course, I'm aware of how dangerous the Russian Mafia is. I read the newspaper and listen to the news, just like you."

He stared at her for a long moment, then rose to his feet. Digging into his pocket, he pulled out a wad of cash, then tossed it onto the table to cover the tab. "Come on, let's get out of here."

Praying her face remained outwardly calm, she followed him outside. Once settled in the passenger seat, she stared out the window in a daze, her thoughts whirling.

Alek Nevsky was suspected of shooting the deputy prime minister. He was also supposedly linked to the Russian mob. Should she mention the family tie to Sloan? No, he would only think she was guilty by association. Then, what should she do?

Nothing. Alek wasn't really her uncle, was technically her adopted mother's cousin. But for all those years Natalia had referred to him as *dyadya*, uncle. He and his wife, Lara, had comforted her at her mother's funeral. Had attended her engagement party before she'd caught her cheating fiancé kissing her former best friend. Alek was always laughing and making jokes. He was her link to her homeland, the kind and gentle part of Russia that she wanted to think still existed. She simply couldn't believe he was part of the Russian Mafia.

Going to the police was out of the question now. They'd

take one look at her relationship with Alek and condemn her.

Thankfully, she had Sloan. The landscape out her window began to change. They were heading south toward Alexandria. She turned toward him with a frown. "Where are you taking me?"

"We're going to stop at my place to pick up a few things." He glanced at her. "Mainly cash. I don't want to use any credit cards or ATM machines."

She was surprised by his answer. "You think it's safe?"

He lifted one shoulder. "I don't see why not. I haven't noticed anyone following us. If a faction of the Russian Mafia is the guilty party, they haven't tagged my car. In fact, they wouldn't likely know about my involvement with you at all."

It bothered her how he chose to believe the Russian Mafia over Josef's own claim that the FBI was responsible for his shooting. The more she thought about it, the more suspicious she became. Uncle Alek couldn't possibly be guilty of murder. She sent Sloan a haughty glare. "The reporter is lying. Why on earth would any faction of the Russian Mafia kill someone from their own country here in the US? Josef was the deputy prime minister of Russia."

"They're always going after their own countrymen, especially those who threaten to put a lid on their extortion efforts." He quirked a sardonic brow. "Trust me, they'd kill their own mother to make a point. For all we know, they killed him because Korolev joined forces with the Feds, especially now that the FBI has opened a branch in Moscow."

His contempt for the country of her birth grated on her nerves, although she had to admit his theory was possible. But then why did Josef say someone from the FBI was out to kill him? "Do you think the Russian Mafia could have infiltrated the government?"

"The Russian government? Yeah. I do. There are many factions of the Russian Mafia, although only two of the groups, the Dolgopruadnanskaya and the Solntsevskaya, pose any significant threat. During my time with the FBI, we suspected most KGB agents had transitioned into members of the mob. So yeah, the Russian government is fighting a losing battle, in my opinion."

She narrowed her gaze. He seemed to know a fair amount about the Russian Mafia. Given his Ukrainian background, she wondered if that had been his area of expertise. If so, it explained why he'd been hired to help protect Josef. "Not the Russian government," she clarified. "Ours. The FBI."

He shrugged, but his expression was one of skepticism. "Anything's possible, I guess. But it's not likely."

"Why not?" She latched onto the idea and refused to let go. "It would certainly explain a lot."

"Like what?" Now, he was irritated. "There's always the chance of an agent going bad, but maintaining secret connections with either of the Russian Mafia groups would be hard to hide."

His faith in his former employer was touching, but Natalia wasn't so sure she agreed. At least, not anymore. After everything that had happened, she thought Josef was right. He'd seemed so certain. His eyes hadn't been foggy from the drugs, they had been clear and intense. She touched the pendant hanging around her neck nestled against her cross. Why had he gotten so agitated when he saw it?

"Since 9/11, the main focus for the FBI and the Department of Homeland Security has been terrorism." Sloan tapped his fingers along the steering wheel as if he was thinking out loud. "The two strongest factions of the Russian Mafia have gotten more involved in money laundering scams, illegal arms dealing, prostitution, and drug running, mostly abroad. We knew they'd targeted Israel, investing billions of dollars in the economy there to have easy access to terrorist groups." His fingers continued to tap the steering wheel. "Although the Solntsevskaya group has expanded into New York, the FBI arrested Radoejev, the man believed to be in charge. There hasn't been a significant infiltration in DC, at least, not that we know about."

"But it's a possibility." Now that he'd talked through the theory, she could easily see it. Why wouldn't they try to expand into DC, right under the Fed's noses? Josef could have been shot by some rogue FBI agent who was trying to cover up his crime by pinning the deed on Alek.

Poor Uncle Alek.

Thank heavens her mother wasn't alive to see this.

He clenched his jaw. "Yeah, I already admitted that much. You could be right; someone inside the bureau might be working with either faction of the Russian Mafia. Anything goes when lots of money is involved."

Of course, she was right. Satisfied, she turned her back on him. Outside, normal traffic surrounded them. In the bright light of day, with the hardworking people of DC going about their business, her fear and panic from the night was difficult to hang on to, even with all the talk of Russian thugs. The men and women driving to work and the families sightseeing seemed so ordinary. Looking at the familiarity of it all, it was hard to believe the horrible events had really happened.

"A shopping center!" She pressed her nose against the window, never had she been so happy to see a discount store in her life. Toothpaste. She wanted toothpaste and a comb. Clothes. "Pull in, I can't stand the thought of wearing these filthy scrubs for another minute."

"Princesses don't shop at discount stores."

She sent him a lethal glare over her shoulder. "I told you not to call me that."

A wry smile twisted his lips. "I don't think stopping for clothes is a good idea. I have some stuff at my place that should fit you."

He did? She sniffed. From one of his many women friends, no doubt. She imagined he had dozens of females in his life. Too handsome for his own good. She knew his type only too well. Hadn't she almost married one?

"Just a few minutes, that's all I need." Begging was not her style, but at the moment she felt desperate. "Please."

"Nope. No can do." He made a series of turns before pulling up in front of a small condo complex.

"Come on." He parked illegally, along the curve of the main drive. As they went inside, she assumed being a former FBI agent came with certain privileges.

Focusing on Sloan was easier than thinking about the tangled mess she'd found herself in, so she glanced curiously over his shoulder as he unlocked his door. He gestured for her to go in, closing the door behind them. The condo was small, but clean for the most part. A few dishes in the sink.

He disappeared into the bedroom, and she cast a glance about the room, curious to know more about the enigmatic man who'd saved her life.

One photograph sat on top of the television. A wedding picture. Sloan was married. The sinking feeling in her stomach betrayed her keen disappointment as she moved closer. She frowned. The couple didn't look at all familiar. The man smiling into the camera, with his jet-black hair and dark skin, certainly wasn't Sloan. The woman shared Sloan's mink brown hair. Could she be a relative?

Ridiculous to feel such an overwhelming relief. She didn't care about Sloan on a personal level, except to be grateful for the way he'd saved her life in the hotel. She wouldn't even go as far as to call him a friend.

Even if he did make her crazy and spoke with a bad Ukrainian accent.

"Here's a box of stuff." He returned to the living room carrying a box, dropping it carelessly on the floor. A fine layer of dust rose from it, making her sneeze. The box and its contents must have been in storage for a while.

She opened the top flap. "Woman's clothes?"

His jaw tightened. "Yeah."

"From your ex-wife?" She couldn't help fishing for information.

"My sister." He turned toward the door, then hesitated and swung back, pinning her with an intent gaze. "If you want to know if I'm married, just ask."

She'd rather bite out her own tongue than admit she'd wanted to know. But a sister explained the woman in the wedding picture. She angled her chin. "I don't care if you are or not. I was only trying to make casual conversation."

"Yeah. Right." He reached for his cell phone. "Stay here. I need to make a few calls."

"Wait!" She abandoned the box, dashing across the room toward him. "You can't just leave me here."

He lifted an arrogant brow. "Sure I can. I won't be long."

"But—" She couldn't think of a good reason not to let him go. Other than the simple fact that she didn't want him to. In the short time they'd been together, she'd grown dependent on his reassuring presence, which only fueled a stab of anger. She didn't want to be dependent on him or anyone. She didn't appreciate the way he barked out orders either.

"Ten minutes," he repeated. He swung open the door and then glanced back over his shoulder, adding, "And, Princess? For the record, I've never been married."

"*Shtob tebya*. Because no one is crazy enough to marry a man like you." Her insult fell on deaf ears as he'd slammed the door behind him before she had time to finish speaking.

Men. She'd learned the hard way they couldn't be trusted. No matter how they whispered sweet words of love, as soon as a younger, prettier specimen came into view, they vanished quicker than a silverfish.

Better to stay single.

The condo seemed unnaturally quiet. Not even the ticking of an alarm clock or the humming noise of the refrigerator broke the silence. Natalia rubbed her hands up and down her arms feeling ridiculously nervous. There was no reason to be afraid. Whatever else she thought of Sloan, she truly believed he'd brought her here because it was safe.

She forced herself to turn back toward the box. Digging out the clothes, she found a few basic things, two pairs of blue jeans and a couple of short-sleeved tops. She wanted to wear the hot pink one, but since they were on the run, she figured the black one might be better.

She disappeared into the bathroom to change. Sloan's scent filled the enclosure. Or rather, the remnants of his soap did. The musky scent intrigued her. After pulling on the borrowed clothes, she pushed aside the shower curtain to see what brand of soap he bought. Not that she was an expert on men's toiletries. She lifted the bar and sniffed. Immediately, she felt her knees go weak. Oh yes, the scent was definitely from the soap.

Stop it. There was no time for foolish sentiments. She didn't even like the man and refused to be attracted to him. She replaced the soap with a firm thud, then picked up her discarded scrubs and left the bathroom.

Five minutes had passed since Sloan left her alone. Why did it seem like fifty? Why did he have to go outside to make his calls anyway? Just to keep her in the dark about what he planned next? No more leaving her out of the loop. Maybe she wasn't an expert when it came to the dangerous factions of the Russian Mafia, but as far as she was concerned, they were in this mess together.

With a scowl, she glanced at his tiny office and the laptop computer sitting there. Fingering her Russian pendant, she wondered if there was any information about it on the internet. Josef had recognized it. Was there some hidden meaning to the symbol of the crescent moon and the three stars with the purple stones in the center? Or could she find the store from where the necklace originated from? The burning need to know about her past wouldn't leave her alone. She needed to find out about her birth mother and the events that caused her mother to give her away.

Natalia strode to the computer desk and sat down. It was probably password protected. Good thing she knew how to work around that pesky little detail. Ivan had taught her well. After turning on the computer, she entered the inner workings of the operating system, then brought up the software.

Her fingers hovered over the commands, more tempted than she cared to admit to snoop through Sloan's personal files. She didn't have much time, though, if Sloan was going to be back in ten minutes, so she quickly bypassed his files in favor of accessing the internet.

With any luck, she could be in and out before Sloan returned.

JULY 1 – 10:19 a.m. – Washington, DC

SLOAN RUBBED a hand along the back of his neck as he walked down to the main lobby of the building. There had been no reason to leave Natalia alone in his condo other than he couldn't stand one more minute of togetherness.

He punched the speed dial for Jordan's number for the millionth time. When Jordan picked up, he almost fell on his butt in shock.

"It's about time you answered my call," Sloan roared. "Took you long enough."

"I've been busy." Ever the rational one, Jordan's tone was serene.

Busy? Was he kidding? He and Natalia had been tripping over dead bodies and dodging bullets for the past couple of hours. Jordan's concept of busy was sure different from his.

"I've been on the phone with my contact at the bureau all morning," Jordan continued as if Sloan's simmering temper didn't mirror that of a raving lunatic.

Sloan jammed his fingers through his hair as he paced the length of the lobby. He struggled to remain calm. "Okay. Fine. What did Bentley have to say?" Jerome Bentley was his and Jordan's source of inside information since they'd both left the agency. Jerome was a good guy, one of the best in the business.

"They're looking for Natalia."

He stopped cold. "Why?"

"Officially? Or unofficially?" Jordan asked in a cynical drawl. "Officially, they have a few questions about last night, both Korolev's death and her rather untimely house explosion."

"And unofficially?"

"They think she's a potential link to the Solntsevskaya branch of the Russian mob."

Ice coalesced in his veins. "Why exactly do they suspect that?"

"I don't know. She's Russian by birth, adopted by a Russian-born woman with dual citizenship in America. Is that enough? Maybe. They're digging for more."

The thought of Natalia having connections to anything as dangerous as the Russian Mafia left a vile taste in his mouth. Every instinct he possessed screamed she was nothing more than a pawn in a dangerous game. Collateral damage. In the wrong place at the wrong time.

Expendable.

But then again, what did he really know about her? The bit of intel Jordan had sent him last night was sketchy but squeaky clean. Or so he'd thought. What would the FBI find when they dug deeper?

"Do they suspect Ivan Rasacovich too?" he forced himself to ask.

"Yeah. They're pretty much linking his death to the mob as well. The friendship between Rasacovich and Natalia isn't helping her case any."

Even if Rasacovich had been guilty of being involved in the Russian Mafia, he doubted Natalia knew anything about it. Still, he didn't need this added twist. "Does Bentley know she's with me?"

"I had to give him something. I told him you'd taken her

into protective custody. I promised him a face-to-face with her soon."

No way would he allow that to happen. Sloan resumed pacing. He had to let Jordan know what they were dealing with. "There was another attempt on her life at the motel room last night." He glanced at his watch. "Rather, this morning."

"Professional?"

"Yes, but it was strange. The single shooter had a strange-looking gun, two pieces, one part worn over the shoulder. The weapon had a silencer and shot multiple rounds in a split second."

"A Russian APB with a silencer." Jordan whistled. "He was working alone?"

"Yeah." A Russian APB with a silencer? Now he really wished he'd taken the few extra minutes to snag the gun. "He had a cross tattoo on the back of his neck, I couldn't see the whole thing, but it resembled the symbol for the Solntsevskaya gang. I left his body there with a dented skull. You'll need to take care of him, unless the locals found him first. If that's the case, you'll need to smooth things over."

Jordan let out a deep sigh. "All right. What else?"

"I need to turn Natalia over to you."

A long, heavy silence hung between them.

"Why?"

Sloan hunched his shoulders. "You know why. I can't do this. She needs to be safe."

"You've obviously managed to keep her safe enough if you're directing me to clean up your mess."

Was Jordan being deliberately obtuse? He wanted to shake some sense into him. "We've been lucky. How much longer do you think I can ride on luck?"

"I'll pull some strings on my end. What do you need? The usual?"

Cash, weapons, new cell phones, transportation, and access to information. Oh, and a headshrink. Sloan sighed. "Yeah, the usual. Only you and I are going to swap places. You can play bodyguard, and I'll pull the strings from the office."

There was another long stretch of silence. "Fine. Meet me at the cabin in four hours."

He closed his eyes in relief. "You got it." Now that he'd gotten his way, he experienced a strange sense of loss. The cabin was a small dwelling in the heart of the mountains two hours from DC. Nice, isolated, and best of all, it couldn't be traced back to either his or Jordan's names. It would be the perfect place to leave Natalia with Jordan.

Princess or not, she deserved to be safe.

And he knew, deep in his bones, he wasn't the right guy to keep her that way.

CHAPTER SIX

July 1 – 11:00 a.m. – Brookmont, MD

WITH HER HANDS smoothing the lump of clay on the potter's wheel, Lara Nevsky tried to ignore the phone, no doubt a telemarketer. But even once it stopped ringing, she couldn't concentrate. The tall, slender vase she'd been shaping lurched sideways, and she muttered under her breath. Always, it had been like this, in the months since she'd left Alek. Her passion for clay, for sculpting, had seemingly abandoned her.

His fault. He'd ruined their wonderful marriage. And now he'd ruined her one true love, sculpting.

The phone rang again, and she gave up, stopped the wheel, and wiped her hands on the towel before picking it up.

"Lara? Please, don't hang up. I can only make this one call. I need your help."

Recognizing Alek's voice, her spine stiffened. "One call?" she repeated. "Why?"

"I've been arrested. I need you to get in touch with our attorney, Stefan Durik."

"Arrested?" Despite her desire to stay far from Alek, away from the temptation to return to their marriage, she couldn't believe what she was hearing. "For what?"

"They think I shot Deputy Prime Minister Josef Korolev. But I didn't do this ugly thing, Lara. I promise you I did not do this. Someone planted that gun under our bed."

A gun under their bed? Lara sank into a nearby chair. "Murder?" No matter how Alek had ruined their marriage, she couldn't believe this of him. He simply wasn't capable of killing a man in cold blood. He was the sweetest, kindest man she'd ever met.

"Please, get in touch with Stefan. Tell him what happened. Tell him to get in touch with FBI Agent Michael Cummings. Please." Alek's tone was desperate.

"I will." She didn't mention she'd already been in touch with Stefan recently, to discuss the possibility of divorce. She wrote down the name of Michael Cummings. "Where are you? Will they allow visitors?"

"No!" His emphatic response shocked her. "Don't come here, Lara. Just call Stefan. *Ya lublu tebya*, Lara."

I love you. She wanted to respond in kind, but the words stuck in her throat.

"Oh, and Lara? You need to find Natalia and tell her the truth."

No. Natalia and the other tainted remnants of his past were the reasons she'd left him. She found her voice. "I can't."

"You must." She imagined the fierce expression on his face. "In case something goes wrong, Natalia needs to know the truth. The sooner the better."

She pressed a hand to her chest. Why couldn't the past

stay in the past? She didn't want to think about it. "Nothing will go wrong."

"If it's God's will," Alek agreed. "Please. Find Natalia."

Before she could open her mouth to say anything more, he disconnected from the line. She quickly searched on the counter for Stefan's number.

Stefan had to get Alek out of jail and fast. Nothing bad was going to happen to him. Nausea churned in her stomach. Everything they'd built was unraveling around them. Nothing would happen to Alek.

Nothing.

Her fingers trembled as she dialed the phone.

Ya lublu tebya, Alek.

JULY 1 – *11:08 a.m.* – *Washington, DC*

NATALIA FOUND dozens of websites with various jewelry designs, so she picked one and scrolled through it. There were many unique pendants—a Royal Crest of the Tsars, a Russian double-headed eagle, and an Etruscan Revival gold necklace for starters. Very interesting designs, but none looking even remotely close to her pendant.

Although, once again, she noticed how prevalent her purple stones were. A few years ago, she discovered the lilac-tinted gem was called charoite and was an unusual mineral named after the Chara River in Russia, the only place to obtain the stone.

Charoite was supposed to contain a healing power, helping the wearer to sleep easy without being disturbed by nightmares. It also supposedly held the power to cleanse and purify one's body as well as getting rid of negative energies within oneself.

She believed in God, not precious stones. But still, the legend was charming. She clasped the crescent mood and cross in her hand. She'd faithfully worn the pendant over these past three years, since her adopted mother had died. Had her birth mother left Natalia the necklace as a way to protect her? Her pulse raced. Imagining how her mother had given her up for a good reason, in order to save her life, made her feel better.

Surely the pendant was harmless. Why on earth would Josef ask who'd given it to her? Why would it matter? None of this made sense.

When the front door opened, she jumped around in guilty surprise.

"What are you doing?" Sloan did not appear happy to see her seated at his desk.

"Nothing that concerns you." She escaped out of the internet site she was on and quickly shut the computer off.

"I can't leave you alone for a minute, can I?" He sounded thoroughly annoyed. "Who were you sending a message to? Another friend? Your father?"

"No one." Although now that he'd mentioned it, she wished she had thought of sending her father an email message. Maybe if Sloan would let them stay here longer, there'd be time. She kept the idea to herself. Knowing Sloan would push until he knew the truth, she admitted, "I was looking at websites of Russian jewelry."

"Jewelry?" He gaped at her as if she'd been searching for sharp sticks to poke in his eyes. "Why, because you need something to match your outfit? Were you expecting to find silk in the box of clothes?"

Durachok. He was pushing this whole princess routine

a little too far. She clenched her jaw and held on to her temper, refusing to divulge personal information from her past for his entertainment. There was no need for him to know about her pendant. Or Josef's strange comment about hiding it. Or her not-so-distant family relationship to Alek Nevsky. Lifting her chin, she eased away from his computer and waved a hand toward it. "I don't care what you think. But if you don't believe me, look for yourself."

JULY 1 – 11:15 a.m. – Washington, DC

SLOAN STARED at her for a long minute. Crossing over to his computer, he booted it up. And immediately noticed she'd bypassed his password protection. He sent her a narrow glare. "Where did you learn to do that?"

Natalia raised an elegant brow and shrugged. He scowled and turned away. Seeing Natalia wearing his sister's things had sent an unpleasant shock stuttering through his system. He missed Shari. She'd been so young, so vital. And it was his fault she was dead.

He'd failed to protect her.

A mistake he wasn't going to repeat with Natalia. With deft motions, he pulled up the internet and checked the sites she had recently visited. Only one URL popped up, a site called The Russian Shop.

He couldn't believe it. The princess really had been surfing for jewelry. Was it a trick? He took a cursory glance through the various menus but didn't find anything suspicious. With a disgusted snort, he abandoned the program. "If you're finished shopping, we have to go."

"Where?" She crossed her arms over her chest, ignoring

his jibe. Her haughty tone turned him on at the same time it annoyed the hell out of him. "If we are safe here, why leave?"

"We won't be safe here forever." He did actually think his place was safe enough for the moment, but he wasn't about to invite her to stay with him indefinitely. Then he'd never get rid of her.

"I'm not moving an inch until you tell me where we're going."

Her mouth thinned in a stubborn line, and he had to glance away or give in to the temptation to steal a kiss.

"I finally got in touch with Jordan. We're going to meet him at a cabin in the mountains."

Sloan couldn't wait to hand the princess off to his partner. Four more hours.

He should be able to do anything for four hours.

"Come on." He crossed over to the door. "Let's go."

"Wait." She hung back. "Can't we take a few things with us? A comb or a brush? Toothpaste? A few clothes?"

This wasn't a vacation outing, but he knew she didn't have anything but the bag she carried like a shield. With a sigh, he turned back toward his bedroom. "Get some stuff out of the bathroom; there should be spare items in the closet. I'll grab a duffel bag."

"Thank you."

Her obvious gratitude was so unprincess-like, he slowed and glanced back at her. But she'd disappeared into his bathroom. There really was something wrong with him if he preferred her haughty tone to quiet acceptance. Shaking his head, he quickly found the duffel he used for going to the gym, emptied the dirty clothes onto the bed, then stuck a spare T-shirt inside for himself before heading back into the living room.

While he waited for Natalia, he used his computer to see if he could dig up any information on Alek Nevsky. Sloan's pulse jumped at the possibility the guy was part of the Solntsevskaya gang. The same gang that was responsible for Shari's death. His fingers shook a bit as he punched the keys to bring up the information the FBI had compiled on the guy. He still had some access, with permission of course. He printed the information, frowning when he noticed there wasn't much.

When Natalia came back into the living room, he gestured to the open bag. She piled in the various items she'd found in his bathroom, then added her canvas bag too. When she lifted the duffel, he hauled it out of her hands.

"I'll carry it." He stuffed in the few sheets of paper, along with his laptop, then slung the duffel over his shoulder. Princess or not, he couldn't stand to watch her lug the thing around.

"Fine." For a minute, the stubborn glint was back in her eye, and he found himself smiling.

"What did you print from the computer?" She glanced at the displayed page on the screen to the duffel he carried.

"Information on our suspect, Alek Nevsky." Sloan strode toward the door, impatient.

"Can I see it?"

"I'll show you later. Let's go."

She scowled but allowed him to precede her out of his condo.

They didn't speak as they rode the elevator down to the first floor. Outside, large puffy clouds temporarily obliterated the sun. Sloan glanced around but didn't see anything out of the ordinary. He waited for Natalia to move down toward his car before stepping behind her. There wasn't much he could do to protect her, but he was more than willing to give up his life if need be.

He would have done the same for his sister too. Gladly. He'd been the one investigating the Solntseskaya. He should have been the one who died, not Shari.

"This place you're taking me, how far is it?" Natalia asked, breaking into his pensive thoughts. He opened the passenger door and glanced down at her.

"A couple of hours, maybe more depending on traffic." He leaned forward to set the duffel bag on the floor of the front seat.

"Thank you." She eased into the car. Something whizzed past his head in the same split second she bent over to unzip the top of the duffel.

A small, round hole gaped at him from the cushioned seat.

"Get down!" He shoved her head toward the floor, then clamored right over her. "Grab the door," he shouted. He smacked his knees against the steering wheel as he slid into the driver's seat. Jamming the key into the ignition, he cranked the engine. Without even looking for oncoming traffic, he floored the gas pedal and peeled away from the curb.

"That was too close." His hands were shaking as he held on to the steering wheel. He kept an eye glued to the rearview mirror but couldn't identify anyone following them. Still, he knew he'd have to dump the car, and soon.

Natalia remained hunched over, hugging the bag at her feet.

"I think you can get up now." Sloan figured he'd get an earful about how he'd nearly gotten her killed. Again. He couldn't blame her. When would he learn? Jordan better meet them at the cabin and soon. Before he managed to screw up even more. "The shooter must have been on the roof or in one of the empty condos."

"I can't." The words were muffled, and she didn't move.

With a frown, he reached over to grasp her shoulder. "What do you mean you can't? Are you sick? Are you going to throw up?"

"No. I'm bleeding."

CHAPTER SEVEN

July 1 – 11:41 a.m. – Washington, DC

SHE WAS HIT? Where? In his haste to reach for her, Sloan nearly rammed into the car in front of him. He was torn between concern over Natalia and putting as much distance as possible from the shooter. He grasped her shoulder, tried to tug her upright. "Show me! Where are you bleeding?"

Slowly, as if she were in extreme pain, she turned toward him and lifted her head. Blood smeared her beautiful skin, running across her cheek from a gash over her ear. Helpless fury flicked through his system.

His fault. He tried not to dwell on the fact that it was his fault.

"Get a shirt out of the bag, press it against the wound." He swerved again to avoid a braking car. A horn blared loudly as he encroached on the next lane. He swerved back into the center of his lane. Where did these idiot people learn to drive? He glanced over at her, dividing his attention between Natalia and the road. She'd found a shirt to use as a bandage, but a thin trickle of blood continued to trail down her face and into her lap. For the first time in his life, a wave of dizziness hit.

He blinked, looked away. What was wrong with him? He was no stranger to blood. Grinding his teeth together, he willed himself to snap out of it. "Are you doing okay? Please, Natalia, say something. Are you still with me?"

"I'm with you." Her voice was low, quiet. "But tone it down, would you please? There's a jackhammer in my head."

"Okay. Yeah." He wrestled his panic under control and dropped the decibel level. If she could joke, things couldn't be as bad as they looked. "Just keep talking to me so I know you're all right." Steadier now, Sloan zipped between lanes, weaving in and out of traffic trying to keep a wary eye out for both the cops and the bad guys.

Was the shooter following them? He couldn't afford to ignore the possibility. A different, untraceable car would be nice right about now. They needed a plan.

His mind went blank.

He couldn't think. He ground the heel of his hand against his forehead as if to stimulate the brain cells to function. *Think!* There wasn't enough cash in his pocket to buy a new car, and he couldn't do that anyway with Natalia bleeding all over the place. Talk about attracting attention.

Jaw tight, he peered at the vehicles behind him. None of them appeared to be following them. But that didn't mean squat. He didn't even know who was after them. If the shooter had been up inside one of the condos or even on the roof, the guy obviously had time to set up for the shot. Who even knew he had Natalia in the first place?

Jordan? No, he couldn't believe it. Jordan was one of the

few he could trust with his life. His buddy had saved his butt on more than one occasion. He thought back to their phone conversation. Jordan had told Bentley about his having Natalia. He frowned, trying to remember the exact words. Something about being on the phone with Bentley all morning and promising a face-to-face meeting with Natalia.

He and Jordan had always trusted Bentley. Was Natalia right in thinking there was a leak in the FBI? After this latest disaster, he realized she might have nailed the truth.

"You're not talking." Risking a quick glance, Sloan grew alarmed. She was resting, her eyes closed, her head on the bundled up shirt. She was too still. "Natalia. Come on, babe, wake up and talk to me."

"Babe?" One green eye opened to glare at him. "I'm not your babe. Don't ever call me babe."

"You don't like babe, you don't like princess." Relieved, he glanced back toward the road. "Geez, you're difficult to please."

"Idiot." The whispered word didn't hold the same punch as when she'd called him a stupid pig earlier, in Russian. She moaned. "Ooh, the hammers are worse."

Worse? A sign that she had a serious head injury? He wasn't a nurse. What was he supposed to do? Get her to a doctor? The ED at Washington University Hospital? No, wait. What was he thinking? They'd be sitting ducks if he did that.

He shut down his spinning thoughts. First things first. A new ride was essential if he was going to be able to move around the city without the possibility of a tail. The only person he could contact was Slammer. The scumbag owed him a favor, and if there was ever a time to ante up, it was now. Slammer could set them up to trade rides, if the guy hadn't gotten himself tossed into prison during these past few months.

Slammer had spent a fair amount of time in jail. Hence the nickname.

Still pushing through traffic, he eased up on the gas pedal and picked up his phone. Normally he didn't call Slammer with his own cell, but these were desperate times. He'd need a new phone, too, before long anyway.

"Who are you calling?" Natalia asked. He shook his head and waited for Slammer to answer.

"Yo."

"This is Dreyer. I need a favor."

"Like what?" Slammer wasn't much for small talk.

"A swap. I need a different set of wheels."

"No way. Get your own ride."

"You owe me. When you were looking at three years, I kept your butt out of jail." Sloan kept his eye trained on the road behind him. So far so good. No way was he letting Slammer off the hook. "If you don't do this for me, I swear I'll hunt you down like the slimy worm you are and toss you into the pen myself."

"I gave you info. I don't owe you jack."

"I'll hunt you down," Sloan repeated in a low, don't-mess-with-me tone. "Meet me at the corner of Fifteenth and King with a new ride in twenty minutes." He hung up, knowing that for all his protesting, Slammer had no intention of ever going back to prison.

"Not a nice part of town." Natalia's soft voice drew his gaze.

"No." His gut clenched at her pale, drawn features. "Are you all right? Do you have a doctor friend I can take you to? Or should we try the hospital?"

"No doctor friend and no hospital. Head wounds bleed a lot and look worse than they are. I'll be fine."

She wasn't fine, and they both knew it. But he had to ditch the car. Then they could stop at a store, get some medication and some bandages, or go to a clinic. There were plenty of options once they'd taken this next step.

"You have scary friends," Natalia whispered.

Slammer wasn't exactly a friend, but the guy would come through. The ride would be there. It had to be. He refused to accept defeat.

Natalia being wounded and narrowly escaping death was failure enough.

JULY 1 – 12:11 p.m. – Washington, DC

HER HEAD POUNDED with a harsh intensity she'd never before experienced. If this was how her patients felt after sustaining traumatic injuries, she'd seriously undermedicated them. Next time, she'd double the dose of morphine. Triple it.

Sloan yanked the car into a hard turn, and she winced, biting back a pathetic moan. Then he stomped on the gas pedal, making the car lurch forward.

Bile rose in her throat. She batted it down. Concussion. She no doubt had sustained a concussion. If she didn't get out of this roller-coaster ride soon, she was going to lose it all over Sloan.

"Natalia? Talk to me."

She swallowed hard and wet her lips. "Not a race car."

"Huh? Are you confused? That's it. I'm taking you to the hospital. Your head injury is worse."

"No. I'm not confused." Natalia strove to project confidence into her tone to help him understand. "You're driving like a lunatic."

"Oh. Not a race car. I get it." Sloan muttered something she didn't catch under his breath. "Sorry. We need to get to the south side of DC, fast."

Sorry? Sloan apologizing? She must look far worse than she'd realized. He actually sounded worried. About her. Unless her concussed mind was playing tricks on her. More likely, he didn't want her to die because then he'd be forced to explain to the authorities what happened.

She closed her eyes again when he stepped on the brakes. She really didn't want to go to the hospital. There wasn't much to treating a concussion besides rest and making sure her symptoms didn't get worse. She winced when Sloan made what felt like another jerky turn. Rest in a nonmoving vehicle, preferably.

Finally, after what seemed like dozens of stop-and-go movements, he pulled up and threw the gearshift into park.

"Slammer's a dead man. I'll kill him."

"What?" She lifted her head to squint through the windshield. "Why?"

"A rusty cargo van. The idiot left us an ancient, rusty cargo van. The stupid thing had better run."

"It's green." There was a liberal amount of rust on the van too, but the actual color of the paint was definitely bile green.

"Yeah." Sloan sighed. "Let's get you inside."

She didn't want to move. The mere thought almost made her cry. But Sloan had her car door open and his hand on her arm, so she forced herself to swing her legs out, then to stand.

"Easy now." Sloan braced her upright when her knees

gave out. She sensed he was about to swing her into his arms, and since being carried like a sack of potatoes would have been humiliating, she commanded her feet to move. One step, then another, until they'd reached the passenger door. She grabbed for his arms when his hands encircled her waist, although he lifted her into the seat with ease. His biceps bunched beneath her fingertips, and she was reminded of his strength when she felt at her most vulnerable.

"The duffel." She leaned back and closed her eyes. The inside of the van smelled like pizza, which only added to her nausea. She tried to breathe through her mouth.

"I'll get it. Sit tight." Sloan closed the door. At least he hadn't slammed it.

Moments later, she felt him climb into the driver's seat and heard the soft thud as he dropped the duffel bag at her feet. He searched for the keys and then started the engine. In a few minutes, they were on their way.

The car rattled like a ghost in chains. The volume of noise increased with every bump and every turn. In the midst of it all, Sloan muttered a constant commentary under his breath.

"I'll kill him. If this thing dies in the middle of the freeway, I promise he's dead meat."

She didn't respond but clutched the armrest to help keep her head centered on her shoulders. She almost felt bad for the man named Slammer. Almost. The sickening scent of pizza and the rattling beneath her feet put a serious dent in her sympathy.

"Okay, as soon as we get out of this neighborhood, I'll take you to the doctor." Sloan's warm hand on her arm made her open her eyes to glance at him. "If we go to Washington University Hospital, will they cut you a break?"

"I have insurance." She frowned, trying to figure out what he was asking. "I won't need to pay."

"No, I mean about your wound. They'll probably be able to figure out it's a gunshot wound, and ED docs need to report them to the police." Sloan scowled. "I'm afraid if your name is linked to any type of report, especially one going to the local law enforcement, the shooter will find you. I don't think we can trust anyone, except for Jordan."

Jordan again. He just wouldn't give up. "Don't take me to the hospital." Between exhaustion and throbbing pain, Natalia honestly didn't care where they went. As long as she was able to get out of this horrible cargo van, soon.

"You have a head injury." Sloan's voice was terse. "You need to be looked at. Get a CT scan or X-rays or something."

"Not a head injury. Just a concussion." She was splitting hairs, because a concussion was a head injury. But not bad enough that she was willing to risk the wrong people finding her. Sloan was right, she couldn't trust anyone.

Even his friend Jordan.

"A concussion?" Sloan's voice betrayed a note of panic. "I don't know how to treat a concussion."

"Like a headache. Except you'll need to make sure I don't get worse." Right now, the pounding in her temple was so bad she couldn't even imagine anything worse. "But you'll need to stop for bandages and extra-strength Tylenol to alternate with ibuprofen."

"I can do that." Sloan was amazingly easy to sway in his present mood. Too bad she wasn't feeling well enough to take full advantage.

Natalia cracked open her window, desperate for fresh air, falling silent. The rattling of the van didn't bother her as much anymore. Soon, Sloan stopped the car.

"I want you to stay here and wait. I won't be long."

"Okay." She closed her eyes, reveling in the silence.

He returned in record time, or so it seemed. Unless she'd lost consciousness? No, she didn't want to believe that. Still, she squinted at her watch, unsure as to how much time might have passed.

Before heading back on the road, he pulled out a small bottle of water from the bag and shook a couple of extra-strength Tylenol into his hand. He held them out to her.

She took the pills and the water gratefully. When she took a tentative sip, the water churned in her stomach, and she forced herself to take a little more. Based on the amount of blood soaking into the T-shirt, she needed to keep hydrated. Praying she wouldn't throw up, she rested her head against the back of the seat. "Thanks."

"Don't thank me." Sloan turned on the van and backed out of the parking space. "I almost got you killed."

She wanted to argue with him, but the effort was more than she could manage. But what he said wasn't true. Sloan hadn't almost gotten her killed. His quick thinking had saved them both.

He'd been right all along; someone was trying to kill her. Without Sloan, she'd probably already be dead.

Sloan was the only person she could trust.

CHAPTER EIGHT

July 1 – 3:39 p.m. – Bedford, VA

SLOAN GRIPPED the steering wheel so hard his fingers cramped. With a concentrated effort, he relaxed them one by one. He needed to hand her off to Jordan as soon as possible.

Scanning the countryside, he frowned. Nothing looked very familiar—not the town, the mountains, or any other part of the scenery. Not a single thing.

He tried to think back, to retrace the route he'd taken two years ago, the last time he'd met Jordan at the cabin. He'd taken a left at some sort of Y juncture in the road, toward Summerville. Then after about another ten miles, he'd taken a left at the dirt road marked Private Property.

There! He saw the Y a few seconds too late and had to yank the cargo van over to the left. Natalia moaned, stirred, then opened her eyes.

"Are we at the cabin?" Her husky voice added a layer to the guilt already strapped across his shoulders. If he hadn't stopped at his condo for cash, she wouldn't have been injured.

Of course, then he wouldn't have known about the inside leak either. Steep price to pay for that bit of information. He couldn't wait to more closely examine the information on Alek Nevsky he'd pulled from the FBI database. If the Solntsevskaya gang of the Russian Mafia was involved, Nevsky would be their best lead. This could be his best chance to avenge Shari's murder.

"Not yet. Another ten to fifteen minutes." He'd let Natalia rest once they'd left the city, only waking her up for a brief moment every half hour or so.

"Okay." Her eyes slid closed.

He tore his gaze from her vulnerable face and turned his attention to the road. He coaxed the van up another hill, ignoring how the rattling grew louder with each mile. The clouds overhead had gotten darker as he headed west, and the resulting gloom suited his mood perfectly. After a few miles, he found the dirt road without difficulty and maneuvered the bulky cargo van down the wooded drive.

There was no one on the road behind him. Hadn't been for the past ten to twelve miles. Even before that, cars either passed him by or turned off the road. He was certain they hadn't been followed, although he'd left his phone in his car along with the keys as a gift for Slammer. The jerk.

A good mile off the road, the cabin loomed before him. He pulled the cargo van around the back, right into the thickest part of the foliage so it wasn't easily seen from the driveway.

"Natalia." He reached over to lay a hand on her slender arm. "We're here."

"Good." She opened her eyes, blinked once. Twice. "What cabin? I only see trees."

"The cabin is behind us. Don't expect anything fancy," he warned as he swung out of the driver's seat and went around to the passenger side. He opened her door. One look at her drawn features confirmed she wasn't walking anywhere. "Put your hands around my neck."

"Hmm?" Her brow furrowed when she realized what he meant. Her lush mouth pulled into a prim line. "No. I can walk."

"Put your arms around my neck. The ground here is uneven, littered with fallen branches and rocks." While he explained, he slid one arm beneath the crook in her knees and the other behind her back, making the decision for her.

"Sloan." The way she murmured his name sent a flicker of longing unfurling deep in his belly. She'd been shot, yet here he was fantasizing about kissing her.

"Shh. I have you." He held her as if she were a fragile Waterford crystal vase as he picked his way through the debris, not willing to risk dropping her. On the small screened-in porch, however, he had to set her down so he could fish out the key.

A small animal scurried out of the way when he felt beneath the bottom step for the metal container holding the key. Within moments, he opened the cabin door and ushered Natalia inside.

"Sit over here." He steered her toward the closest kitchen chair. "I'll be right back with the supplies."

She hadn't moved by the time he'd covered the green van with tree branches and hauled the duffel bag inside. His stomach knotted. Was she worse? He honestly couldn't tell.

Pulling the bandages out of the drugstore bag, he set the packages on the counter. Moving through the cabin, he found the fuse box and hit the master switch so they'd have water and electricity.

Armed with soap, water, and bandages, he sank down next to her and pulled on the hand holding the shirt to her head. "Let me see."

She winced as he tugged the shirt out of the way. He swallowed hard when fresh blood oozed from the wound. Up close, it looked better than he'd expected. The gash was shallow but extended a good two inches long and had missed the top of her ear by a fraction of an inch.

He dabbed a clean corner of the T-shirt into the water and used it to wipe away the excess blood. She didn't make a sound as he ministered to her wound. There was blood caked in her beautiful blonde hair, but he did the best he could with the soap and water at his disposal. Then he coated the gash with the antibiotic ointment.

Bandaging the wound was tricky, considering he couldn't exactly tape gauze to her hair. He finally wrapped a long strip of thin gauze all the way around her head to keep it in place. When he was finished, she looked like the survivor of a low-budget slasher movie.

"Can you hold on for a few more minutes?" he asked, pushing away from the table. "I need to make up the bed."

Her skin was so pale he wondered just how much blood she'd lost. He hurried upstairs. Within a few minutes, he'd tossed some sheets on the bed, found an old quilt to throw on top of them, and returned downstairs.

"Water," she whispered.

He wrapped an arm around her shoulders while she drank from the cup he held to her mouth. He'd have to get some soup into her, too, but first things first. "Come on, you'd better lie down. There are two bedrooms upstairs in the loft."

When he bent to lift her into his arms, she stiffened against him. "Wait, I can walk."

"Stop fighting me, Natalia." Ignoring her protests, he held her close and headed for the stairs. "Don't I get brownie points for playing nurse and taking care of your wound?"

"Ha. Some nurse." But she relaxed against him as if he'd been carrying her around for years.

He elbowed open the door of the closest bedroom and gently placed her in the center of the queen-size bed. Looking down at her, his heart twisted. This was his fault. He hesitated and glanced at her bloodstained sweater. "Do you need help getting undressed?"

Her eyes flew open, and her hands came up to grab his. "No. I can take care of it."

He nodded and stepped back, knowing she deserved privacy but loath to leave her alone. What if she fell? Hurt herself worse?

"Natashen'ka." The endearment slipped before he could stop it, and he bent closer to press a chaste kiss on her cheek. "Rest now. I'll bring you something to eat soon."

Eyes wide, she didn't say another word, about the kiss or anything else.

He fought a lopsided grin. He'd finally rendered her speechless. He turned and walked back downstairs.

JULY 1 – 6:00 p.m. – Washington, DC

ALEK CLOSED his eyes and tried to ignore the dank, sour scent clinging to the walls surrounding the bed of his cell. He hoped Lara had called Stefan. And Natalia. The public shooting of Josef Korolev had been an act of desperation. Who could have done such a thing? He couldn't afford to ignore the tie to his country. Especially since he was being framed for the murder.

How ironic the FBI would think him guilty of murdering his childhood friend. The same FBI that had turned its back on him.

For a moment, self-pity caught him by the throat. First his wife separating from him, now this. He wished he'd never left Kazan all those years ago. Memories of how he'd grown up in Kazan, the son of a poor merchant but carefree and happy. How easy to pretend he was back there, with the sun reflecting off the water in the Bulak Canal, his house crowded between dozens of others along the bank of the river, the busy boats bringing needed goods or carting their wares away.

Kazan was a time of innocence. A good place to grow up, he thought with a pang of nostalgia. He shouldn't have been so eager to leave. But he'd had no intentions of staying amidst the merchant ranks, so as soon as he was able, he'd escaped the area of poverty.

The price of success had been high, loyalty given more so than received. Yet he couldn't completely regret the course he'd taken, the choices he'd made. The dark years, as Lara called them, were in the past, or so he'd naively thought. He and Lara had been lucky to escape, to arrive here in the United States, seeking the very precious freedom they'd longed for. Life had been good.

Until now. He opened his eyes, staring at the pocked cement ceiling above his bunk. The past had finally caught up to them, but they weren't beaten yet. Stefan would get him out of prison, and Lara would warn Natalia of the danger.

He could only pray to the dear Lord above that it wasn't too late. For Natalia. For Lara.

And for himself.

JULY 1 – 6:15 p.m. – Bedford, VA

SLOAN STIRRED THE BEEF BROTH, holding on to a vain hope that the hearty stock would help bring some color back into Natalia's cheeks. He'd checked on her every hour, torn between relief that she was sleeping and bone-rattling fear that her concussion might turn worse as a result of his misreading the signs.

Only another hour or so and Jordan should be here. Good thing, too, because he'd scoured the kitchen for food but, other than dried soup and several cans of beef stew, hadn't found much to eat.

They needed basic provisions to go along with the other high-tech supplies Jordan was bringing.

Logs crackled and popped in the fireplace, the scent of burning wood filling the cabin. He'd taken the time to clean the place up, to sweep out the mice, and to start a fire in the fireplace. Despite being summer, the mountain air was cool, and he didn't want Natalia to catch a chill.

Listen to him. Catch a chill? It had been a long time since he'd had to take care of someone. And the last time, his sister had paid the price. He stirred the soup realizing this was why he needed Jordan's rational brain here and pronto. One measly bullet wound had morphed him into a nursemaid.

He poured the broth into a bowl, added a few stale saltine crackers he'd found deep in a cupboard, and carried the meal upstairs to the loft. When he saw Natalia thrashing in the covers, he quickly set the bowl on the nightstand.

"Natalia?" He leaned close and placed a soothing hand on her head. "Open your eyes, Princess. Can you hear me?"

"Too much blood." Her whisper was followed by a heartrending moan. "Dead. Ivan's dead."

He should have known the nightmares would haunt her. In all honesty, she'd held up better than he'd had a right to hope. "Wake up, Natalia. Wake up. It's just a bad dream."

Her beautiful green eyes opened, focused hopefully on his face. "Alive? Ivan's alive?"

He winced. "No, I'm afraid he's not. But dreaming about it won't bring him back." Sloan wanted to kick himself for raising her hopes. "Here, I brought you some soup and a couple of crackers."

"I'm not hungry." Her green eyes slid closed, and she turned her head away. He could see a small bloody stain on the dressing he'd wrapped around her head, but it was only the size of a dime. Nothing to worry about, he hoped.

"Too bad, Princess, because you're going to eat." He wasn't in the mood to play games. Didn't she realize how his patience was stretched to the max? "Whether you like it or not."

Her eyes snapped open at his tone. "Nurses don't force-feed their patients."

"So sue me. Move over." He nudged her from the side of the bed far enough so he could sit beside her. Taking the bowl from the nightstand, he glared at her. "What's it gonna be? The easy way or the hard way?"

"I'll throw up." The way she said the words made it sound like a threat.

"Go ahead." If she thought a little puke was going to put him off, she was crazy. He'd seen far worse. Had done far worse. Setting his jaw, he put the spoon in the bowl, scooped up some broth, then held it out as if she were a baby. "Open up."

"*Durachok*. Give it to me, I'll do it." Clutching the sheets to her chest, she winced and tried to lever herself upright.

With a sigh, he set the soup down and then slid his arm around her shoulders so he could prop a second pillow behind her back. She looked fragile, but he knew there was a core of steel underneath her soft exterior. He found himself glad she'd gone back to calling him dumbhead in Russian.

"Better?"

"Yes. Thank you." She tucked the sheets and quilt beneath her arms and held out her hands.

He placed the bowl of soup in her outstretched hands, fighting the insane urge to kiss her again. He needed his head examined. Time to get out of Dodge. He left, heading back downstairs, all the way outside, staring up at the stars flickering overhead.

She was vulnerable. He didn't have the right to kiss her. His priority was to keep her safe, then to find the scumbags who'd killed his sister.

Taking a deep breath, he peered through the darkness.

Jordan, where are you?

After a few minutes, the silence of the mountains and the rustling of the trees calmed his rioting emotions. Okay, Jordan wasn't here yet, but that didn't mean he couldn't work. He needed to work or he'd go right out of his ever-loving mind.

He had his computer, but there wasn't an internet connection. Wait a minute, he snapped his fingers. He'd almost forgotten the information he'd printed out on Alek Nevsky.

Thrilled with something constructive to do, he strode to the duffel bag and unzipped it. He pawed through the clothes with a frown. He'd set the papers right on top, where were they?

Turning the duffel upside down, he shook the contents onto the kitchen table. He pulled apart the folded clothes. Toiletries rolled out; a round container of deodorant hit the floor with a thud.

Nothing.

He looked inside the duffel again, poked and prodded to make sure there weren't any side pockets or false bottoms where the papers might be trapped. Then he tossed the empty bag aside and hiked back out to the cargo van to make sure the papers hadn't slid out somewhere along the way. Without much light, the search took longer than it should by far.

Still nothing.

He trudged back inside. The information he'd printed was gone. Missing. He remembered the moment Natalia had gotten into his car, how she'd bent over to unzip the bag a fraction of a second before he saw the bullet hole in the back of his seat. The innocent action had saved her life.

Simmering anger unfurled in his gut. Innocent and vulnerable? Yeah, right. She'd taken them. What in the world had she done with his information on Alek Nevsky?

And more importantly, why?

CHAPTER NINE

July 1 – 6:53 p.m. – Bedford, VA

AFTER NATALIA FINISHED THE SOUP, she set the bowl aside with shaky hands. The hammering in her head had settled to a dull throb, and her stomach seemed to accept the small bit of nourishment. Steps in the right direction.

Maybe Sloan was doing a fair job acting as her nurse. She reached up to touch the bandage wrapped around her head, a hint of a smile tugging at her mouth. He'd been uncharacteristically sweet, carrying her inside, more worried about her wound than he'd wanted to admit. He'd called her *Natashen'ka*, the Russian version of sweetheart. Then he'd kissed her cheek, not like a man interested in a woman, but in comfort. As a friend.

As Ivan once would have.

She shied away from the thought. No more dreams. No more nightmares. Closing her eyes against the horrible vision of Ivan lying in a pool of blood, she focused on the present. She needed to get better, to help Sloan figure out who wanted her dead. She also longed for a shower to rinse the remnants of dried blood from her hair. Did the rustic cabin even have the luxury of a shower? She'd forgotten to ask.

She inched down and rested her aching head on the pillow that carried the barest hint of Sloan's soap. Turning her head, she buried her nose in the softness and inhaled deeply. For some reason, Sloan's scent relaxed her, lessened the force of pain reverberating along the inside of her skull.

The thud of footsteps on the stairs leading up to the loft made her freeze. Then she relaxed. She had to stop seeing danger at every corner. They were safe here. She lifted her head, reassured when Sloan's broad-shouldered frame filled the room.

"Where is it?" Sloan's blunt question caught her off guard.

"What?" She hated feeling helpless as she sat upright, clutching the quilt to her chest. His harsh tone wasn't helping the pounding in her head.

"The information I had on Nevsky. What did you do with it?" He took a determined step toward her.

She hid the flash of guilt and tried to brazen her way out of this, which would be easier to pull off if she weren't lying half naked in bed with a gunshot wound across her temple. She lifted her chin. "Nothing. Your precious papers must have fallen out of the duffel bag when I pulled out the T-shirt for my wound."

"They didn't fall out. You bent to look for them at almost the exact moment you were shot." Sloan leaned so far over the bed she worried he'd lose his balance and fall on top of her. "But what's even more interesting is your motive. Why did you take the information, Natalia? Because you know

Nevsky? Because you were afraid I'd find something out about you and Nevsky being involved in this thing together? Are you a part of the Solntsevskaya group too? Did you finish off Josef Korolev that night you took care of him in the hospital?"

"Don't be ridiculous. Why would I do such a thing? Someone blew up my house. Then they tried to kill me, remember?" He'd put two and two together to come up with ten. If she didn't tell him the truth, he'd continue to think the worst.

And for some idiotic reason, she didn't want Sloan to think the worst.

"Lying won't help." Gone was the man who'd cared for her wound so tenderly. His eyes glittered with suppressed anger. "Jordan will be here any minute, and he's bringing computer access. I'll know all your secrets in the space of a few keystrokes."

She swallowed hard. He couldn't possibly know all her secrets, but he was right about one thing, lying wasn't helping. She needed to tell him about Uncle Alek. "Fine. Give me a minute to get dressed and I'll tell you what I know."

He stared down at her for a long moment, before taking one step back. And another. "I'll be right outside the door."

She nodded, waiting for him to do as promised. The minute the door closed softly behind him, she tossed the covers aside and swung her legs around to sit at the side of the bed. The room undulated around her, and she gripped the edge of the mattress to keep from falling on her face.

After pulling on her jeans, she hesitated. The sweater she'd been wearing was bloodstained. Using the wall for support, she made her way to the door. "Sloan? I need a different shirt to wear."

There was a long moment of silence. Then she heard

his heavy footsteps taking the stairs down to the main level. Seconds later, he returned, cracked open the door, and held out a clean shirt, likely from the duffel.

Pulling the garment over her head made her wince, but she refused to give in to weakness. She opened the door, facing him. "Thanks."

He grunted, then stepped back so she could head downstairs. Keeping her balance wasn't easy, and when her feet hit the landing at the bottom of the stairs, she wanted to weep with relief. By sheer will alone, she walked into the kitchen.

He kept his distance as if he regretted his earlier kindness. She sat in the closest chair before her rubber knees gave out completely.

"What is your relationship with Nevsky?" he asked. Almost reluctantly, he set the open package of crackers and a glass of water in front of her.

"He's my adopted mother's cousin." She nibbled the stale crackers and sipped the water, feeling marginally more human. Sloan paced the room like a caged animal.

"Alek Nevsky is your adopted mother's cousin," he repeated in that surly tone of his that doubted every word.

She narrowed her gaze. "Yes. But I haven't seen him in a few years."

"Define a few."

"Three years. Since my mother's funeral."

That news made him pause. "And you claim to know nothing about his link to the Solntsevskaya?"

She ground her teeth, struggling for patience. "Uncle Alek is a kind and gentle Christian man. He didn't shoot Josef Korolev, and he certainly isn't linked to the Solntsevskaya or any other faction of the Russian Mafia."

"Uncle Alek?" Sloan spun toward her. "I thought he was your mother's cousin?"

"He is. I've addressed them *Dyadya* and *Tetya*, Uncle Alek and Aunt Lara, since I was a little girl."

Sloan set his palms on the table and loomed over her. "So if you have nothing to hide, why did you steal the papers?"

Refusing to be intimidated, she told him the truth. "At first I did want to see what was printed about Uncle Alek, but when I realized I was injured, I shoved them under the seat. Forgive me for not thinking clearly when we switched cars. Despite my concussion, I should have asked you to pull them out."

He ignored her sarcastic jab. "You shoved them under the seat because there might be incriminating evidence against him."

She shrugged. "What does it matter? I wouldn't believe anything written by the FBI anyway. If there's a leak, the incriminating evidence, as you put it, is no doubt fabricated from lies."

Sloan's jaw tightened, and he stared at her as if she were the enemy. "You're the only one who's been caught lying."

"As if you wouldn't do the same?" Irritated now, she leaned toward him. "If your family was a target, wouldn't you try to protect them?"

Their gazes clashed, and tension pulsed like a tangible force. After an eternity, Sloan broke away. "Princess, my family isn't part of the Russian Mafia."

She closed her eyes in a wave of exhaustion. Nothing she could say would make him believe her. Why was she trying so hard? Her head hurt, her stomach churned, and she wanted very badly to take a shower.

A noise outside caught Sloan's attention, and before she

could blink, his long strides covered the distance to the door. He flashed a look, warning her to be silent, and doused the lights.

"Stay here," he whispered in Ukrainian. She heard a slight creak as he opened the door and stepped outside.

She swallowed the automatic protest, telling herself he was just being cautious. As a former agent he would, of course, be careful not to make assumptions. But she refused to sit there like a frightened rabbit and wait.

Holding her breath, she stood and groped for the furniture as her eyes adjusted to the darkness. When she could see, she crossed the room to the fireplace. The fire had died down to a few glowing coals. After grabbing the poker, she hefted the iron weight in her hand, before making her way to the door.

She heard the muffled footsteps outside, then the murmur of low voices. Her palms were slick with sweat as she tightened her grip on the weapon. As the voices grew closer, she recognized Sloan's.

"About time you got here. Maybe you can keep me from killing her myself and saving the assassin the trouble."

"Come on, Sloan, can't be that bad." Heavy footsteps sounded on the wraparound porch surrounding the cabin.

"You have no idea." Sloan's reply held deep resignation.

The door opened, and light flooded the room.

Sloan and another man entered the cabin. Sloan closed the door and stared at her. "What in the world are you doing with that thing?"

"Backing you up, in case the bad guys found you." She lowered the poker to the floor, feeling foolish.

"See?" Sloan glanced at the man she assumed was Jordan and threw up his hands. "I give up. I told her to stay put, and as usual, she didn't listen. She's all yours. From here on out, it's your job to keep her safe."

Jordan raised a sardonic brow. "Seems to me she was doing a pretty good job on her own."

JULY 1 – 9:15 p.m. – Bedford, VA

NATALIA EMERGED from the small bathroom to find that the men had transformed the kitchen into a high-tech office while she'd made use of the shower. She paused, marveling at the transition. Sloan had never looked more like an FBI agent. Dressed completely in black, his T-shirt clung to his chest, emphasizing his lean, muscular frame. Sloan and Jordan wore shoulder harnesses and guns, weapons Jordan must have brought with him. She noticed a pair of cell phones sitting on the table. Sloan and Jordan were deep in conversation that abruptly ceased when she entered.

No stretch to imagine they'd been discussing her.

She'd been somewhat reassured to recognize the tall black-haired Jordan as the man in the wedding photo in Sloan's condo. She should have been glad; Jordan Rashid had treated her with nothing but kind politeness since he arrived. Yet the thought of Sloan leaving her with the stranger made the knot in her stomach tighten in a painful jerk.

With an effort, she shook off the sensation. Maybe when this was all over, Sloan would let her use his equipment to help find her birth mother. The idea cheered her up.

"Sit down. We have a few questions for you." Sloan's

flat tone proved he was still not happy with her.

Curiosity, more than anything, nudged her forward. "How did you get computer access here?"

"Satellite," Jordan responded absently, his gaze focused on the laptop screen, his fingers flying across the keyboard.

She'd heard of such technology but had never seen it up close. Apparently, she wasn't going to get a good look now, either, because Sloan pulled out a chair with the toe of his shoe in a wordless command.

Muttering something unkind in Russian under her breath, she sat.

"How is it that you were the nurse assigned to Josef Korolev?" Sloan wanted to know.

"I was chosen because I was scheduled to work that day and happened to speak Russian."

"So you didn't volunteer for the job?" Sloan pressed.

What was he getting at? "I certainly would have volunteered, but as it turned out, my supervisor asked me to take care of Josef before I'd even heard about what happened." She thought back for a moment to the start of her shift and the flurry of activity the VIP had brought to the routine day. She'd been honored to help one of her fellow countrymen.

Then Josef Korolev had died.

And her nightmare had begun.

"What's your supervisor's name?" Sloan asked.

"Margaret Baker."

"How long have you worked for her?"

"Four years, why?" He must be crazy to think her nursing supervisor was involved in this. Maybe Sloan should leave her with Jordan. If Sloan checked himself into a psych hospital, they'd no doubt be happy to provide treatment for his paranoid delusions.

"Exactly how did Josef die?"

"His heart went into a life-threatening arrythmia called V-tach. We did CPR and shocked him, but we couldn't convert him." Her shift at the hospital seemed like weeks ago instead of a mere twenty-four hours. "Most likely, he suffered a severe heart attack as a result of his surgery."

"When will we get the autopsy results?" Sloan turned to Jordan.

"They're doing the autopsy in a few days, under the watchful eyes of both Russian and US officials," Jordan informed him.

"Even then, you'll only get preliminary results," Natalia added.

Both men glanced over at her. Sloan scowled. "Why is that?"

"Takes thirty days to get all the pathology reports back, including the tox screen. At least in a normal case. Even with a rush job ordered by the government, you're looking at a couple of weeks, maybe more."

"Great." Sloan dragged his hands over his face. "That figures."

"After Josef died, there was a lot of discussion around one of the housekeepers who was in the room with him moments before he died." Natalia glanced at Jordan who seemed more interested in what she had to say. "His name was Ray Johnson. They asked me for a description, but the man I described as Ray Johnson didn't exactly match the guard's description of the man he saw entering Josef's room."

"Didn't they pull up his picture from their computer files?" Sloan asked.

"No, the computer program was down." Natalia glanced between the two men. "I've tried, but I don't remember seeing Ray Johnson at all during my shift. I was busy, I could have missed him. But what if the person claiming to be Ray Johnson was really someone else? Someone who stole Ray Johnson's identity?"

Sloan didn't laugh off her suspicions but jotted more notes next to the name of her supervisor.

"Go on," Jordan urged. "What happened after you went home?"

Natalia dropped her gaze to the table, wishing she didn't have to relive this part. "I'd just gotten out of the rideshare when the explosion went off. My home—my cat—everything I owned was gone."

"Did you smell anything? See anything?" Sloan persisted.

"No." She shook her head. "I ran. I saw the creepy guy from the Metro on the street coming toward me, so I ran. I don't know what caused the explosion."

"A bomb, maybe with a motion sensitive detonator," Sloan mused. Then he swung back toward her. "Did you say cat?"

"Yes. Peety was old, arthritic, but I still loved him." She angled her chin, daring him to poke fun at her.

"The cat must have accidentally triggered the bomb." Sloan rubbed the back of his neck. "Whoever set the bomb must have missed knowing about your cat. Lucky for you as it saved your life."

Peety died for her. She curled her shaky fingers into fists. She'd saved him from the shelter, now he'd saved her. Her heart squeezed. The people who had done this awful thing had to be found and punished.

"We know the how, but we still don't know the reasons why." Jordan abandoned the computer. "Maybe we're going at this all wrong."

Sloan nodded. "Motive. Why take out Natalia? First a bomb, then two assassination attempts. For what gain?"

"Nothing." Natalia shivered. The way they spoke so casually of her possible death was not reassuring. "I'm just a nurse."

"She knows someone or something." Jordan ignored her protest and gazed at her pensively. "Nevsky?"

"Maybe. But why try to kill her? Doesn't seem logical since they already have him in custody," Sloan argued.

"It does if he's being framed." Natalia was sick of hearing them bash Uncle Alek. Uncle Alek was a Christian; he and Aunt Lara had given her the cross she wore around her neck years ago. He wouldn't hurt a mouse.

"She has a point." Jordan sighed. "Think bigger. The attempt at Korolev in a public place had to be a message. To whom? Someone in the US government or farther across the globe to someone in Moscow?"

"I agree the hit was a message. Korolev was here to promote his International Middle East Peace Conference. The US hasn't publicly denounced the idea, but everyone knows we're not supportive, especially with Russia taking the lead. So why shoot the deputy prime minister? As a message to back off the conference?" Sloan sat down in front of the computer and began typing in commands.

"A sanctioned assassination attempt?" Jordan shook his head. "I just can't see it, not in DC. It's too close to home."

"I agree with you. Frankly, shooting Korolev would have the opposite effect. The US can't afford to publicly disclaim the Middle East peace talks. Not after we went to the mat for Iraq."

"And how does the Solntsevskaya fit in?" Jordan asked with a frown. "None of the Russian Mafia factions have gotten involved in the political arena."

"True." Sloan glanced over. "Let's hope this isn't the start of a bigger plan."

"I can't see it. There has to be something we're missing," Jordan mused. "Some connection between all these threads."

"I'll work on digging a little deeper for information before I leave," Sloan offered. "No sense driving back to DC this late."

"Considering the last attempt on Natalia's life was right outside your condo, I wouldn't recommend heading home anytime soon," Jordan said dryly.

"Which reminds me, Bentley was the one who knew I had her. Do you think it's possible he's the leak?" Sloan asked.

Jordan sighed. "I wouldn't have thought so. Bentley is high up in the organization as an assistant director. He's always been a trustworthy guy. Besides, he could have talked to someone else who is the real leak. You'd better be careful."

"I can take care of myself, don't worry." Sloan never took his eyes from the screen.

"I'm hungry." Jordan stretched and glanced around. "Good thing for you I brought food too. I have a bag of groceries outside in my car. Give me a few minutes and I'll throw something together to eat."

"No eggs," Sloan muttered, typing furiously on the computer keyboard. "Natalia hates eggs."

"Good thing I didn't buy any." Jordan disappeared outside. Natalia sat quietly, appreciating the silence. She was just reaching for another cracker when Sloan groaned loudly.

"What is it?" she asked.

Sloan's grim gaze met hers. "There's a message from

Jerome Bentley, our FBI contact, on my email. He's ordered us to bring you in now or they'll put out a federal warrant for your arrest. The charge is treason."

An icy chill settled in her bones. She swallowed hard. "Are you going to take me in?"

"Not a chance." Sloan gave a harsh laugh. "If there's a leak inside the FBI, you'd be dead before you ever got to trial."

CHAPTER TEN

July 1 – 9:55 p.m. – Brookmont, MD

LARA NEVSKY STARED in horror at the charred remains of Natalia's house. A scream locked in her throat, struggling to get free. She clasped a hand to her mouth to keep from giving in to the hysteria, but her gaze remained glued to the blackened remains.

There could be no doubt the devastation had been deliberate. Someone had targeted Natalia.

A soft whimper escaped as she turned back toward her car. *Belgi*. She had to run away. Now. In case they were watching.

Her fingers trembled so badly she had trouble starting the car. Clutching the steering wheel in a deathlike grip, she drove away from the scene.

Natalia. Where was Natalia?

Blindly, she groped in her purse for her cell phone. Alek had programmed Natalia's number into her phone prior to their separation, but she'd never called it. She willed her hands to stop shaking as she pressed the speed dial labeled Natalia's cell phone.

There was no ringing on the line, just the canned message claiming the phone number was out of service.

Her stomach tightened, convulsed. Had something happened to Natalia? Was she too late? Had they killed her?

She cut off the car trying to make a left-hand turn, and she swerved just in time to miss the front fender. She pulled off onto the side of the road. Gulping deep breaths, she tried to remain calm. What should she do?

If only she could talk to Alek. He would know what she should do. But Alek was still in jail. Stefan had informed her Alek was due to go before the federal judge at nine sharp tomorrow morning. No matter what Alek said, she intended to be there.

The dark years had returned. Alek would protest if he were to hear her saying this, but it was true. Alek and Katya had both risked their lives to sneak Natalia out of Russia. Katya had been more than happy to adopt the young child to keep her from harm. If Katya were still alive and knew about Josef Korolev's murder, she would agree with Alek about telling Natalia the truth.

But Natalia's house had been burned.

And Natalia's phone wasn't working.

Darkness closed about her, stealing her breath so she couldn't breathe.

She prayed it wasn't too late. That God was protecting Natalia. That He'd helped her to escape, that she wasn't already dead.

Because if that was the case, surely she and Alek were marked for death too.

. . .

JULY 1 – 9:59 p.m. – Bedford, VA

SLOAN TORE his gaze from Natalia and turned his attention back to the computer screen. How could she think he'd be so stupid as to turn her in? Didn't she know he'd already climbed out on a very narrow limb for her? "Don't worry. We're going to keep you well hidden until we find out what's going on."

"I can't believe this." Natalia's stunned expression made him want to haul her into his arms. Earlier he'd been so angry he'd wanted to shake her until her teeth rattled. Now her obvious vulnerability made his chest ache.

"You're safe here, Natalia." Sloan cleared his throat, anxious to get back to the investigation. He and Jordan had already pulled up the information on Nevsky but hadn't found squat. He found grim satisfaction in knowing Natalia had filched the papers for nothing. If Nevsky was pulling in extra money from the Solntsevskaya, it wasn't showing up anywhere they could find it. He supposed he should be glad the papers were harmless, or who knew what Slammer might have tried to do with the information. He wouldn't put anything past Slammer. "All we have to do is figure out why someone wants you dead."

"Can we prove there's a leak in the FBI?" she asked, wrapping her hands around her soup bowl as if seeking warmth.

He rose to his feet, then walked over to break up the logs at the base of the fire. "Someone shot at you outside my condo, but right now, I can't prove it was the FBI." He trusted Bentley and figured the guy was only following orders. He needed information from Natalia but wondered how much to tell her. "What do you know about Rasacovich?"

"Ivan?" Bewildered, she brought her gaze to his. "I don't know what you mean."

"Could he be involved in the Solntsevskaya? Or any other branch of the Russian Mafia?" Sloan returned to his seat. "I know you're certain Nevsky's innocent, but two men are dead, and someone's trying to make this look like a mob hit." He paused, then added, "If you know something, then please tell me so I can get the evidence I need to keep you safe."

"Ivan couldn't tolerate violence or criminals." Her voice was barely above a whisper. "He'd never partake in anything related to the Mafia."

"How did he earn his living?" From what he remembered, Rasacovich lived in a fairly decent house in an upscale part of DC. A nicer place than his, anyway. Crime generally paid better than serving the public.

"He was a Russian interpreter for the hospitals in the area."

"Hospitals, plural?" Sloan pressed.

She nodded. "Yes, I met him at Washington University Hospital, but I knew he also responded to calls at Georgetown Hospital, others too."

Sloan made note of the second link to Washington University Hospital where Korolev had died. "Does interpreting pay enough for him to afford the house he lived in?"

"It pays well enough, but I believe he inherited the house from his father."

Hmm. A father who was part of the Russian Mafia? "What was his father's name?"

"Gregory." She rose from her seat, wrapped her arms around her stomach, and wandered toward the remains of the fire. "How can you ask me to do this? Ask me to look at someone I've known and loved and wonder if he's guilty of some horrible crime?"

He squelched the spurt of sympathy. "Listen, Princess, from this point forward you need to think of everyone as a suspect. Do you understand me? You can't afford not to."

"No. I don't understand." Her tone lacked conviction as she stared at the dancing flames. "I can't live this way."

"You'd rather die?" Sloan leveled her with a hard, flat glare. "Because that's the alternative."

Thankfully, the flat statement shut her up. Taking advantage of her silence, he concentrated on the screen in front of him.

"Think bigger," he muttered half under his breath. "Jordan suggested we think bigger."

The possibility that the attempt on Josef Korolev might somehow link to the Solntsevskaya haunted him. He could admit he was obsessed with the faction because of his sister's death. He knew very well she'd died because of his participation with the investigation of the Solntsevskaya crime ring. He was supposed to protect her, but they'd killed her anyway. He refused to give up this second chance to bring them down.

"Where is Jordan?" Natalia asked with a frown. "He's been outside for a while now."

"Probably walking the perimeter of the cabin," Sloan answered absently, excited to see he got another hit on Korolev's name, this time in a press conference between the president of Russia speaking with the Palestinians. The article had been printed several months earlier, and the subject was, once again, the Middle East peace talks at the International Conference in Moscow. Russian President Vladimir Putin was quoted as speaking out against the use of nuclear weapons, but he did say using nuclear technology for civilian use was acceptable. There was also a statement about how Russia was willing to provide arms to the Palestinian leadership to assist with fighting terrorism. Hmm. Very interesting. Could it be that some factions intended to use the International Conference as a front for something more nefarious? FBI and CIA officials were no doubt wondering the same thing.

He scrolled back to the top and read through the list of press conference attendees. Besides the Russian president and Deputy Prime Minister Josef Korolev, there was Russian Minister of Defense Boris Tereshkova and his wife, Anya. He scribbled those names, along with those of the Palestinian leaders, on a notepad to do a cross-check on them later.

"What if something happened to Jordan?" Natalia asked, her voice full of concern. "I don't care if he is walking the perimeter, it's strange he hasn't returned."

Frowning, he glanced at his watch. Actually, Jordan had been gone longer than the fifteen minutes it should have taken to grab groceries from the car, even if he had decided to check out their surroundings. Sloan stood and moved toward the door.

"Stay here." He scowled at her. "And I mean it this time."

"Fine." She crossed her arms over her chest, but her wide eyes betrayed her concern.

He opened the door and slipped outside, waiting for his eyes to adjust to the lack of light. When he could see well enough, he crossed the porch and took the steps down to ground level.

Slinking along the cabin, staying close to the wall, he headed around back to where they'd stashed Jordan's car, a staid nondescript Chevy Lumina. He frowned when he saw the empty space where the car used to be. Had Jordan moved it?

Or had something happened to his partner?

His chest tightened as he carefully looked for signs of a struggle. Then he widened the scope of his search to include a good twenty feet around the cabin.

Nothing. When he headed back to the area behind the cabin where they'd stashed the cargo van, he looked again at the empty spot where the Lumina should have been. It took a moment for the reality to set in.

His partner had left him! Just up and left him. *Alone with Natalia.*

Acid anger burned his gut at Jordan's betrayal. They'd agreed to switch places, that Jordan would stay here and he'd go back to work the investigation from their office. He'd been counting on his partner to take care of Natalia.

Anger quickly morphed into helplessness. Sloan dragged his hands through his hair, warding off the bitter taste of failure. He wasn't nearly good enough to protect Natalia from the assassins who hunted her.

He wouldn't survive another innocent death on his conscience.

JULY 1 – 10:37 *p.m.* – *Bedford, VA*

NATALIA LOOKED up with a rush of relief when Sloan strode into the cabin, a brown bag of groceries tucked under his arm. He kicked the door behind him, and she winced as the sound echoed through her aching head.

"You found him?" She rose to her feet.

"He wasn't there to find." Sloan dropped the groceries onto the sideboard with a thud. "At least he left us the food."

"What do you mean?" She wished he'd stop speaking in riddles.

"I mean he's gone. Took the car and left." Scowling, Sloan pulled canned goods from the bag with jerky movements. "I suppose I should be thankful he didn't take the rest of the equipment too."

Jordan left? "Why?"

"How should I know?" Sloan's tenuous mood made her think once again of the caged grizzly. "The jerk hasn't answered his phone."

She gasped. "Oh no. Something's happened to him."

"Bull." Sloan crushed the empty grocery bag in his hands and tossed it on the fire. The flames licked greedily at the dry paper. "He left a text message on my phone. Said to stay here and he'd return in twenty-four hours."

Twenty-four hours. A single day. A lifetime. Ironic to think she'd only known Sloan for a little over twenty-four hours. After everything that had happened, she felt almost as if they'd known each other for months. Time stretched endlessly ahead of them. The cabin wasn't nearly big enough to keep out of each other's way.

Apparently, Sloan shared the same sentiment because he returned to his seat behind the satellite computer, his brow pulled into a dark frown. "You'd better go upstairs and get some sleep."

What? No more interrogation? No more threats? She raised a brow. Or maybe he was looking for a way to get rid of her. Ha! He'd discover she wasn't so easy to get rid of.

"I'll help." She pulled her chair over to sit beside him.

"No!" His emphatic outburst made her eyes widen. He

must have realized he sounded like a madman because he quickly lowered his tone. "Natalia, you can help me by getting some rest. If we need to leave in a hurry, I want you to be at your best. Not suffering from a concussion. I'm sure your head is still pounding."

It was, but she didn't care. "My life is at risk."

His expression turned solemn. "I know. Mine too. I promise I'll do whatever is necessary to keep you safe."

She believed him. Knew he'd sacrifice his life for hers. How could she argue with that? She hesitated, and then realized there was only one computer anyway. They both couldn't work at the same time. Dejected, she turned away.

"I wish there was something I could do to help." Instead of going upstairs to the bed, she curled up on a corner of the sofa, across from the fire.

"Think back to the moment you began taking care of Josef Korolev and see if you can remember anything else that might help give us a clue as to what's going on," Sloan advised. "Somehow, you're the key. We just have to figure out how and why."

She stared at the fire, thinking she didn't feel like a key. If anything, her brain felt like a fuzzy black box with no real memories of what her quiet, calm life used to be like. She tried to think back, she really did, but despite her best efforts, her eyelids drifted closed. Her last conscious thought was that she hadn't told Sloan everything Josef Korolev had said to her.

She'd failed to mention Josef's strange reaction to her pendant.

JULY 1 – 11:35 p.m. – Bedford, VA

. . .

SLOAN JUMPED in his seat when his brand-new cell phone rang. He grabbed it and hit the answer button before the noise woke Natalia.

"You traitor." Sloan kept his voice low and headed outside to the wraparound porch, seeking privacy.

"Bad news." Jordan ignored his insult. "I picked up a tail."

"Serves you right for leaving me with the green cargo van. I thought we had a deal? You'd protect Natalia and I'd work the investigation from the other side." Sloan thought it was a good thing Jordan wasn't within touching distance or he'd deck him. Then, after his initial burst of anger faded, his interest sharpened. "A tail? When?"

"Just inside the DC city limits."

"Any idea who it is?"

"My best guess? Our former employer."

Not good. The theory of a mole in the FBI was growing stronger and stronger. Bentley? Saunders? Wilcox? Harper? He ran the list of agents who'd touched this case through his head. It could be any of them or none of them. There was no way to know for sure. Good thing Jordan was the best in the business. "Is Natalia's location at risk?"

"No. You're safe for the moment." Jordan's voice sounded weary. "But I'm not going back to the office. I'm going to lie low. We'll have to keep in touch."

Sloan couldn't maintain his anger at how Jordan had left him with Natalia. He sighed. "Fine. I'll let you know if I come up with anything concrete." Sloan stared out at the dark woods surrounding the cabin. Isolation was good. He desperately wanted to believe they were safe here.

"You also might want to come up with plan B, because I sense we're in serious trouble here. If they're tailing me, I can only assume they have our respective homes and the office covered as well. If someone inside the FBI is somehow linked to one of the main factions in the Russian Mafia, they're going to do everything in their power to find you and Natalia. And we both know the lengths they'll go to get what they want."

As much as he hated to admit it, Jordan was right.

Things were getting more serious. Using the cabin as a safe haven was probably only good for another twenty-four to forty-eight hours.

"Take care of yourself, Jordan." He tried to mask his worry.

"Yeah. I'll be in touch." Jordan rang off.

Sloan snapped his phone shut. His partner was right. They needed a plan B.

If he could manage to come up with one.

CHAPTER ELEVEN

July 2 – 2:13 a.m. – Bedford, VA

SLOAN STARED at his computer screen, trying to make the pieces of the puzzle fit. The Solntsevskaya was all about making big money; they didn't usually get involved in the political arena. Yet something political had caused the Solntsevskaya to risk taking out Korolev here on US soil. Kazakhstan, a province of Russia, had opened the oil pipeline to China just a few years ago, a move that bothered the US. The US government considered China to be a political sleeping giant. What if the Solntsevskaya planned to expand into China? Combining China and Russia's power base would have a disturbing impact on the US. Especially since the world trade deficit had tanked and the US owed China millions of dollars.

Then there was the ongoing stalemate between the US and Russia in reaching an agreement to dismantle and protect Russia's vulnerable nuclear, biological, and chemical weapons. Most of the nuclear weapons had been brought to a central location in Moscow, but the chemical weapons storage facilities were still scattered; one was located close to the new oil pipeline. Sloan was interested to note Boris and Anya Tereshkova were mentioned again in one article about why the weapons hadn't been destroyed yet, mostly because Russia claimed they needed funds from the US in order to complete the project as outlined in the Chemical Weapons Convention.

The threat of nuclear, chemical, or biological weapons falling into terrorist hands was really bad news. He could easily imagine the Solntsevskaya selling them to the highest bidder. And if the highest bidder was some country in the Middle East? Years ago, he'd considered the Solntsevskaya to be one of the biggest threats to the US, but his bosses in the bureau didn't agree.

Abandoning his computer, Sloan drew a large triangle on a blank paper. He labeled one point as the Kazakhstan oil pipeline to China. The second point he labeled as the dispute between Russia and the US regarding the dismantling of weapons, and the third point being the International Middle East Peace Conference scheduled in Moscow. Three political issues in which the US and Russia were on opposite sides of the political debate. Inside the triangle he wrote the words terrorism, money, and power. On the outside of the triangle he wrote the names of Josef Korolev, Natalia, and Alek Nevsky along with the Solntsevskaya.

Was there a link between the three points of his triangle? Could the Solntsevskaya or some other faction be involved? Or were they merely a smoke screen to keep attention diverted from what was really going on? If the link was world power, was the mole in the FBI connected too? Or was the mole in the FBI working through the Solntsevskaya on some unknown agenda? The idea that anyone living through the horror of 9/11 could coldly betray their country for terrorism was difficult to comprehend.

But then again, greed knew no boundaries.

He had a bad feeling everything was connected somehow. In each of the three major issues, the one common theme was the Solntsevskaya and a heightened threat of terrorist activity. But how Korolev's assassination, Natalia's house bombing, and the murder of Ivan Rasacovich all fit into the equation was still a mystery.

Normally, he loved fitting the puzzle pieces together. But this particular picture was so full of more holes than swiss cheese. He had plenty of theories and suppositions, but not one shred of anything resembling real proof.

Grinding his palms into his eye sockets, he fought a wave of fatigue. No sleep in well over twenty-four hours was catching up with him. He needed at least a few hours of downtime before his brain would start filtering through the information for useful patterns again.

Sloan shut the computer down and pushed himself to his feet. He caught sight of Natalia still curled up on the sofa, and despite his bone-weary exhaustion, his heart squeezed at the sweet innocent vision she made.

Don't think about it. Natalia is off-limits. Way off-limits.

Jerking his thoughts from that dangerous path, he took a step back. He was somewhat surprised she'd actually fallen asleep. The woman defined stubborn. With a frown, he noticed her head lay at an awkward angle against the sofa's armrest. Bad enough she'd suffered a concussion, but when she woke up, she'd have a stiff neck too.

Leave her, he told himself. She's sleeping. Just leave her alone.

He made it as far as the foot of the stairs leading to the loft before he stopped. Telling himself he was nothing more than a softhearted fool, he spun around, went back to the sofa, and gently lifted her into his arms.

"What?" she murmured when he picked her up.

"Shh. Go back to sleep," he whispered. "Everything is fine," he added in Ukrainian. "You're safe."

Miraculously, she did nestle against him. He climbed the stairs to the loft bed he'd made up for her earlier. Without turning on the lamp, he put her on the bed and tucked the quilt around her.

He caught a whiff of her vanilla scent. It oddly reminded him of home. Why he was so attracted to a woman whom he didn't fully trust and called him names, he had no idea. He forced himself to back away and find the other bedroom. Pulling sheets and blankets out, he deftly made the bed, then dropped onto the mattress. He instantly fell asleep.

The sound of moaning woke him up what seemed like less than five minutes later. Natalia! He bolted upright and made a mad dash into her room.

Like earlier, she was suffering a nightmare. He helplessly watched her for a moment, then sat on the edge of the bed. "Natalia, wake up."

"No, please. No! Blood, so much blood . . ."

"Natalia, please. Wake up." When she continued thrashing, he reached out and gathered her close. "It's just a bad dream."

To his surprise, she nestled against him. He sat with his back against the headboard, holding her close, hoping she'd fall back asleep.

He hadn't expected to fall asleep, but the overwhelming exhaustion must have done a number on him because the early morning light was peering through the windows when she abruptly moved away from him.

"What are you doing here?" Natalia's voice was sharp.

He blinked. "I, uh, you were having a nightmare—"

"You crawled into bed with me? Is this the sort of sneaky behavior I can expect from you?"

"No. You were moaning. I was worried." Although, he should have figured this wouldn't go well. He sighed and slipped off the bed, turning his back to provide a modicum of privacy. "I didn't mean to fall asleep, for three lousy hours," he muttered, glancing at his watch. "Which sums up the total amount of sleep I've had since the moment I tangled with you."

When she didn't answer, he shot her a glance over his shoulder. The uncertainty in her gaze made him pause. She looked uncertain and vulnerable. He preferred her spunk.

"Did you find anything on the computer?" she asked.

He rubbed the back of his neck. "Yeah, I think so."

"Will you show me?"

He stared at her for a long minute, then shrugged. "Why not? You can either poke holes in my theories or add to them."

If Natalia was the key, the more information he sifted through her, the better. The sooner they could identify who wanted her dead, the sooner he could get rid of her.

His job was to protect Natalia, not to think about ways to make her feel better. The first rule of protection was to keep an emotional distance, a rule he hadn't followed with his sister. You'd think he'd learn his lesson.

As long as Natalia continued to find him irritating and annoying, he figured he might be okay.

JULY 2 – 5:45 a.m. – Bedford, VA

. . .

NATALIA TRIED to ignore the lingering awareness of Sloan. The man was annoying, no reason to remember the few times he'd been sweet and kind. She followed him down to the kitchen turned office. At least the few hours of sleep had worked wonders in taking the edge off her constant headache.

Now if she could just get rid of the ridiculous attraction she had for Sloan, she'd be in business.

She told herself to get a grip as she took a seat at the table. Sloan didn't sit but stood behind her as he pointed to the triangle drawing he'd made. She tried to focus on the information before her, but she was far more aware of his clean, musky scent. Waking up being cradled in his arms had felt nice. Until her sheer survival instinct had pushed him away.

Her heart knew what her brain didn't want to acknowledge. Sloan had the power to hurt her just as deeply as her cheating fiancé had.

Maybe worse. The thought was sobering.

"These are the three hot topics between the US and Russia right now," he said, indicating the various points of his triangle. "Think back to when you were taking care of Korolev. Did you hear anything about these issues?"

Natalia tried to go back in time, to when her life seemed normal and she'd been at work taking care of her patients. "There was some talk, of course, about how the International Middle East Peace Conference was the likely motive for Josef's shooting," she admitted.

"Nothing else?"

She couldn't seem to tear her gaze away from Sloan's large block-printed words: terrorism, money, and power written in the center of the triangle. She'd seen firsthand too many victims of violence in the ICU, most for far less important reasons than what Sloan had written. This was different somehow. Certainly premeditated. Calculated. Cruel. "Not that I can recall. By the time Josef was admitted after surgery, the biggest concern was when to transport him back to Russia. The Russian countrymen were trying to decide if they should take the president up on his offer to return Josef on Air Force One."

"I'm not surprised the president made such an offer. Korolev's assassination isn't exactly good for our image, especially with all the political strife between our countries." Sloan moved away from the back of her chair to pace the room again. His sleep-tousled hair gave him a softer, more approachable image.

Had he really only slept for three hours since they'd met? It hardly seemed possible, but the first night in the motel room he'd sat in the chair, watching over her. The same night he'd saved her life when the assassin burst into the room firing at the rumpled mass of covers on the bed still warm from her body.

She knew next to nothing about this man. Yet she felt safe with him.

She pulled her wayward thoughts together with an effort. Just because Sloan had saved her life, twice, didn't mean she had to fall for him. No, if she wanted to escape this nightmare with her sanity intact, she'd best stay away from Sloan at all costs.

"You're right, the attempt on Josef Korolev doesn't make our country look good." Natalia fought to keep her tone even. "Yet I can't believe even the Solntsevskaya would take out one of their own just to put the US government in a bad light."

"Maybe I haven't picked out the right pieces to fit this

puzzle," Sloan muttered under his breath. "There could be hundreds of possibilities I haven't even thought of."

"There was some grumbling about how the deputy prime minister wasn't scheduled to speak at the White House the way most dignitaries are." Natalia tapped her finger on the triangle. "And if I remember correctly, part of the reason for that decision was because this trip to the United States had been put together without a whole lot of advance notice, which made our government officials wary."

Sloan stopped midstride, then swung around to face her. "You're right. If the deputy prime minister had given his speech at the White House, the chance of anyone shooting him is slim to none. Although, the security at The Washington Center wasn't anything to sneeze at."

She arched a brow. "But you're forgetting Josef claimed he was shot by the FBI. If that was the case, they'd have had access to him inside the White House too."

"But the Secret Service would be there, too, in a larger force than at The Washington Center. And now the FBI is busy pointing the finger at some faction of the Russian Mafia," Sloan argued. "A difficult theory to believe if the shooting had taken place inside the White House."

"True. So maybe we need to figure out why this little speech was thrown together at the last minute?"

Sloan stared at her. "You may be onto something. Wait a minute." He bent to shuffle through the papers scattered over the table. "Here it is." He pulled out a note and placed it in front of her. "This is about Russian Minister of Defense Boris Tereshkova. He and his wife, Anya, are named as being present at the opening ceremony of the Kazakhstan oil pipeline to China. Then they're both mentioned in this article here, defending Russia's refusal to dismantle their weapons of mass destruction due to financial constraints. Wouldn't it be interesting if our friend Boris was also involved in Josef Korolev's impromptu trip to America?"

Natalia slowly shook her head. "I don't see it as a major connection. As the minister of defense, Boris Tereshkova is going to be involved in governmental issues regarding security. I don't see how that proves anything."

Sloan's shoulders slumped. "You're probably right. I'm grasping at straws."

The name Anya Tereshkova drew her gaze. Anya was a very common name in Russia, yet it was also her birth mother's first name.

"What's the matter?" Sloan asked when she continued to stare. "Did you find a connection?"

"Not really." Her fingers reached for the pendant she wore around her neck, smoothing her fingers over the crescent moon and tiny stones, seeking comfort. "The name Anya drew my attention."

"Why?"

She shrugged. "A few months ago, I worked with Ivan to try and trace my heritage. I have been trying to find the true identity of my Russian birth mother. Long after my adopted mother died, I found her personal journal hidden in the bottom of her dresser, but all the entries were in Cyrillic Russian." She grimaced. "I can read Russian, but not as well when it's written in Cyrillic. Anyway, I took the journal to Ivan and, with his help, discovered my adopted mother had actually known my birth mother. She mentioned my birth mother by the name Anya." She pushed the paper aside, feeling foolish for telling Sloan all of this. As if he really cared how lost she'd felt since discovering she was adopted. "A coincidence I'm sure. Anya is as common in Russia as Ann or Anna is here in the US."

Sloan pursed his lips as he picked up the paper with his notes scribbled on it. "You're right. A first name doesn't tell us anything. I don't suppose your mother mentioned a last name?"

"No." She shook her head. She and Ivan hadn't gotten very far through the translation. And now all her notes were gone. "Although, she did leave me one thing." Pulling the two pendants out from beneath her T-shirt, she lifted the crescent moon one for him to see.

"A necklace?" He leaned closer to look at the crescent-shaped moon and the three purple stones in the shape of stars. "It's nice, but I'm not sure it will actually help us."

"Maybe not," she conceded. "But when I was taking care of Josef Korolev, he seemed to recognize it. He wanted to know who gave it to me."

CHAPTER TWELVE

July 2 – 8:45 a.m. – Washington, DC

ALEK'S HEART soared when he saw his wife seated in the courtroom, but shame quickly overwhelmed his joy. Lara should not be here to see him with his hands cuffed behind his back. She should not be here at all. Those who'd framed him for this crime would take note of his weakness and exploit it.

"Make her leave," he whispered to Stefan. "She shouldn't be here."

"When can anyone make Lara do something she doesn't want to do?" Stefan asked irritably. "You should be more worried about how we're going to get you out of here. The evidence they have mounted against you is staggering."

"Planted evidence. All of it. Planted to make me look guilty." Alek knew he sounded like a madman, but it was true. "I need to speak to one of the FBI agents, a Michael Cummings. Can you find him for me?"

"I tried. Seems no one has heard of him." Stefan scowled. "At least that's the runaround I'm getting."

Alek felt his last vestiges of hope slipping away. No one had heard of Michael Cummings? What did that mean? Nothing good for him, that was for sure. "If I don't get out of here, you need to promise me you'll protect Lara." On this he would not budge. "Promise me, Stefan."

"Shh," Stefan warned. "The judge is coming."

"All rise," the bailiff intoned.

He and Stefan both stood. He imagined Lara had as well, but he couldn't bring himself to turn around to look.

The legal mumbo jumbo flowed back and forth between the prosecuting attorney, the judge, and Stefan. He entered his plea of not guilty. When the federal prosecuting attorney asked the judge to keep him incarcerated while awaiting trial, Alek was shocked. Stefan argued Alek's record was clean, he was an upstanding citizen of the community, and he was hardly a flight risk. But the prosecuting attorney pulled out several papers detailing how many times over the past year Alek had traveled to Russia. With a sinking sense of hopelessness, Alek watched the judge examine the papers, fearing the outcome.

"No bail." The judge hammered his gavel, indicating there was no going back.

"Alek!" Lara cried as he was led away. "No, Alek! I need to speak to you. Alek!"

He didn't turn his head, didn't acknowledge her presence at all. He was too ashamed.

Maybe Lara had been right to leave him. He'd brought this upon himself, taking those trips back home at Michael's request, even when Lara had begged him to leave well enough alone. After the second trip, he'd returned home to discover she'd moved out of their house into an apartment.

Even then, he couldn't stop himself from trying to put things right.

He wasn't guilty of killing Josef Korolev, but his life hadn't been completely virtuous either. God may have forgiven him, but others hadn't. The sins of his past would be impossible to escape.

At least there might be time to warn Natalia of the truth. He knew full well he deserved his fate.

Natalia, however, did not. She was no more than an innocent pawn in a deadly game.

JULY 2 – 9:30 a.m. – Bedford, VA

SLOAN PUSHED AWAY from the computer and scrubbed his hands over his eyes, trying to clear his blurred vision.

So far, Natalia's necklace was a dead end. He hadn't found anything even close to the design of the pendant on the internet. After an hour of searching, he'd switched his focus to Anya and Boris Tereshkova but hadn't found much about the pair either. Anya had been born in Kazan but had moved as a young woman to Moscow. She married Boris at age twenty-four and had remained married for the past twenty-five years. Natalia was twenty-six years old, so the math worked in favor of Anya being her mother. The only picture he'd been able to dig up had been a grainy profile shot. Anya had dark hair while Natalia's was blonde, but he thought there might be a slight resemblance in their facial structure.

Was he losing his mind? Just because some forty-nine-year-old woman's name was Anya and bore a slight resemblance didn't make her Natalia's mother. And even if by some stretch of the imagination Anya was really Natalia's birth mother, so what? What did the connection mean? And where did the pendant fit in, if at all? The woman had given Natalia up for adoption years ago. Why would someone try to kill Natalia now? As a way to get back at Boris and Anya? Didn't seem like enough of a motive, even if they were working with the Solntsevskaya.

He must be losing his touch. This angle was nothing more than a dead end.

"Did you find anything helpful?" Natalia asked from her position on the sofa.

"No." He'd been grateful when she'd stopped leaning over his shoulder as he worked. Ignoring her presence across the room was difficult enough when her scent still lingered in the air. He cleared his throat. "I didn't find anything on your necklace at all. As for Anya Tereshkova, she was born in Kazan but moved to Moscow when she was eighteen. She's been married to Boris for twenty-five years." He shrugged. "Either of them could belong to any faction of the Russian underworld. There isn't a lot of information."

"Kazan?" Natalia echoed in a strangled tone. "My adopted mother was born in Kazan too. How ironic. From what I've read, Kazan wasn't a very large city."

"It's not, at least if you go by what you find on the internet." Sloan frowned. "Wait a minute. What was I just reading about?" He turned back to the computer, using the back button to retrace his steps. After a few minutes, he found the article. "Here. Guess who else was born in Kazan?"

"Who?"

He met her gaze with a grim one of his own. "Deputy Prime Minister Korolev."

Natalia stared. "I don't understand. What does it mean?"

"That they're friends? That one helped out the other? That they all have the same Mafia connection?" Sloan went back to his notes. "Two people living in Moscow working in positions of power to have come from the same small town can't be a coincidence."

"No, probably not," Natalia agreed. "Especially since you need a certain amount of money to gain a position of power. Or have friends in high places. Which is exactly how the Russian Mafia works." She frowned, and then added, "But how does the necklace fit in? Even if Josef saw it back then, why on earth would he remember?"

"I don't know. The design of your necklace doesn't match any of the symbols of the known Mafia factions. I've studied them at length, and it's not even close. I think if we can find some sort of connection between them, we'd have more answers." Sloan turned back to his computer.

"Kazan did have royalty once, even had their own Kremlin," Natalia pointed out when he pulled up information about Kazan on his computer. "It's not used now, of course, but there continues to be two classes of people who live in Kazan, the very rich and the very poor. Maybe this necklace came from the rich group."

Sloan wrote more notes. "Yeah, but that only makes me wonder which person came from the rich side of town. Anya or Josef?"

"I don't know. My adopted mother was from Kazan, and she wasn't rich. Her name was Katya Sergeyevna Sokolova." Natalia's gaze held a faraway expression. "She gave me her middle name as well because I didn't have a father of my own. So my full name is Natalia Sergeyevna Sokolova."

Sloan frowned. "You have a father. You called him from your cell phone the night we stayed in the hotel room, didn't you?"

"My adopted father," she corrected. "I didn't know my birth father. My adopted father is American and was born in DC, I think. He's a history professor and loves Russian antiques. That's how he met my adopted mother."

Natalia's past couldn't get any more complicated. "Do you know where you were born?" he asked.

"Kazan, according to what Ivan and I found in my mother's journal."

"Do you have your mother's journal with you?" He glanced around for the canvas bag she'd carried around for the past day and a half but didn't see it lying around. She'd no doubt left it upstairs.

"No." Her face clouded. "The journal was lost in the explosion, along with all the rest of my things."

"I see." He drew another picture to help frame things in his mind as he thought out loud. "You were born in Kazan and might have received your pendant from there. We have your adopted mother from Kazan here in the US, we have Josef Korolev who was born in Kazan and died here in the US, we have Anya Tereshkova who was born in Kazan and still lives in Moscow, working closely, we assume, with Korolev." More coincidences. "I bet they knew each other as children. Ironically, they're all within a similar age range, give or take a few years."

His cell phone rang, interrupting his train of thought. The only person who had the number was Jordan. "Yeah?"

The line was so full of static he could barely make out the words. "They found me. I'm injured. Stay hidden."

"Jordan? What happened? Where are you?"

Silence. The connection was broken.

Ice coalesced in his veins. Sloan swiftly punched the redial feature to call him back.

But Jordan didn't answer.

JULY 2 – 10:13 a.m. – Washington, DC

A BEAD of sweat rolled down the center of his back, despite the cool, air-conditioned temperatures in the room.

Clarence Yates, director of the FBI, banged his hand on the table. "I want answers! Why is Nevsky's lawyer trying to set up a meeting with a missing FBI agent? What's going on?"

Keeping calm wasn't easy, but there was no sense in risking everything for the brief satisfaction of ramming his fist into the director's face.

"It's nothing but a weak ploy, sir." He kept his tone calm, controlled. "Nevsky's been pleading innocence all along, claiming he's been framed." He shrugged. "Just remember, he's the one taking numerous trips to his homeland. Don't fall for his lies. I'm sure if we dig further, we'll find he's the key link to one of the more powerful factions of the Russian Mafia."

The director stared at the group of men seated around the table. "I don't like it. I don't like that Nevsky knows the name of our agent who mysteriously disappeared on his way to the US embassy in Russia. An agent we've pretty much written off as dead."

He didn't so much as bat an eyelash. "It's looking more likely that Michael Cummings was the leak we'd suspected."

The director didn't like hearing that. "This meeting is

adjourned. I want an update on the location of Korolev's Russian nurse ASAP."

"Of course, sir." He stood and followed the others out of the room.

The only report he'd give once he found Natalia was the details of how she died. The woman seriously annoyed him. He'd already taken care of the major part of the problem he'd been assigned, but the job wasn't complete yet. Not until he'd found the woman.

And he would find her. She couldn't hide forever.

Not from him.

JULY 2 – 10:18 a.m. – Bedford, VA

NATALIA WATCHED the color drain from Sloan's face, a stunned expression in his eyes. "What's wrong?"

"Jordan's hurt." With a jerky movement, he tossed the phone onto the kitchen table next to the computer. "I can't believe they found him."

"Who found him?" Natalia rubbed her arms, aware of the sudden chill.

Sloan raked his hand through his hair. "Either the FBI or the Solntsevskaya, take your pick."

"The FBI wouldn't hurt him, would they?"

"Why not, if the mole really shot Korolev?"

Fear was bitter on her tongue. If Sloan was this upset, it was bad. Very bad. Would this nightmare never end? A wave of helpless frustration washed over her. She tried to remind herself they were doing everything possible to figure out what was going on.

Sloan's face was drawn into harsh lines, so she rose from her seat on the sofa. "I'm sorry. I know he's your friend."

"If I had any idea where to find him, I'd go." Sloan was clearly upset. "Why didn't he give me his location? He could be anywhere in DC. *Anywhere.*"

"Because of me." Because Jordan wouldn't risk dragging her into the line of fire. Jordan had protected her. The realization made her sick to her stomach, and she held on to the back of the chair to steady herself.

Sloan didn't answer but grabbed his hair as if he would yank it out of his head in frustration. She crossed over and put a hand on his arm in a feeble attempt to soothe his pain. And hers.

"Don't," he said in a low, raspy voice as he turned from her. "Leave me alone."

She couldn't. Things were going from bad to worse, and she felt responsible, although she was as much a victim as anyone. Yet right here, right now, she and Sloan only had each other. Ignoring the hard set to his shoulders, she wrapped her arms around him, resting her cheek along the smooth muscles of his back.

He stiffened for a moment, then unclasped her hands from his waist and swung around to face her. She didn't utter a single word of protest when he hauled her into his arms and kissed her.

Never had she been kissed like that before. He devoured her mouth like a dying man taking his last breath. He was so intense, so overwhelming, yet she wasn't afraid. Instinctively, she knew he'd never hurt her.

The kiss went on and on. As if he'd never stop. Finally, he lifted his head, resting his forehead against hers. Breath sawed in and out of his lungs as if he'd run a marathon.

She felt the same way.

The tenderness vanished when he lifted his head, his gaze boring into hers. "I hope you're not looking for an apology."

"*Durachok*," she muttered, pulling away from him. "I'm not. It was just a kiss. I don't expect anything from you."

He went still, and for a moment she thought she'd actually hurt his feelings, until he said, "Good. I'm glad we understand each other."

She sighed. This situation was her own fault. What possessed her to attempt to offer Sloan comfort? She should have known he'd toss her efforts back in her face.

"You need to go upstairs and pack."

"Pack?" Taken aback, she stared at him. "Why?"

"We're leaving." His no-nonsense tone told her he wasn't in the mood for an argument. "As soon as I can gather our equipment together, we're out of here."

"To go where?"

He didn't answer but stalked over to the table holding the equipment.

"I'm not going anywhere." She didn't understand what he was thinking. What he planned to do.

"Suit yourself." Sloan focused on disconnecting the computer equipment.

Calling his bluff would backfire. She had absolutely no doubt he'd leave without her. Jordan was his closest friend; she was only a nuisance. She wanted to rail at him, to scream and shout that they were safe here in the cabin.

But safety was an illusion.

And no matter how much she wanted to stay, she feared being left alone even more.

CHAPTER THIRTEEN

July 2 – 10:39 a.m. – Bedford, VA

SLOAN KNEW he shouldn't have kissed Natalia like a man possessed. When she'd finally disappeared upstairs, he'd collapsed into a chair, dropped his head into his hands, and wondered if God had completely given up on him.

This wasn't the time or place to fall for a woman. Especially one he'd vowed to protect. But all he really wanted was to kiss her again and again.

He scrubbed his hands over his face and turned his attention back to disconnecting the computer. He needed to forget about how sweet Natalia had tasted. Jordan was hurt, or worse. As much as he didn't want to admit it, there was a good chance his partner was dead. Hiding out at the cabin wasn't going to help get them out of this mess. They needed to draw out the FBI mole, to figure out who was behind all the killing. And why.

Natalia needed to be safe, but he couldn't guarantee

anything. Especially not after he'd crossed the line and managed to become emotionally involved.

No more. He wasn't tripping down that dangerous path again. From here on out, he was staying as far away from the tempting Natalia as possible.

"I'm ready."

Her husky voice sent a wave of awareness washing over him. He closed his eyes and tried to maintain control. "Haul the duffel out to the van, then give me a hand with this stuff."

For once she did exactly as he asked, walking past him to go outside. He closed down the satellite portable computer and returned it to the carrying case, then followed her out. She avoided all physical contact as he stored the equipment in the back of the cargo van.

Between the two of them, they managed to get everything worth taking packed in the van. Ten minutes later, they were back on the road, driving toward DC.

Neither of them spoke. The tension grew so thick he thought he might suffocate from the pressure.

"Do you have a plan?" she asked, finally breaking the interminable silence.

"Yeah." A half-baked one, but a plan. "When we get closer to the city, I want you to call your Aunt Lara. Tell her we need to talk."

Natalia frowned. "Won't the FBI look for us there?"

"Probably." He kept his eyes on the winding country road. "I'd be surprised if they didn't have someone watching her place. But we should be fine if we arrange to meet somewhere public."

"Do you really think Lara knows anything?"

"She'd better. We desperately need a lead."

"Did you try Jordan again?"

He clenched his jaw. "His cell phone isn't on. He probably got rid of it after he called me."

"Oh."

This time, he was glad when she lapsed into silence. He glanced at his watch. They still had a couple of hours of driving before they were close enough to put his plan into motion.

Hours in which there was nothing to do except try to forget Jordan possibly lying injured or dead while at the same time remembering exactly how sweet Natalia had tasted and how perfectly she'd fit into his arms.

While longing for more.

JULY 2 – 1:19 p.m. – Alexandria, VA

NATALIA KEPT HER EYES CLOSED, feigning sleep. Sloan had withdrawn from her with a painful finality. As if he couldn't wait to get rid of her once and for all.

Too bad she was far from actually getting any rest.

"Wake up, Princess. It's time to make your call."

She stifled a sigh, lifted her head, took in their surroundings, and glanced at him. "She lives in Brookmont, we have a while yet."

"Not if she's going to meet us in DC, we don't." Sloan handed her his cell phone. "Talk to her in Russian. Tell her we want to meet outside the Washington Monument in an hour."

An hour was barely enough time. She stared at the phone, then dialed the number.

"Hello, Stefan?"

She blinked back a surprising dampness at Lara's sweet

and achingly familiar Russian voice. "No, *Tetya*. It's me. Natalia."

"Natalia? You're alive? Where have you been? We've been very worried about you."

"I'm alive and safe." At least for the moment. "But I need to talk to you. Can you meet me at the Washington Monument in an hour?"

"I can try." She imagined Lara was already wiping her clay-stained hands on a nearby towel. There was a hitch in her aunt's voice when she asked, "Did you hear about Alek?"

"Yes. I know he's innocent, *Tetya*. We'll clear his name, you'll see."

"Don't say anything more," Sloan warned. "Just get off the phone."

"I have to go, *Tetya*. See you soon." Natalia quickly disconnected the call, then tossed the phone back to Sloan. "There is no reason to be rude. I haven't seen or spoken to my aunt in a long time."

"I wasn't being rude, but if the FBI has a tap on her phone, they might be able to trace the call to this new cell number. Or they might try to meet us at the Washington Monument." He shrugged. "If they don't understand Russian, we should have bought ourselves a little time."

"I hadn't thought of that," she admitted with a sigh. Being constantly on the defensive was difficult.

"Who was she expecting to call?"

Natalia frowned, then realized he'd overheard the beginning of their conversation. "Oh, Stefan. Her lawyer, I think."

"You know her lawyer?"

"Not exactly, but I know my mother's lawyer was Stefan Durik. He's from Russia too." Stefan had handled her mother's estate, and since they had all spoken at her mother's funeral, she assumed Stefan must also be working with Alek and Lara.

"Where is he located?" Sloan wanted to know.

"Just outside DC. Why?"

"Because we might need to pay him a little visit."

"I don't think he's going to tell us anything," she objected.

"Figures."

She rolled her eyes in exasperation. "What did you think? That Stefan would betray his attorney/client privilege?"

"No, not that." Sloan divided his attention between the road and the rearview mirror. "I think we may have picked up a tail. There's a dark blue sedan that's been behind us for the past couple of miles."

She shot a nervous glance over her shoulder. "Can you assume that so quickly?"

"Maybe not." Sloan's expression was grim. "But make sure your seatbelt is tight, because I'm going to try to lose him."

The ancient cargo van was hardly a low-slung race car, but with Sloan behind the wheel, it did a good imitation of one. With a sharp turn of the wheel, he careened across several lanes of interstate traffic and flew off the nearest exit ramp.

"Look out!" she shouted at the moment he swerved around the car in front of them stopped at the red light. Ignoring the light, he barreled through a right turn, merging into the lane of oncoming traffic. Horns blared from all sides.

She didn't breathe easy until he slowed down, once he'd

gone through several turns along the back roads. "We can't get to DC without taking one of the main bridges."

"I know." He continued to drive through Arlington County while avoiding the main highways. "I figured we might make it across if we use the Chain Bridge."

"And if we don't?" She was almost afraid to ask.

Sloan didn't answer.

Natalia let out a deep breath and tried to think positive. If anyone could get them into DC without detection, Sloan could. He was good at his job, even if she wanted to strangle him more often than not.

Or kiss him. It was a toss-up as to which she wanted more.

The traffic thinned out a bit once they managed to cross the Chain Bridge and get into DC. Within a few miles, Sloan pulled over and parked the car.

"What are you doing?" she asked.

"We're going to take the Metro to the monument." Sloan locked up the cargo van and pocketed the keys. "For one thing, we're less conspicuous as pedestrians than driving around in the green cargo van. And for another, parking in DC is impossible."

She couldn't argue with his logic. When he took her hand, she caught her breath in surprise, then quickly figured out he just wanted her to keep up as he strode through the crowd of people to the nearest train station.

As she sat on the subway, Natalia realized it had been two days since she'd come home from work on the Metro. Two days and an entire lifetime ago. She wasn't the same person, not after everything that had transpired in those forty-eight hours. From losing her home to an explosion, Ivan's death, the attempts on her life, to kissing Sloan.

She didn't know who she was anymore, especially with the big gaping hole in her past. For too long now, she'd done nothing but try to discover the real identities of her birth parents.

Would she ever know the truth?

JULY 2 – 2:37 *p.m.* – *Washington, DC*

SLOAN SLOUCHED in the seat beside Natalia, scanning the people on the train for anyone who might be FBI. Despite his lack of sleep, every muscle in his body was on alert. His gut told him they were on the right track, meeting with Lara Nevsky.

When the train stopped, he stood and took Natalia's hand again, to keep her close to his side as they disembarked from the train. The Washington Monument wasn't far, so they walked.

"Let me know if you see her," he murmured, his mouth close to her ear. He wished he'd had time to pull up a picture of Lara Nevsky, but he hadn't. He'd need to depend on Natalia to pick her out of the crowd.

She nodded, glancing around at the people around them. He swept his gaze over the area as well to make sure they weren't being followed.

"Over there," Natalia told Sloan. "The woman wearing a light-blue and white short-sleeved blouse and navy blue slacks."

"I see her." Sloan noticed an empty park bench and steered Natalia toward it.

"Natalia!" Lara hurried over. "It's good to see you."

"For me too, *Tetya*." Natalia gave the woman a warm

hug, then turned to introduce Sloan. "This is Sloan, my protector. He used to work for the FBI."

"The FBI?" Lara's eyes rounded, her gaze turning hopeful. "Do you know Michael Cummings?" When Sloan shook his head, she continued, "The morning after his arrest, Alek asked me to call Stefan so he could get in touch with someone from the FBI, a Michael Cummings. I'd hoped you'd help me find him."

The name wasn't at all familiar. "I'm afraid I don't know him. Why was Alek in contact with someone from the FBI? Were they working together for some reason?"

Lara twisted her hands together. "Alek and I haven't been together for the past year, so I don't know much. Only what Stefan told me. Alek claims he was taking trips home to Russia because this Michael Cummings asked him to meet with some people there."

"But he didn't say why?" Sloan pressed. Interesting, from what Lara was describing, he suspected Alek was functioning as a source of inside information. But for whom? And to what end?

"No." Lara shrugged. "Stefan asked me if I'd ever heard Alek talk about this Michael Cummings, but since I moved out, I hadn't."

"*Tetya*." Natalia frowned and took her aunt's hand in hers. "I'm sorry. I know moving out must have been a difficult decision for you. Why didn't you call me?"

"You had enough troubles of your own." Lara patted Natalia's hand with a sad smile, averting her gaze. She subtly withdrew from Natalia's touch. "I didn't want to burden you with mine."

Sloan wanted to get back to the point. "I'd hoped you'd let us look through Alek's papers, but I guess that's not possible if you weren't living together."

"No." Lara blushed, embarrassed. "I don't have anything of his." Then she lifted her gaze. "But I do have a house key I can give you." She rummaged in her purse, then pulled out a key and handed it to Natalia.

"Do you think Stefan Durik would talk to us?" Sloan knew he was pushing, but he didn't want to sit out in the open any longer than necessary. The last attempt on Natalia's life had been outside his condo in the bright light of day. He wasn't about to take any chances.

"I don't know. Maybe." Lara didn't sound overly hopeful. She turned toward Natalia. "There is much I need to discuss with you."

"We don't have time now," Sloan warned. As much as he wanted to hear more, the nagging itch along the back of his neck warned him they needed to move. He glanced over his shoulder, hoping the Feds weren't out there with listening devices picking up their conversation. "We'll get in touch with you later. Set up another meeting."

Lara switched to Russian. "Natalia, you must be careful. I saw what happened to your house. You are in much danger."

"Sloan understands part of our language," Natalia replied gently in English. "But don't worry, I'll be fine."

He wished he could sound as confident; instead, he stood and drew Natalia to her feet. At least they had a name and a key, it was more than he'd expected. "Don't tell anyone you spoke to us. Especially anyone from the FBI."

Lara sucked in a quick breath, her eyes widening in alarm. "But why? I thought you worked with the FBI?"

"There isn't time to explain, but you must trust us on this." Sloan's instincts were clamoring at him to leave, and he tugged on Natalia's hand. "Please, don't tell a soul."

"Goodbye, *Tetya*," Natalia said over her shoulder. "Take care."

"You too. I hope and pray God will watch over you, Natalia."

"And I pray He will watch over you and Uncle Alek too."

"Come on." Sloan dragged Natalia behind him through the crowd. "We're going to head back to the Metro."

"Back to where we left the car?" Natalia asked.

"No, we're going to ride to the southeast side of DC." Sloan took the steps down to the Metro.

"Why would we do that?" Natalia stumbled a bit, so he slowed his pace.

"To go to Pike's Pub." Sloan breathed a little easier when he didn't pick out anyone who looked to be a tail. "A place Slammer hangs out."

"Slammer?" Natalia wrinkled her nose at the name. "Don't tell me we need another car?"

"Maybe." He could admit he might have overreacted to the navy blue sedan that he'd thought was following them, but another vehicle couldn't hurt. And he also wanted to know more about the Russian Mafia, and Slammer was the guy who might be able to give them a name. The guy had more connections than the hub of an airline. "I'm hoping he can help with our other problem, if you know what I mean."

Natalia nodded, although her expression was uncertain. He waited until they were settled on the next train before filling her in.

The train filled up quickly as they grew closer to rush hour. At least the mass of people would make it difficult for anyone to follow.

They arrived at Pike's Pub, a tiny hole-in-the-wall joint, an hour later. The outside of the building was falling apart, and he knew the inside décor wasn't much better. Natalia didn't belong anywhere near the place, but he didn't dare leave her outside alone. They wouldn't stay long, but with any luck, they'd find Slammer inside.

The stale scent of cigarette smoke and beer greeted them as he opened the door. Several men sat around the bar, most of them drinking. His hopes dropped when he didn't see Slammer's familiar face amongst the few patrons.

Sloan headed for the bar, keeping Natalia close to his side. She wasn't dressed provocatively, but a few of the men leered at her anyway. He ignored them with an effort, ordered two soft drinks, and put cash out for the bartender. "Hey, you see Slammer around lately? The dude owes me heavy coin."

The bartender, a large Asian man, scooped up the money, then shook his head. "Don't hold your breath on seeing your money."

"Why not? Slammer land in the joint again?"

"Nah." The bartender slapped two lukewarm soft drinks on the bar.

He reached for his glass, eyeing the bartender over the rim.

"He's not in the joint," the Asian man continued. "He's dead."

"Dead?" Startled by the news, he stared at the bartender, his glass halfway to his mouth. He tried to cover his reaction. "How? What happened?"

"Blew up when that new car of his exploded about a mile from here." The Asian shook his head and snickered, leaning one elbow on the bar. "Whoo-hee, you should'a seen the way that fire lit up the sky. I'm telling you, that Slammer sure knew how to go out with a bang."

CHAPTER FOURTEEN

July 2 – 4:12 p.m. – Moscow, Russia

"I WANT AN UPDATE." The rain continued to pelt the earth, and the river outside was rising to a dangerous level. If the rain didn't stop, the banks would flood. Again.

"There isn't anything to update you on. We're still searching for her."

Svoloch. The job needed an expert, not an incompetent idiot. Was a trip to the US in order? No, it was too soon after Korolev's death to take the risk. The threat of a flood made staying in Moscow a priority. "How hard can it be to find one woman?"

No response.

Stupid man. Remaining calm was difficult. The incessant rain didn't help. "Is Nevsky still in jail?"

"Yeah. They didn't let him out on bail."

Good. At least one part of the plan was working. Soon all the power would be within grasp. But the woman needed to be found.

And silenced. Permanently.

A task that should have been done years ago or they wouldn't be in this situation now.

"Find her. Call me every day until you find her."

"Sure thing. Don't worry, the next time we talk I'm sure I'll have good news."

"I hope so. Otherwise I might assume you are no longer of any use to me."

"Don't get hasty." The underlying panic in his tone was perfect. "There are still a few days left before the deadline. I'll get the job done."

"You'd better. Or I won't hesitate to replace you."

Of course, the mole would be replaced soon anyway, but he didn't need to know that. Not until the job was finished.

Not until Natalia was dead.

JULY 2 – 4:13 p.m. – *Washington, DC*

"GREAT. Now I'll never get my money." Natalia couldn't believe the way Sloan casually sipped his beer as if nothing were wrong. "Jerk."

"Hey, at least you know he's not spending it." The mammoth Asian man behind the bar actually laughed. "The fool was bragging about the sweet deal he'd made for the car too. Guess the car had the last laugh."

The car. A sudden icy coldness slid down her spine. Sloan's car? The one they'd traded for the awful rusty cargo van?

"When did this happen anyway?" Sloan set his half-full

beer on the bar. "Didn't see any cops or fire trucks outside when we pulled up."

"Late last night, close to bar time." The Asian puffed out his chest. "Did my best business last night, right under the nose of all those cops. You shoulda seen it. 'Twas a beautiful thing."

"You're the man." Sloan grinned back at him.

"You bet." The big Asian nodded. "You ever need anything, come to me. I'll set you up, sweet."

She poked Sloan in the ribs. Were they going to stand here in this filthy bar all day? Slammer had died because they'd switched vehicles. She felt sick at the thought of indirectly causing another man's death. Not that Slammer was completely innocent, but he certainly didn't deserve to die.

"Whad'ya want?" Sloan frowned at her, then gave an elaborate sigh. "Guess the old lady wants out of here. Catch you later maybe, for that sweet deal." Sloan sent the bartender a sly wink.

Old lady? She narrowed her gaze and held her tongue. Barely.

The Asian shrugged, then picked up her untouched soft drink and downed it himself, emptying the glass with one chug. "Yeah, sure. Later."

With relief, she headed toward the door as Sloan stayed protectively behind her the entire time. The moment they were outside, she turned to ask him about the car. He shocked her by covering her mouth with his.

"Not here," he whispered before drawing away. "Come on, let's pick up the Metro."

Irritated at how he'd managed to leave her breathless with his unexpected kiss, she followed him to the subway station. Sloan had grabbed her hand again, keeping a brisk pace. At the train station, they had to wait for the next train, so she found an isolated spot where they could talk.

"Slammer died because we gave him your car, didn't he?" Natalia kept her voice low.

"Yeah." Sloan glanced around, making sure no one was close enough to overhear. "Whoever torched him didn't do their homework though. They should have known we weren't in the car. Which is a piece of the puzzle that doesn't fit. Even a rookie Fed would have made sure before taking such a drastic step." He shrugged. "Maybe we're not responsible after all. Slammer could have ticked off one of his low-life customers. Wouldn't be the first time."

She didn't ask what sort of customers Slammer had because she suspected she didn't want to know exactly what wares he'd sold. "This is horrible."

"No different than the other deaths." Sloan gripped her hand in his. "We didn't do anything, Natalia. Remember that. We're victims here. You and I didn't set that bomb."

He was right. She let out her breath in a sigh. They hadn't blown up the car. And if Sloan's observations were correct, she wasn't sure who had.

"What did the bartender mean? About doing his best business under their noses."

Sloan grimaced and sent her a sidelong glance. "He pulled one over on the cops, selling drugs while they were right outside."

Drugs? It bothered her that Sloan knew about that. Why not call the police? Let them know what was going on? "Oh."

"Don't get all bent out of shape. I've had to hang around these guys to get intel I needed about the Russian Mafia. It's not like I'm involved in any criminal activity."

"Are you sure about that?"

Sloan narrowed his gaze and changed the subject. "We need to go through Alek's things, see what we can come up with. Do you know how to get to his house?"

"Yes." The subway train pulled up, the noise making it impossible to say anything more. She followed Sloan onto the very crowded car. Seeing how easily Sloan slid into the buddy role with the bartender had bothered her more than she wanted to admit. Not that she was a total prude, but she'd never actually chatted with a known drug dealer before. On occasion, she'd get an ICU patient who had drugs in their possession, but that was the extent of her interaction with the criminal population of DC.

Until now. Drug dealers probably weren't as bad as violent murderers, she reminded herself. Soulless murderers like the Solntsevskaya. So what if Sloan fit in? She trusted him to help find the man who'd killed Ivan. Which was all that mattered.

Uncle Alek's house wasn't far from hers, but it was more than a few miles from the nearest Metro station. "It's close to Langdon Park. We can't take the train the whole way though, and it's too far to walk."

"We can take a taxi from the Metro station. Can't use a rideshare, as that's a credit card transaction easily tracked. Regardless, I'm not ready to go back for the van yet."

Because he was afraid that vehicle might explode too? She touched the cross at her throat. Lara was right to remind her to have faith in God. He'd watched over her and Sloan for the past few days. She needed to continue to place her faith in His plan.

Her knuckles pressed against the crescent moon pendant. She wished they'd found some answers about her past. Had her parents given her up to avoid being tainted by the Mafia? Why had Josef recognized the pendant? Was her mother out there somewhere, thinking of her? And what about her birth father? Had her mother known who he was? In truth, Natalia knew there was a possibility both her birth father and birth mother were dead, but somehow she couldn't make herself believe it. Did she have a brother? A sister? The need to know gnawed at her.

Natalia closed her eyes, the throbbing in her head seeming to grow worse. She couldn't help thinking about Slammer. Ivan. Josef. So many deaths. Such a senseless loss of life. Who else besides the Mafia could be behind all this? And why? For nothing more than money? She didn't want to believe it.

She didn't know what Sloan expected to find at Uncle Alek's. Evidence he was being framed for Josef's murder? She doubted he'd find anything of the kind. Anyone smart enough to pull that off wasn't going to leave a bunch of obvious clues behind.

They disembarked from the subway at the Rhode Island Avenue stop, then flagged down a taxi. Before they got in, Sloan asked her for the address, and then told the taxi driver to drop them off at Langdon Park.

They didn't talk until the taxi driver had let them off at the corner of the park. Sloan paid, in cash, then ushered her toward the picnic area where there was an empty table. "Have a seat. We need to go into your uncle's house the back way, in case they've got someone watching out front. Do you have the key?"

"Yes." She handed it over. "If they're watching the house, how are we going to get in?"

"I don't know." Sloan glanced around. "Tell me about this area. Is it mostly residential?"

"Yes, except for the Amtrak tracks running along the

back of his house. Uncle Alek used to complain about the noise."

"Okay, tell me exactly where his house is."

"This would be easier if we had a paper and pencil." Natalia sighed and drew imaginary lines on the top of the picnic table as she described the layout of the houses on the street. "His is the middle house in the cul-de-sac. It's red with white trim."

"All right. We're going to walk past the back of the house. If things look clear, then we'll go inside the back way."

She nodded, anxious to get this little trip over with. "Let's go, then."

They walked east a few blocks, then crossed the Amtrak train tracks near Franklin Street. Glancing around the area, she didn't see anything suspicious. There was a line of trees between Alek's property and the railroad tracks, no doubt planted in an attempt to minimize the noise.

She and Sloan crept up to the trees. Peering through, she recognized the back of Uncle Alek's house. There wasn't anyone around as far as she could tell.

"I bet they're sitting out front, if at all. There's no place to park a car back here to watch the back door."

She had to agree. "Let's just hope the key works for the back door."

They crossed the lawn, moving quickly. "When we get inside, no lights and no talking, in case they have the house bugged."

She widened her eyes and nodded. Sloan slid the key into the lock and opened the door. They stepped inside, and Sloan closed the door behind them.

Moving silently, they crept through the house. Natalia took the lead since she knew the layout. There was a small room that her uncle used as a study, so she took Sloan there first.

The place had already been searched, Natalia noted with dismay. Her uncle's neat and orderly office was a mess, papers everywhere, and the computer that usually sat on the desk was gone. Sloan's expression turned grim, but he went through the paperwork anyway. She picked up a few of the papers scattered on the floor and noticed one was a medical bill from Washington University Hospital.

She didn't recognize the doctor's name but noticed the bill was for laboratory work. She couldn't help wondering what was wrong. Normally Uncle Alek sought her out when he came to Washington University Hospital, but apparently not this time.

Sloan was still going through papers. He then went down on his hands and knees to examine the area around the desk. He pulled out a piece of paper that was trapped between the desk and the wall. Grabbing her arm, he thrust the paper into her hands.

It was a letter written in Russian. Cyrillic Russian. She didn't understand everything written in the note, but one thing was clear.

The letter was dated three weeks ago, addressed to Alek Nevsky, and was signed by Josef Korolev.

Stunned, she stared at the undeniable connection. Uncle Alek had corresponded with Josef Korolev.

And was now in jail for Josef's murder.

JULY 2 – 5:38 p.m. – Washington, DC

"YOU SHOULDN'T BE HERE." Alek stared at his wife,

wishing he could break through the barrier separating them to gather her in his arms. "Don't do this to yourself. Stay away from me."

"I can't stay away, Alek." Lara gave him a watery smile and put her hand up onto the glass. "I had to come. I needed to see you. To talk to you."

He placed his hand over the glass too, in the same spot as hers. Since he'd been about to die of loneliness, he couldn't argue. Even though he knew Lara's coming to the jail where he was being held was risky.

"Did you talk to our favorite relative?" He was aware law enforcement officials were watching and listening to their conversation. He dropped his hand. For all he knew, they'd tapped the phone too. If so, they already knew about Natalia.

"Yes. She's doing wonderful. She has a new man in her life." Lara's smile was strained. "I think you'd like him."

A new man? Was she trying to tell him Natalia wasn't alone? He wasn't sure if the news was a good sign or a bad one. "So you told her what she needed to know?"

Lara bit her lip and shook her head. "There wasn't time, they were in a rush, but I will. I promise. If you could see how happy she is, you wouldn't worry."

They were in a rush? Because they were on the run? He couldn't help but worry. Natalia was in terrible danger, but he didn't dare speak of it now.

"I'll try not to worry. But it's difficult. She's so special to me. Like a daughter."

"I know." Lara tightened her grip on her purse. "They will only let me stay a short time. But it's not nearly enough, Alek. I want to get you out of here. I wish there was something I could do to help."

He swallowed a groan because he very badly wanted

the same thing. To get out of this awful place amongst real criminals. To have one more chance with Lara.

This time he'd make a better choice. This time he would put his marriage first.

But it was too late. They weren't going to let him out. Once there was room in the federal prison, he'd be transferred over there and held until his trial. Hopelessness washed over him.

"I know, *milaya moya*." My darling. "I wish I could have a second chance too." He drew himself upright. "But there is nothing you can do. You must not come here again. This isn't healthy. You left me, and now you must continue to make a life for yourself without me."

"You ask too much," Lara whispered.

His heart soared. Did she really mean it? He forced himself to look stern. "I only ask you to live your life. And if I'm proven innocent of this horrible crime, then we'll start over again. From the very beginning."

"Yes." Lara sniffled, her eyes bright with tears. "I'd like that, Alek."

Having Lara so near yet so far was torture. He couldn't stand for her to see him like this, so he stood, indicating he was ready to return to his cell. "Go home, Lara. Don't come back here again."

She was openly crying as he walked away.

By the time he'd reached his cell, his cheeks were wet with tears too.

JULY 2 – 5:56 p.m. – Washington, DC

SLOAN DIDN'T KNOW how much of the letter Natalia

could read, but he knew they were finally onto something. He took the letter from her and tucked it into his pocket. There would be time to talk about the contents later. For right now, it was enough for him to know Josef and Alek knew each other at least enough to respond to letters on a one-on-one basis. What else had the FBI missed? He bent over the desk, intent on continuing the search.

Outside the study, the floor creaked loudly from the weight of a footstep.

He froze. Natalia's eyes widened with fear, and she grasped his arm in a tight grip. He quickly scanned their options. The closed door was the only exit from the room, unless you counted the small window across from the door. One glance confirmed the window faced the back of the house with a clear view of the line of trees separating the yard from the railroad tracks.

They could make a break for it. If there weren't agents already swarming the perimeter of the house, waiting and ready to pounce.

He tried not to think the worst, slid his gun out of his shoulder holster, and stood behind the door to listen. If there was only one person on the other side, they had a good chance of getting away.

Natalia let go of his arm and crossed over to the window. Pushing up on the sill, she eased the frame upward. He held his breath, waiting for the telltale noise to alert the intruder to their presence.

Maintaining his stance behind the door, he waited. Natalia sent him a panicked look when the window stuck, only halfway up.

He nodded, indicating she should continue to push it open.

She hesitated, obviously torn. From the corner of his

eye, he noticed a slight movement. He quickly gestured for her to get away from the window as the doorknob continued to turn.

Natalia didn't move fast enough. The door opened, and she was caught against the window like a rabbit in a snare. Sloan saw a hand holding a gun as the intruder came through the door. Natalia gasped, diverting the attention of the intruder long enough for him to attack.

He grabbed the hand holding the gun and yanked the guy off balance, using the door as a weapon, slamming it against the guy's face.

"Omph." Their assailant groaned but shoved the door back at him in an effort to get free.

Knocked off balance, Sloan nearly lost his hold on the guy's gun hand. He reared forward, putting all his weight behind the action, pressing his thumb into the sensitive area between the guy's thumb and forefinger.

"Argh!" The guy opened his hand and dropped the gun at the same time he kicked Sloan in the stomach, breaking his grip. Sloan didn't go down but steadied his grip on his gun.

"Don't." Sloan aimed his gun square in the center of the guy's forehead. "I have nothing to lose. I won't hesitate to kill you."

The assailant must have believed him because he went completely still. Sloan kicked the gun out of his reach.

"Natalia. Pick up the gun." He didn't take his eyes off the FBI agent. Ethan Wilcox. He recognized him as one of the agents working the Josef Korolev event. "Who sent you here?"

"The same people who hired you, originally." Wilcox smirked. "Only now you're on the FBI hit list, Dreyer. We have orders to shoot to kill, you know."

Behind him Natalia gasped, but he wasn't surprised. The FBI hadn't liked him much when he worked for them either, especially his boss, Saunders. Something about the way he didn't care to follow their precious rules. "So why didn't you?"

Wilcox's smirk faded. "Hey, all we want is the woman. Turn her over and I'll let you go, pretend I never saw you."

Yeah. Right. He believed that like he believed in the tooth fairy and happily ever after. "No way."

Wilcox raised a brow. "So now what? Are you going to shoot me?"

It was tempting. Very tempting. "Why do you want Natalia?" Sloan stalled for time. Was Wilcox working alone? He braced himself for reinforcements.

Wilcox sneered. "She's a suspect."

Yeah, but there was more to this whole thing. Much more. And he wanted to know details. "You want the woman? Fine. Maybe we can make a deal. Trade information."

Behind him, Natalia sucked in a harsh breath. He didn't so much as glance at her.

Wilcox narrowed his gaze. "What kind of information?"

"Who told you to bring Natalia in for questioning? Saunders? Bentley?"

Wilcox stared at him.

"Are you working this case alone? Where's your partner? Isn't his name Harper?"

Wilcox crossed his arms over his chest. "You're wasting my time. I'm not giving you jack."

Sloan swallowed a burst of anger. Arrogant jerk. Clearly, Wilcox wasn't going to talk. Maybe he just didn't know anything more than what his superiors told him. One of the things he hated the most about the FBI was everything was on a "need to know" basis. For all he knew, the guy was just following orders.

The way all good agents were supposed to.

Sloan glanced over at Natalia. She stood, holding Wilcox's gun, her expression uncertain. One of them was going to have to tie Wilcox up while the other held a gun on him. He suspected Natalia didn't have the nerve to do either. Nor was he willing to let her get too close as he was afraid Wilcox would try to use her as a hostage.

Stalemate.

By the smug expression on the agent's face, Wilcox knew it.

"Put your hands behind your head." Sloan ordered, taking a careful step back.

Wilcox did as he was told, but Sloan could see he was waiting for the chance to break free.

He lowered the gun a few inches and pulled the trigger.

Natalia screamed almost as loud as Wilcox who grabbed his leg. "What in the— You shot me!"

"Go out through the window, Natalia. Now."

"But—"

"*Now!*" He reached behind him to push her toward the window. "He won't die, I promise. But I'm sure there are several agents already on the way. If we stay, you'll be caught."

Natalia gave the injured man one last look, then crawled through the window. Sloan followed, shoved the gun into his waistband, and grabbed her hand.

"Run. We need to get out of here."

CHAPTER FIFTEEN

July 2 – 6:09 p.m. – Washington, DC

NATALIA GASPED, sucking oxygen, running alongside Sloan as they burst through the row of trees. The telltale sound of an oncoming train made her stumble to a stop.

"Let's go!" Sloan tugged on her arm. "There isn't much time."

"We can't!" Horrified, Natalia watched the oncoming train. Surely he couldn't mean to cross now?

"The train will slow them down." Sloan tugged on her hand again, hauling her toward the tracks. She worried that if she didn't follow, he'd leave her behind. With a murmured prayer, she followed him, jumping across the tracks seconds before the train sped past, narrowly avoiding being hit. The train let loose with a shrill warning honk, the wind whipping against her back as the train roared past.

"Come on, we gotta move." She could barely hear him over the noise as Sloan continued to run, heading back toward Langdon Park. Natalia didn't have energy to waste speaking, but she understood that Sloan was trying to find a way to lose themselves in the crowd.

The image of Sloan shooting Ethan Wilcox in the leg stayed with her as they slowed down to a walk, mingling with the groups of people, anxious to fit in. What if Sloan had hit the agent in the femoral artery? What if the poor guy bled to death before he could get medical treatment? What if he lost his leg?

What if she were charged as an accomplice in the crime?

Impervious to her consternation, Sloan whistled and waved a hand, flagging down a taxi. With relief, she climbed inside when he held the door for her. "Union Station," he told the driver.

Why Union Station, she had no idea, but she didn't ask.

The cabbie had the air-conditioning cranked, and the air seemed twice as cold against her sweat-dampened skin. She shivered, rubbing her hands along her bare arms.

"I remember Wilcox. He was the one who questioned me the night Josef died. It's time we go to the police. Tell them what happened," she murmured to Sloan in a low tone.

"Yeah. There's a stellar plan." His whisper didn't hide his sarcasm. "Because we have such a good reason to think they'll believe us over the Feds."

"They might." She darted a glance at their cab driver who was bobbing his head to static-filled music from the radio. "I heard the local police hate working with FBI agents. Maybe they'll take our side just for that reason."

Sloan groaned and scrubbed a hand over his face. "Get real. This isn't a TV show. Have you forgotten everything I've taught you? Don't trust anyone. And right now that includes the police."

Maybe he was right. What did she know about this sort of thing? She was a nurse, not a cop. And never before had she been on the run like some common criminal. Never before had people wanted her dead. She fell silent, staring out the window as the taxi driver negotiated the traffic to get to Union Station.

When the taxi slowed to a stop, Sloan pulled cash from his wallet and handed it to the driver. "Thanks."

They climbed from the taxi. Sloan immediately headed for the train station.

"Wait." She dug in her heels, tired of following him everywhere like some faithful puppy. "Where are we going?"

"Taking the Metro to where we left our car." Sloan gave her an impatient glance. "Why?"

"We need to take the letter to Stefan." Natalia grasped Sloan's arm. "The letter may help to prove Uncle Alek's innocence."

"You need to worry about yourself, not your Uncle Alek. Or have you forgotten how someone's trying to kill you?" Sloan shook off her hand. "Come on, we're going to catch the next train."

She followed him down to the lower level, waiting while he purchased tickets. Going back to the car served her purpose at the moment. They could drive to Stefan's house easier than taking public transportation.

The height of rush hour had faded, so Sloan was able to sit close beside her. Too close.

"May I see the letter?" she asked.

Reluctantly, he pulled it from his pocket and handed it to her. "Will you read it to me?"

"I'll try. I learned a little Cyrillic with Ivan but not a lot. Some parts are easy though." She took the letter and scanned the words. "Sir," she began, "As I sit here to write this I am still shocked from the news—something. I don't want to believe you, but I do. I can't deny the truth and—something." She shrugged, unable to figure out some of the words, then continued, "I will arrange a trip to the States to visit your city within two weeks so we may discuss this matter further." She glanced at Sloan. "I guess this explains the sudden speaking engagement here in DC."

Sloan was looking at her oddly. "Is there anything else?"

She turned her attention back to the letter. "I can't make out everything, but there is information about his travel arrangements and the hotel where he planned to stay."

"Unbelievable." Sloan raked his hand through his hair.

"What?" She folded the letter carefully. "You seem upset." She frowned. "More upset than when you shot that man in the leg. We need to talk about that. What on earth were you thinking? What if that man dies as a result of your reckless behavior? You'll end up in jail, right next to Uncle Alek."

Sloan rolled his eyes. "Get over it already. I'm sure Wilcox is fine. This letter is far more important."

"Yes, to help prove Uncle Alek's innocence."

"No. Don't you see?" Sloan stared at her. "Don't you get it? This could be used as evidence against your uncle, Natalia. The FBI could twist this letter to prove Nevsky was in fact working for the Solntsevskaya. And frankly? I'm not convinced he's not."

JULY 2 – 6:38 p.m. – Washington, DC

. . .

"WHY WOULD YOU SAY SUCH A THING?"

Sloan could tell Natalia was upset, but he wasn't about to sugarcoat the truth.

"Just because they corresponded about some sort of shocking news," she continued, tucking a strand of her silky blonde hair behind her ear. "It doesn't mean either of them worked for the Solntsevskaya."

Sloan sighed. "Do you think it's a coincidence that your uncle corresponded with Korolev just before he died? You don't think that the FBI can twist that around to mean whatever they want? Like maybe Nevsky drew Korolev out here just for the sole purpose of killing him?"

Her shoulders slumped in defeat. "I don't know. Maybe."

They fell silent as the train ate up the miles. When their stop came up, he plucked the letter from her hand and tucked it safely in his pocket. "We're getting off here."

Natalia nodded, her expression listless as if all the will to fight had drained from her body. Knowing her uncle really could take the fall for this bothered her. Sloan couldn't blame her for being exhausted, especially since they'd spent hours running around DC without finding the proof they needed. Annoyed at how he wanted to protect her, to keep her cushioned from the truth, he stood and prepared to get off the subway. She followed his lead, her eyes lacking the sparkle and spunk he preferred. He shoved his concern aside, although he hoped his feisty Russian princess would return soon.

"How do you know the van is safe?" Natalia asked, once they'd climbed up from the train station. "That someone hasn't tampered with it or rigged some tracking device up to it?"

He glanced at her with admiration. "Hey, now you're

starting to think like a cop. Good job. We don't know the van is safe. Actually, all I really want to do is retrieve our stuff, then pick up another car."

"Pick up another car?" She looked confused. "You mean, like buy another one?"

"No. I mean like steal one." He led the way toward the spot where he'd left the van, but instead of stopping, he purposefully walked past it, checking several of the other cars to see if anyone had done something obvious, like leaving their keys in the ignition. He saw an older model, a rather beat-up convertible that had a soft top he could easily cut through. It wouldn't be the first car he'd hot-wired.

"Anyone watching us?" Sloan asked as he attempted to pry his fingers up underneath the soft top of the convertible and the hard, unforgiving window.

"Not that I can tell." Natalia sounded anything but certain. Her previous listlessness had vanished, leaving her tense, alert as she stood beside him.

"Good. Keep a sharp eye out. I need a few minutes here."

Natalia turned her back toward him as if to protect him from being seen. He winced as he tried to wiggle his hand into the miniscule opening. When that didn't work, he pulled out his pocketknife and tore a slit in the soft convertible top, just large enough for him to reach the lock. He pulled it up by his fingertips and then yanked the car door open. Sliding into the seat, he used his knife to break open the casing beneath the steering wheel, quickly pulled out the ignition wires, and tested them by touching the red one and the green one together.

The engine roared to life. With a satisfied smile, he disconnected them. "We're ready. Let's go." He turned and strode toward the spot where he'd left the van.

She grasped his arm, her nails biting painfully into his flesh when he approached their car. "Don't. I'm scared."

"We're just grabbing our stuff," Sloan soothed, heading around to the rear of the vehicle. He hesitated and looked carefully around for any sign of tampering before reaching for the doors. "Stand back."

"Lord, keep us safe," she whispered.

He echoed her sentiment, despite the fact that he hadn't prayed in a very long time. Since his sister's murder to be exact. He pulled open the doors and felt his heart leap into his throat when he saw a bruised and bloody man lying inside on top of their stuff. The familiar dark hair and skin made his stomach clench painfully. "Jordan?"

"About time you showed up." Jordan peered up at him from his swollen and bruised face. "I need a ride."

JULY 2 – 7:09 p.m. – Washington, DC

"JORDAN?" Natalia wondered if Sloan was hallucinating. But no, when she stepped closer, she saw Jordan sprawled in the back of the cargo van.

"Get him into the convertible," Sloan ordered, helping Jordan out of the car. He propped him on his feet, but Jordan didn't look too steady, swaying from side to side like a willow in the wind. "We have to get out of here."

Since Jordan looked to be in dire need of medical assistance, she didn't argue but slipped her arm around Jordan's lean waist and grabbed onto the waistband of his jeans. "Lean on me."

Jordan could barely walk, and he was a lot heavier than he looked. They'd made it halfway to the convertible when

Sloan jogged past them, carrying everything from the van. He opened the convertible door, stashed the duffle, the computer case, and the bag of food in the back, then turned back to meet them.

Jordan's knees buckled, and Natalia feared she would have dropped him if not for Sloan's quick reaction, grabbing Jordan's arm above the elbow and hauling him upright.

"Come on, buddy. We're almost there." With Sloan's help, they managed to drag Jordan the rest of the way to the car they were about to steal. Strange how stealing a car didn't bother her a bit now that Jordan's life was at risk. Not when all their lives counted on transportation.

One look at the cramped back seat made Natalia grimace. "Put him up front. I'll climb into the back."

"No, I want him in the back, to keep him out of sight." Sloan pushed and shoved until Jordan was lying along the back seat. Breathing heavily, he gestured to her. "Get in. We need to get out of here."

Natalia climbed into the passenger seat and shut the door. As Sloan climbed in and started the car, she turned in her seat to get a better look at Jordan. "What happened? Where are you hurt?"

"Everywhere." His lips curved in a heartbreaking semblance of a smile. "You're cute, Natalia. Really cute." His eyes slid closed.

Sloan hit the gas, and she grabbed onto the back of his seat to maintain her balance. "He's confused, Sloan. I think he must have a head injury."

"He's not confused." Sloan scowled as he glanced at Jordan through his rearview mirror. "You are cute. But I think your nursing skills must be rusty. Can't you tell when someone has had the snot beat out of him?"

Offended, she narrowed her eyes at him. "Of course, I

can tell someone beat him up. *Durachok*, a monkey could tell he's been beaten up. And that's exactly why I think he may have a head injury. I happen to know how that feels, remember?"

Ignoring Sloan, she leaned over the front seat to examine Jordan more closely. "Any other injuries I need to know about? Bullet wounds? Knife wounds?"

"No." Jordan's eyelids opened a slit. "I think I have a couple of broken ribs though. My chest hurts like a son of a gun."

She sucked in a quick breath. Broken ribs were extremely painful, and if his head ached anything like hers had, the poor man had to be in agony. She sat back down in her seat. "We need to make another stop at a drugstore."

"Yeah, okay. Give me some time though. I want to get far out of DC."

"Are we going back to the cabin?" Natalia almost hoped so, because despite what had happened there between her and Sloan, she found herself longing for the peace and quiet of the mountain cabin. So much for being a die-hard city girl.

"No. We have to risk a hotel." Sloan didn't look at her. Was he remembering the intimate embrace they'd shared at the cabin too? He slipped the cell phone from his belt loop and tapped it with a finger. "Jordan called me from his cell phone right after he was jumped. There's no way to know for sure that someone didn't trace the call. We have to assume the cabin has been compromised."

"Speaking of which." Natalia snatched the phone out of his fingers, then tossed it out the window, imitating his actions from the other day. "Cell phones have GPS tracking devices on them."

"Yeah, I know," Sloan drawled, shooting her a skeptical

glance. "I'm pretty sure that phone was clean since Jordan bought it for me, but we'll pick up another one. I gotta say, Natalia. You're starting to think like me."

Was she really? "Scary."

"Tell me about it." Sloan switched directions, turning onto New York Avenue heading east as if they were going back into town.

"What are you doing?" Natalia thought he'd wanted to get out of DC, a sentiment she wholeheartedly shared.

"We need to change directions a bit, to pick a new place to go. I've decided on Baltimore."

She couldn't exactly follow his logic, but at least Baltimore wasn't too far. "What about the drugstore?"

He shook his head. "Not now. We'll wait until we hit the city. Once we reach Baltimore, we'll stop at a drugstore and then find a cheap hotel to spend the night."

JULY 2 – 7:58 p.m. – Moscow, Russia

"IS EVERYTHING IN PLACE?"

"Yes. The pipeline will blow in the next few minutes while the rest of Moscow sleeps."

"Good. And the American will be found guilty?"

"Yes. We have arranged for him to be discovered with traces of explosives in his hotel room. His guilt will not be in question."

"Excellent. I'll wait to hear the news of the bombing before sending the money."

There was a heavy silence. "Fine. But if you don't, I'll make sure the finger of guilt points directly to you instead of to the American."

Rage, hot and white, slashed deep. How dare he threaten to expose the truth? He didn't possess the brains to be in charge of this scheme.

"You'll get the money when the deed is done to my satisfaction and not before." Setting down the phone without throwing it against the wall was a major accomplishment.

Everything was unfolding according to the grand plan. The Kazakhstan-China oil pipeline would be destroyed, and the crime would be blamed on the Americans. As would the murder of Korolev. The taste of power and control was sweet.

Success was within reach. Nothing could stop them now.

Except for the woman.

Natalia.

CHAPTER SIXTEEN

July 2 – 10:24 p.m. – Baltimore, MD

NATALIA WAS ACUTELY aware of Sloan watching her as she sat beside Jordan on the edge of one of the hotel room's two double beds. She critically examined Jordan's chest covered with an array of colorful bruises, especially along the right side of his rib cage. He winced when she gently palpated the area. Had a broken rib sliced the pleural cavity? She wished she had her stethoscope so she could listen for breath sounds.

Sloan paced, muttering under his breath. How irritating to be in tune to Sloan's presence lurking behind her when she needed to concentrate on more important matters, like the state of Jordan's physical health.

"What happened?" Sloan pelted Jordan with questions. "What did the guy want? Can you recognize him?"

Ignoring Sloan, she bent over to peer at Jordan's eyes. At least his concussion appeared to be mild, his pupils reacted evenly and brisk. No other cranial nerve damage that she could see. Although the bruise over his one eye was swelling at an alarming rate.

"Well?" Sloan demanded irritably. "You must know something."

Natalia rounded on him. "*Poshi*. Leave him alone. How am I supposed to do a complete physical assessment with your constant badgering?"

Sloan eyes narrowed. "I need to know what happened. We have to figure out what's going on."

"At Jordan's expense?" She curled her fingers into fists, trying to control her temper. "Give me at least ten minutes to examine him."

Jordan groaned and shifted on the bed. Grateful for the excuse, she turned back to her patient. "I can bind your ribs, which should help stabilize them. You'll need an ice pack for your eye. And I can give you over-the-counter pain medicine." When they'd stopped at the drugstore, she'd insisted Sloan purchase more acetaminophen and ibuprofen. She hoped they'd take the edge off his pain long enough for him to get some sleep. She picked up the Ace wrap.

"Let's get it over with, then," Jordan said in a resigned tone.

He groaned again when she helped him upright. Swaying slightly, he sat at the edge of the bed while she wrapped his ribs with an extra-wide elastic wrap. She had to practically hug Jordan in order to get the bandage all the way around his torso.

"I'm taking a shower." Sloan disappeared into the bathroom, shutting the door rather loudly behind him.

"Thank heavens," she muttered as she wrapped Jordan's chest. Sloan's dire expression and incessant questions were driving her crazy.

"He doesn't like the way you're caring for me. He's protective of you."

She raised a brow at Jordan's observation. "No. It's you he's worried about. He went nuts when we lost contact with you." The way he'd kissed her had likely been an attempt to forget his friend's dire condition. "I get the feeling he doesn't have much confidence in my nursing ability."

"He hasn't cared about a woman for a long time. Two years." Jordan's eyes were focused on some spot over her head as if he hadn't heard a word she'd said. "Since Shari died."

After smoothing one end of the elastic wrap over his chest, she unwrapped another roll. She remembered the picture of Jordan with the brunette woman in Sloan's living room. "Shari was your wife."

"My wife. His sister." Jordan's tone was flat. "Sloan took her death very hard. He feels responsible even though he isn't. The past two years has been difficult for him."

"For both of you, I imagine." Strange how Jordan seemed to be concerned about his partner when he could barely sit upright under his own power. Why did he act as if something romantic was going on between her and Sloan? She hadn't given Jordan any reason to think she was interested in Sloan on a personal level. Or was her awareness of him more obvious than she realized? She hoped not. "I'm sorry for your loss," she murmured, placing the second elastic wrap around his chest.

"Thank you."

She wanted to ask more questions, about Sloan, about how Shari died, and about Jordan himself, but the fatigue etched in his face made her swallow her curiosity.

The poor guy needed sleep. "Here." She dropped four

pills into the palm of his hand and gave him a glass of water. "Take these, they'll help you rest."

Surprisingly, he did as she asked, downing the medicine and handing the glass back. He groaned as he lay down against the pillows.

She covered him with the light blanket, then doused the light. She left the room long enough to fetch some ice from the machine down the hall. She made a cold compress and then placed it on Jordan's forehead. The lamp on the other side of the room was still on, and she stared at the second bed wondering where Sloan planned to sleep.

Her thoughts were interrupted when the bathroom door opened and Sloan emerged, looking more attractive than she cared to admit, with his hair damp from his shower and his T-shirt clinging to every contoured muscle. Her pulse leaped erratically in her chest, a sensation she tried to ignore.

Sloan glanced over at Jordan, noticing he appeared to be asleep. He didn't try to wake him but turned back to where she stood awkwardly between the beds.

"You can rest in the second bed," he said as if reading her mind. "I'm going to hook up the computer to see what I can find out about Michael Cummings."

According to Aunt Lara, Michael Cummings was the FBI agent Uncle Alek was working with during his trips back to Russia. Her interest piqued. She'd like to know more about the man herself. "I'd like to help."

"No need." He took up residence in the chair closest to the door and set up his satellite computer on the small table nearby. "Better for you to get some rest."

She wanted to argue because he needed rest as much if not more than she did. But she was too tired to fight. The open bathroom door reminded her it was her turn to use the shower. She brushed past Sloan to head toward the bathroom, her skin prickling in awareness at the slight touch.

After shutting the door behind her, she leaned against it, staring at her reflection in the mirror over the sink. Her skin was pale, and the wound along her hairline was beginning to scab over. She looked terrible but not as bad as Jordan.

The brief closeness she'd shared with Sloan—was it only earlier that morning?—had completely vanished. She shouldn't have cared, should have known the situation would only become more complicated the longer they were forced to be together.

Jordan's presence had altered things between them. Why didn't she feel a welcome relief?

Because she missed him. Missed the closeness they'd shared, the intimacy of being held in his arms.

More than she would have imagined.

JULY 2 – 11:07 p.m. – Baltimore, MD

SLOAN SCOWLED at the computer screen, trying not to be distracted by Natalia. He'd acted like an idiot when she was taking care of Jordan. There was no excuse, except that the brief flash of jealousy had caught him off guard.

He'd never been jealous over a woman before in his life. But watching Natalia caring so tenderly for Jordan had dropped a green haze over him.

Since when did he care more for a woman than he did his partner? Since never. He shook off the unwelcome thought and scrolled through his email. There was another urgent message from Bentley, their FBI contact. "Bentley isn't too happy with us," he muttered, deleting the message without replying. "He's demanding we turn over Natalia."

"And you're surprised?" Jordan asked, his voice weaker than Sloan liked.

He glanced over at his partner, who was now awake. Sort of. "No. For all we know, he's the mole." Not that they could prove it.

"I hope not."

Sloan knew his partner needed rest, but he burned with a need for answers. "Did you get a good look at the guy who jumped you?"

Jordan tilted his head, looking at him with his good eye since the other was pretty much swollen shut. "No. But there was more than one. Three guys were waiting for me after I'd stopped to grab something to eat."

"Three?" His stomach clenched at the unfavorable odds. "How on earth did you manage to get away?"

The corner of Jordan's mouth curved in a smirk. "I'm good."

Sloan shook his head in disgust. "Yeah. I know. Good thing, too, or I'd be angry." Jordan's close brush with death set his teeth on edge. He honestly didn't know what he'd do without his friend and partner. "I can't believe you found us."

"Divine intervention? Maybe. When I stumbled across the green cargo van, I thought I was hallucinating at first." Jordan frowned. "Until I looked inside and saw your stuff. I jimmied the lock and then climbed in to wait, hoping you'd be back for the gear."

"And you're sure you couldn't identify them?"

"I didn't recognize a single one, but that doesn't mean much, they could still be members of our former employer. Or hired thugs." Jordan shifted, winced, and rubbed a hand over his sore ribs. "I'm sure the only reason they didn't kill me right away was because they wanted information about you and Natalia."

"Natalia?" Sloan's heart dropped. What if they'd gotten their hands on Natalia?

"Yeah. Every one of their questions centered on her. Which makes me believe the mole is getting antsy to get his hands on her."

He imagined he could sense the hot breath on the back of his neck as the enemy closed in. If only he knew who exactly the enemy was. A group the size of the Solntsevskaya was difficult to pin down. He needed specific names of people to target. If the Mafia had branched their operation into the DC area, who was in charge? If he and Jordan could find out that much, they'd have a place to start.

The bathroom door opened, and Natalia stepped out, wearing one of his T-shirts. He averted his gaze, thinking he liked the idea of her wearing his things a little too much.

With an effort, he turned back to his computer and typed Michael Cummings's name into the database he and Jordan had created in the year they left the FBI.

"Do you mind if I turn on the television?" Natalia asked as she settled on the empty bed, sliding beneath the covers and propping herself up against the headboard.

"Suit yourself." He glanced at her from the corner of his eye, relieved she looked relaxed and calm.

"Turn on CNN," Jordan whispered, obviously fighting to stay awake. "See if any information on Korolev or Nevsky is out there yet. Maybe we'll learn something."

Natalia obliged, and Sloan listened as he typed in commands. He found what he was looking for when Cummings's name popped up as an FBI agent. He read the brief bit of information they had on the guy. His picture didn't look familiar.

"I need to find where he is now," Sloan muttered as he redirected his search. He, of all people, knew how much could change over the course of a year.

"Sloan? You have to see this." Natalia's horrified tone pulled his concentration from the computer.

"What is it?" he asked as he turned toward the television. "Turn it up."

She hit the volume button on the remote.

"In breaking world news tonight, we've just learned there's been an explosion along the Kazakhstan oil pipeline, cutting off the flow of oil to Beijing, China. We've been told the explosion went off about four in the morning, Moscow time. And as you can see by the film footage behind me, the fire is still blazing out of control."

"I don't believe it." Sloan stared at the grainy picture of the fire behind the CNN news reporter's head.

"This feeds into your theory, Sloan," Jordan spoke up. "First the assassination of Josef Korolev and now the destruction of the Kazakhstan oil pipeline."

"But I don't understand. How are they related?" Natalia asked in a bewildered tone. "The prime minister was here to talk about the International Middle East Peace Conference. How does the peace conference relate to the pipeline?"

"I don't know." Sloan felt sick as he abandoned the computer to stare at the ongoing news coverage. "But there has to be a link. We need to figure it out and soon."

"Both events compound the strained relationship between the US and Russia," Jordan commented. "With a bit of China thrown in."

Sloan nodded. "Yeah. Except that I keep coming back to terrorism."

"Why terrorism?" Natalia asked. "I don't understand."

Jordan stared at him, unmistakable sympathy in his lopsided gaze. He averted his head, knowing how Jordan worried about his obsession with the Solntsevskaya. He knew the Russian Mafia was branching into terrorism but couldn't prove it.

"It's just a feeling I have. The third point in the triangle is the dismantling of Russia's stockpiled nuclear, chemical, and biological weapons. Russia has the largest stockpile of chemical weapons in the world, over forty thousand tons. I can't help worrying that the pipeline explosion is just a prelude to something more. Something bigger."

"Bigger? Like 9/11?"

"Yeah." Sloan definitely had a bad feeling about all of this. "The assassination of Korolev here in DC was a warning. A message." He stared at Jordan. "Think about it for a minute. The Solntsevskaya has brought their operation to DC. What if they really are setting up a terrorist attempt?"

"Dear Lord, please have mercy," Natalia whispered.

"Exactly. I'd say the city most likely to be a target is none other than Washington, DC."

JULY 3 – 2:20 *a.m.* – *Washington, DC*

ALEK HEARD A SOUND, just the lightest brush of fabric, and was instantly wide awake. Tense, he held his breath, not wanting to alert the guards. In the past day and a half, he'd caught a couple of them staring at him with frank, undisguised hatred. Lying perfectly still in the dark jail cell, he focused his senses on his environment.

Another brush of fabric. The scent of sweat made his gut clench. As he strained to listen, he heard what sounded like a muffled footstep, close. Too close. He imagined he could hear someone breathing just a few feet away.

Someone was inside his cell.

He tensed and sprung, throwing his arm up just as his opponent struck. Using every bit of his advantage, he thrust the other man back a step as he leapt to his feet. There wasn't much room for him to maneuver though, so the assailant's next strike found its mark, and searing pain burned where the blade of a knife sliced his arm.

It had been years since he'd been in a street fight, but some skills were never forgotten. He didn't bother calling for help, knowing that only someone with a key could have gotten inside in the first place. He tried to remain calm, but his heart thundered loudly, impeding his ability to hear.

His assailant rushed forward, and Alek tried to dodge the left hand holding the knife as he slammed a fist into the man's face. Bones crunched and pain burned again as the knife slashed along the vulnerable flesh of his side. Ignoring the searing pain, Alek drove the heel of his foot toward the guy's kneecap, sweeping outward to draw him off balance. Something clattered to the floor, and he felt a surge of satisfaction knowing the guy dropped his knife.

They struggled, locked in an equally matched embrace as each tried to unbalance the other. Finally, Alek found a good grip on the man's face, and he shoved him backward with all his might.

A loud crack reverberated through the room as his assailant crumpled to the floor in a heap.

Blood seeped from his various knife wounds as he

stared at the dark shape of his opponent who hadn't moved since hitting the floor. Putting a hand over the worst of the injuries, the wound along his side, he moved forward.

He bent over the body, peering through the darkness to see what had happened. Then he realized he'd knocked the guy's head against the steel edge of the toilet.

Alek's knees buckled, and he sank to the edge of the bed, his fingers sticky with blood still seeping from the open slice along his side. He stripped off his shirt and pressed it against the wound. Was God still watching over him? He couldn't be sure.

How long did he need to wait before daring to raise the alarm?

How long before he bled to death if no one came?

JULY 3 – 2:31 *a.m.* – *Baltimore, MD*

SLOAN CONTINUED to watch the CNN news coverage of the Kazakhstan pipeline explosion long after Jordan and Natalia had fallen asleep. He pulled out his notes and stared at the triangle he'd created.

Jordan was right, these events were tied together. He didn't believe in coincidences on a good day, and especially not now. The pipeline explosion and Korolev's assassination were somehow linked. Most likely by the Solntsevskaya. Maybe the Solntsevskaya's infiltration into the Russian government was deeper than anyone knew. What he couldn't quite figure out was how Natalia fit into the picture.

He glanced over to where she was curled up on the bed, her beautiful facial features relaxed in sleep. Her uncle,

Alek Nevsky, had to be the key; he'd been in correspondence with Josef Korolev. But why had she become a target? Because of something she knew? Or because of something she saw? He wished he knew.

Tearing his gaze from her, he tossed his notes aside and stood to stretch. Exhausted, he blinked, trying to concentrate. Maybe he'd better use Natalia's spare pillow and stretch out on the floor to get some sleep.

Just as he was about to hit the button on the remote, he saw the headline, *American Suspect in Pipeline Bombing* flash across the television screen in true CNN style. Narrowing his gaze, he turned up the volume to hear more.

"There is a suspect in the Kazakhstan pipeline bombing, and we've learned this person of interest is actually an American citizen. Apparently, this suspect was found dead in his hotel room just moments ago, from what police suspect is a self-inflicted gunshot wound. Our on-site reporter has also discovered that there were traces of explosives found in the room."

"I don't believe it," Sloan mumbled beneath his breath. What else could go wrong? "First the FBI is accused of killing Korolev, and now this. Team USA is really racking up the points." Things were going from bad to worse. The White House officials had to be going nuts over this latest news.

"The suspect's identity has just been released. The Russian authorities believe a man by the name of Michael Cummings created the bomb that destroyed the Kazakhstan oil pipeline. And their theory is that once he set off the explosion, Michael Cummings took his own life."

CHAPTER SEVENTEEN

July 3 – 3:31 a.m. – Washington, DC

HE TRIED to slide into a vacant seat unnoticed, but FBI Director Clarence Yates glared at him for a long moment before sweeping his gaze over the rest of the leadership team. They'd been called in for an emergency meeting in the middle of the night, and it was clear the director was fuming with anger.

"Someone tell me how in the world we allowed Cummings's name to be blasted all over the national news?"

Silence. None of the team members wanted to be the first to speak up, fearing their boss's wrath.

Gathering his courage, he took the plunge, keeping his tone neutral. "Sir, so far, all they've said is that he's an American citizen. His role as an international FBI agent assigned to the Moscow office has been kept quiet."

"Quiet? For how long?" Yates roared, a vein bulging at the temple of his red face. "I'm surprised CNN hasn't already been banging on our doors. And where has Cummings been for the past few weeks? Someone has to know something. Isn't this why I pay you? I want answers, and I want them now!"

He resisted the urge to smile. The director's reaction was proof at how well he'd pulled this plan off. He tamped down the feeling of euphoria. "I don't know, sir. But I'll say this again, Cummings is most likely the leak we've been searching for."

Yates stared him down for a long minute. When he spoke, his voice was dangerously soft. "I assume you have proof of your allegations?"

Proof? Really, what more did the stupid idiot need? Hadn't they already wrapped it up in a neat package a blind man could have opened? "Sir, you can't ignore the fact that Cummings has been out of direct contact for almost a month. Now he's dead in a Kazakhstan hotel room with traces of explosives present. This type of extreme setup is hardly the Russian Mafia's style. No matter which faction you're talking about, their statements are generally blunt and to the point."

"If he was the leak, then we won't see any more information going outside this office, will we?" Yates's eyes glittered with fury. "We need damage control in a big way. I want you to prepare a statement with our public affairs department in preparation for the worst. If we can keep this thing under wraps, we will. I have a meeting with the president in ninety minutes."

So Yates figured his job was on the line. Too bad. As if he cared.

The only thing he cared about was finding the woman before the deadline.

So close. They'd almost had her at Nevsky's place. He

couldn't believe Wilcox had let them get away. The jerk deserved to be shot.

Nevsky. He straightened in his seat as the realization took hold. Maybe they'd missed the obvious. There was one sure way to draw Natalia out into the open.

And he had no problem using a pawn as leverage.

JULY 3 – 4:15 a.m. – Baltimore, MD

NATALIA AWOKE WITH A START, her heart thundered in her chest, her breathing short and choppy. For a moment she was disoriented, peering through the dark hotel room. After a few seconds, she realized the man who chased her through the forest surrounding the cabin had only been a part of her dream.

A nightmare.

She wasn't lost in the forest surrounding the cabin with a crazed lunatic at her heels. She was in a Baltimore hotel room with Sloan and Jordan, her reluctant protectors. Taking deep, gulping breaths, she sat up at the edge of the bed and let out a small scream when her feet touched the soft yet muscled plane of a man's body.

"What's wrong?" Sloan shot upright, glancing around for signs of danger.

"Nothing." Natalia closed her eyes in relief as her heart settled back into a normal rhythm for the second time. "I didn't know you were down there."

Sloan dragged himself to his feet, glancing over to the second bed where Jordan was still sleeping. He scrubbed his hands over his weary face. "Once again, I only managed to get a couple of hours of sleep."

Natalia stiffened. Was he implying that was her fault? "I didn't ask you to sleep on the floor between the two beds where anyone might step on you."

Even in the dim light, she could see his reluctant grin. "Is that an invitation to swap places with me?"

"No." His teasing made her want to smile. "I'll stay where I am, thanks."

He shrugged and lowered himself to the pallet he'd made on the floor. "Suit yourself. But try not to wake me up when you have another nightmare."

She sucked in a quick breath. How had he known about her nightmare?

Lying back down, she stared at the ceiling above her bed. Sloan hadn't known; most likely he'd made a lucky guess. Only now that she was awake, she couldn't fall back to sleep.

She listened to the faint rustling noises as Sloan tried to get comfortable. Another flash of guilt caught her off guard. She was beginning to care about him, far more than she should.

When Jordan began to snore, she smiled, reminded of the way her father had snored, in those early years when her adopted parents were still married.

Her father. She sat up in bed again, her eyes wide. Good grief, she'd completely forgotten the hasty message she'd left him that first night in the motel room. The same phone Sloan had tossed out the window just a few hours after she'd made the call.

If her father had gotten her panicked message, he'd be wondering why she hadn't answered her phone, or at least tried to call him again. She eyed Sloan's computer, thinking about her earlier plan. Should she try sending an email?

She hesitated. There was always the chance her father

hadn't received the message. The twins, Daryl and Daniel, were finished with school for the summer, and her father usually took his family to Canada during this timeframe for their annual summer vacation.

He'd never included her in those trips. Not that she'd been terribly interested in going. As a city girl, the idea of camping and hiking through the woods hadn't held much appeal. Yet, it would have been nice to be included, at least once.

With a sigh, she looked from the computer and lay back down. Maybe later she'd figure out a way to get in touch with her father.

"Can't sleep?" Sloan's whisper sent her heart back into her throat.

She turned her head and leaned over the side of the bed where he'd made his pallet on the floor. What was the point of lying? "No."

"Me either." Sloan once more rose to his feet and, this time, planted himself on the foot of her bed. "Things are heating up. We're running out of time. Remember the FBI agent Lara claimed Alek Nevsky was working with?"

"Yes." She peered at Sloan in the darkness. "Michael Cummings."

"Yeah. Well, good ole Michael just happens to be the suspect in the Kazakhstan pipeline bombing. Not only that, but he's dead. Took his own life, according to CNN."

"You can't be serious." Natalia stared at him. "I don't believe it."

"Neither do I," Sloan responded. "No one is that stupid. As a trained agent, he would have done a better job of covering his tracks. It's a clear setup."

Her heart sank. "So you think this is the work of the Solntsevskaya? For what gain?"

Sloan sighed deeply. "I don't know what to think. None of the puzzle pieces make a whole lot of sense. Except, I keep coming back to your theory. The Solntsevskaya must have an inside source in the FBI."

"Is there any way to get more information on the Solntsevskaya?" Natalia leaned closer to Sloan so her voice wouldn't carry over and wake Jordan. "I'm assuming we can't just look them up on the internet."

His mouth slashed in a grin. "You'll find a little information there, but all of it old. None of the depth the FBI intelligence group has. Our problem is that we need to know about the Solntsevskaya activity here in DC. We can't go to the FBI for information, since we don't know which agent is the inside leak. So, we have to watch out for both the Russians and the Feds as we try to investigate."

"There aren't that many Russians in DC," Natalia said dryly. "Where would we begin?"

Sloan lifted a shoulder. "Most of the illegal activities are hidden behind legitimate ones. Like banks, restaurants, and other private businesses, specifically those which had Russian connections."

"You mean like an antique shop specializing in Russian merchandise?" Natalia stared at him as the realization sent a shiver down her spine. As much as she didn't believe her father participated in anything illegal, she couldn't deny the connection. "My adopted father and his wife actually run an antique shop like that in Alexandria, which is how he met my mother."

Sloan reached out to lightly grasp her arm. "Why didn't you say something sooner?"

She didn't shake off his hand, liking the warmth of his palm against her skin just a little too much. "I did. When you and Jordan were grilling me about my family. I explained all about them."

"You're right, I remember now. I agree, it's worth a try." Sloan let go of her and stood. "We'll need to move carefully though, considering our only method of transportation is a stolen car."

"You're serious?" Natalia wished she could see his expression to understand what was going through his mind. "About going to see my father?"

Sloan nodded. "Yeah. But I want to get a look inside his antique shop first. How far does he live from the shop?"

"Not very," Natalia admitted.

"Good. Let's leave now to give ourselves plenty of time to make sure the Feds aren't staked out at his place. Or to get around them if they have."

JULY 3 – 4:32 a.m. – Baltimore, MD

SLOAN FIGURED the best way to keep from kissing Natalia was to get out of the miniscule hotel room. Sleeping on the floor on a good day wasn't fun. And he was having trouble getting Natalia out of his mind.

Before they left, he'd woken Jordan to explain their plan. Leaving Jordan in the hotel wasn't nearly as risky as it sounded. He and Natalia would have the stolen car, which would be the easiest way someone could have pinpointed their location. They'd paid for three days under Jordan's fake identity. More than enough time for Jordan to lie low and recuperate. His partner would need his strength for when they went back on the move.

Driving back to Alexandria, he kept a sharp eye out for

cops. Luckily, the highways were pretty quiet at this hour of the morning. He glanced over at Natalia, seated like a prim statue on the passenger side of the car. Her regal profile was so beautiful his gut ached. Although, at the moment, she looked too fragile to touch. Remembering how she'd melted against him when he'd kissed her proved she wasn't fragile at all.

Don't go there, he warned himself, dragging his gaze away. He sighed and tried to think of something else.

"What sort of questions will you ask my father?" Natalia asked. "Just because he has a legitimate business connected to Russia doesn't mean he's involved in anything illegal." By the look of uncertainty on her face, he figured she was having second thoughts about the wisdom of agreeing to this expedition.

He shrugged. "I don't suspect him of anything illegal. But I am curious about his contacts for Russian antiques and his regular customers because they could lead us to something or someone else."

She nodded and relaxed. "I understand. I'm sure my father has never heard of the Solntsevskaya, unless he'd read about it in the newspapers."

Sloan raised a brow. "The Solntsevskaya doesn't often get named in the media." He rolled his shoulders, fighting a wave of fatigue. "What's your father's name? You mentioned he remarried too. What about the rest of his family?"

"His name is Gordon Polaski, and his wife's name is Darlene. They have twin boys, Daryl and Daniel."

Gordon Polaski? The last name made him frown. He glanced at her. "You don't use his name at all, do you?"

"No. My mother preferred to keep her maiden name. I legally changed mine to match."

He raised a brow, unable to imagine her using the name Natalia Polaski. Natalia Dreyer? No, adding his last name wasn't much better. He shied away from the disturbing thought and changed the subject. "There's our exit. Let me know if you see anything resembling a cop."

"I will."

After getting off the interstate, he followed Natalia's directions to her father's antique shop. He parked several blocks away, shut off the engine, and tried to plan the best approach.

"You stay here," he said finally. "I'm going to check things out on foot first."

"Wait." She put out a hand to stop him. "Why go into his antique shop without him? I'm sure he'd be happy to give us copies of whatever you need."

Sloan wanted to laugh, but she was completely serious. "I just want to see if the Feds are here watching the place. We'll go to your father's house next, I promise."

"If you're sure," Natalia said doubtfully.

He couldn't explain his gut instincts telling him the antique store was the place where he'd get the information they needed. "Just wait here," he repeated. "If I see any sign the Feds are hanging around, I'll return to get you."

"Fine." She crossed her arms over her chest, clearly not happy with him. "I'll wait here, but you'd better hurry."

"Scoot down in the seat so no one can see you."

She scowled at him but did as he asked, scrunching low enough that not even the top of her head was visible.

He slid from the stolen convertible and melted into the shadows. Glancing back at the car, he was glad when it appeared empty. He scanned the area, looking for signs of surveillance. There was a car parked suspiciously close, about thirty feet up the road. For a moment, he wished

Natalia was here to give him an idea what other businesses lined the street. He firmly believed the Feds were stashed someplace close by.

There was a small, ancient church on the corner, surrounded by a wrought iron fence with a tiny cemetery in the back. Natalia's father's antique shop was next to the church, so he started there.

All previous traces of fatigue vanished as his blood hummed with repressed energy. He took his time, checking all the hidden spots he'd have used if he were the one keeping an eye on the antique shop. When he didn't see any sign of life in the church, he crept through the cemetery until he was alongside the brick building of the antique store.

He stared at The Antique Shoppe. Natalia's father's store was located in the heart of Old Town Alexandria. The windows were dark, and the closed sign was on the door. He tried to think back. Yesterday was Sunday. Today was early Monday morning. Had the shop been open yesterday, on a Sunday? His fingers itched to go inside, to look through Natalia's father's client list.

Turning around, he decided to go around to the back of the building. He continued to proceed with caution just in case someone was watching the place, but he was curious to see if there was an easier way into the shop from the back.

Thankfully, the door along the back wasn't under the bright streetlights. In fact, the more he looked around, the more he liked the setup. There was enough cover that he could chance getting in and out without being seen. At least if they moved fast, before daylight broke.

He glanced at the sky. The horizon was already starting to lighten in the east.

Making a quick decision, he gauged the distance to the

door. Just when he was about to make his move, he heard a noise from behind him. Reaching for his gun and primed to fight, he swung around and came face-to-face with Natalia.

He yanked her deeper into the shadows. "What are you doing here?" he whispered harshly, his mouth right next to her ear.

"I knew you were going inside," she accused in a low voice. "I'm coming with you."

He should have expected it. Why he continued to underestimate her, he had no idea. There wasn't time to argue, so he clamped a hand on her arm and led the way to the back door. He was fully prepared to work the lock, but to his surprise, the doorknob turned as if the lock were broken.

The hairs on the back of his neck lifted. He eased the door open and crossed the threshold, keeping Natalia close to his side. Inside, the darkness was more pronounced, so he pulled a tiny penlight from his pocket, keeping the pencil-thin beam aimed at the floor. The back door led directly into a hallway, with an office on one side and a larger storage room on the other.

He crept toward the office, holding his breath as he turned the corner. Finding the room empty, he breathed a little easier. It would have been just his luck to have come across one of his former FBI colleagues going through Polaski's things.

Going straight to the desk, he began a methodical search. Natalia stood close by, her expression uncertain. He couldn't explain what he was looking for, but he'd know it when he found it. He discovered a key to the tall file cabinet and began going through Gordon Polaski's haphazard filing system.

Invoices. He pulled the folder out and held the penlight

in his mouth as he flipped through them. When he saw several invoices from the same Russian vendor, he knew he'd found a lead.

"Sloan?" Natalia whispered.

He took the pencil-thin flashlight from his mouth. "What?"

She pointed to the edge of the desk, where there was a dark rusty smear about the size of a man's palm. Her voice trembled. "I'm pretty sure that's blood."

CHAPTER EIGHTEEN

July 3 – 5:21 a.m. – Alexandria, VA

NATALIA SWALLOWED HARD, trying not to think the worst as Sloan played his penlight around the room. It wasn't as if there were bloodstains all over, not anything like the horror she'd witnessed at Ivan's house. One tiny smear of blood didn't mean anything. Maybe her father or his wife, Darlene, had accidentally cut themselves with a letter opener.

"We have to find my father," she whispered as Sloan tucked the file folders under his arm and headed around the desk toward her.

"We will. That's our next stop." Sloan put his hand in the small of her back to guide her outside. Following his lead, they made their way back to the stolen convertible.

She slid into the passenger seat and clasped her hands together to hide their shaking. Adrenaline, she told herself. All this sneaking around was getting to her. Sloan stuck the file folders in the space between the seats before starting the engine and shifting into drive.

As he pulled away from the curb, he glanced at her. "Are you all right?"

"Of course." She refused to think the worst. The blood had been minimal, nothing to worry about. "Turn left at the next light."

He manipulated the turns as she directed him toward her father's house. She wasn't surprised when he ignored her last directive and instead went several blocks out of the way before pulling over.

"Please, Natalia, I'm begging you to wait here for me." He killed the engine by untwisting the ignition wire.

"I can't. Please don't ask me to." She couldn't sit here alone, wondering what was going on. "I'm coming with you. The blood . . ." She didn't even want to think about what the smear of blood meant. "I'm a nurse. I want to be there, just in case."

Sloan clenched his jaw. "You have to give me at least a few minutes to make sure there isn't anyone watching the place."

"Ten minutes." She held up her watch to the faint hint of dawn peeking through the early morning clouds. "Then I'm coming to find you."

He sighed and pinched the bridge of his nose. "Fine. Ten minutes. You'd better hope the house isn't under surveillance, because your life is on the line if we're caught."

His too, she thought bleakly as he slid out of the car. But even knowing she potentially put Sloan in danger couldn't convince her to change her mind. Especially now that she was close to seeing her father.

Dawn brought light, removing the shadows that offered a bit of protection from prying eyes, but he made use of the trees and shrubs of neighboring yards. When he disappeared around the corner of a house, she stared at the watch on her wrist, half expecting she'd need to go looking for him. But Sloan returned well within his designated timeframe.

"I haven't seen anything obvious as far as anyone watching the place. Your father's house looks deserted, but the family to the right is up and awake, so we'll need to be quiet and try not to draw their attention."

If he thought she'd change her mind, he was wrong. "Let's go, then."

He grimaced but didn't argue as she got out of the car, leaving him little choice but to let her accompany him. They moved quickly, going around to the back of the house to keep from being too noticeable.

As they approached her father's home, Sloan whispered, "The place is locked up tight with a pretty impressive security system. I've bypassed the alarm, so we should be able to break in through the back door." He sent her a sidelong glance. "Unless you have a key?"

"No key." The thought of Darlene giving her a key almost made her laugh out loud. The woman would have had a conniption fit if her father had even suggested such a thing. "Why can't we just walk up to the door and knock?"

"Because I don't know for sure the house isn't being watched." Sloan steered her left with a hand on her arm. "This way."

Rounding the house, he made his way to the back door. She couldn't tell how he'd bypassed the alarm but held her breath when he picked the lock and opened the door.

As they entered the house, Natalia winced and glanced around in apprehension. What if one of the neighbors saw them and called the police? At least the alarm hadn't sounded.

Stepping over the threshold, he hesitated. "I don't suppose you'd consider waiting out here?"

"No." She followed him inside, into the laundry room. The room was clean, with a hamper half full of dirty clothes. She imagined the twins went through a lot of clothes, especially during the hot summer months. There was a stale, sour smell hanging in the air that made her wrinkle her nose. Darlene was normally a neat freak.

"Stay behind me," he warned in a low tone.

She didn't argue but followed him as he crept along the wall toward the kitchen. The air grew cooler as they moved into the main part of the house, her father obviously had central air-conditioning. Sloan glanced around, and she figured he was looking for either her father or his wife.

The kitchen was empty, the interior of the house smelled even more stale and rank, as if it had been closed up for a while and someone had forgotten to take out the garbage before they left. Maybe they'd had to leave in a hurry? There was no sign that someone had been there recently—no coffee in the coffeemaker, no dirty dishes in the sink, nothing left on the pristine white countertop.

No signs of life at all.

She frowned. "Do you think they're still upstairs, sleeping?"

"I'll check." Sloan turned, but she was right behind him.

"We'll both check." His commanding attitude was starting to wear thin. Hadn't she proved herself capable of keeping up with him over the past few days?

Shivering in the coolness, she followed him as they headed through the empty living room to the stairs leading up to the second floor. Natalia frowned when there didn't seem to be anyone up there either. By this time of the morning, she'd expect at least her father to be up and in the shower.

Unless they were on vacation, which would explain a lot.

Except the bloodstain on the corner of the desk.

The twin's room was on the left, the door hanging ajar as if they'd left in a hurry. Sloan pushed the door open and stepped inside. After a quick moment, he swung around to face her.

"Empty."

She let out a breath she hadn't been aware she was holding. "Good. That's good."

"Let's check the master bedroom."

She followed Sloan, feeling certain her father had gotten his family out safe. But when Sloan opened the door, a foul smell hit hard.

"Go back." Sloan tried to stand in her way, but she shoved past him to see her father lying on the bed, his throat slit open.

"No! Dad!" She would have run to him if Sloan hadn't caught her by the arm. She didn't realize she was crying until Sloan grabbed her and hauled her against him. "Shh, Natalia. I'm sorry." Sloan cradled her face against his shoulder, muffling the sound. "It's too late. He's been dead for a while. There's nothing we can do."

The horror of Ivan's murder came tumbling back. She squeezed her eyes shut, but the images wouldn't go away. She didn't understand. Couldn't comprehend why anyone would do this. "Why? What kind of monster does this?"

"I don't know. We have to get out of here." Sloan physically pushed her from the room, shutting the door behind them. He took a minute to wipe off the door handle with his shirt and then did the same thing on the boys' door, along with the doorframe and wall.

"Don't touch anything. Do you understand me?" Sloan kept a hard arm around her waist. "We're getting out of here."

She nodded, still unable to speak. A scream was lodged in her throat, and if she let it out, she'd lose it completely. She stood in the kitchen watching Sloan wipe off the door handle as he had the two bedroom doorknobs upstairs.

Suspects? Her mind tried to make sense of his actions. He was worried they'd be considered suspects in the slaying of her father?

He opened the back door using his shirt and relocked it before closing the door behind them. She tripped, almost fell to the ground, but Sloan hauled her upright, held her against him as they made their way back to the car.

She couldn't erase the image of her father lying dead in his bed. They hadn't been close, but now they never could be. Her fault. She should have made amends before now.

Her fault.

A deep coldness invaded her limbs. She tried to find comfort in her faith but couldn't. Numbly, she wondered how much longer before she was dead too.

"Natalia?" Sloan took her arm, shook her. She tried to concentrate, but everything was fuzzy. She could hear Sloan talking, but his voice was faint, hollow, as if at the end of a long tunnel. "Come on, don't do this. I need you to stay with me."

"I'm here," she whispered. Although, she knew that couldn't be right because she didn't feel like she was there.

She didn't feel anything.

On some level she knew Sloan was driving her back to

the hotel in Baltimore, but she didn't care. What did it matter? Dead. Almost everyone she knew was dead.

Maybe she should just give up. Go to the police. Then someone would kill her too. And the walking, talking, living, breathing nightmare would end.

"Natalia!" Sloan swerved, nearly hitting another car on the highway as the early morning DC traffic clogged the streets. "Look at me. We need to find your stepmother, Daryl, and Daniel. Your father probably helped them escape. Who would know where they are?"

Sloan's voice was faint. Had he mentioned the twins? She frowned. "I don't know."

"Come on, think. Where would your father go for help?"

The image of her dead father returned in full detail, and she winced, wishing for the return of blessed numbness. "Stop it. I don't know! To the police?"

"No, he didn't go to the police, not if his body is still in the house. There'd be yellow crime scene tape over the doors." Sloan sounded certain.

It took a minute for the words to penetrate her fog-filled brain. Against her will, the fog dissipated and sharp, painful, confusing emotions filled her chest. "What are you saying? That my father did something to them? To his own family? Impossible. He couldn't have murdered his own family. Never!"

He shot her a quick glance. "No, I don't think your father did that. But he might have known he was in danger and had taken steps to get his wife and kids into hiding. And for that I think he'd need help."

"No." She shook her head, not wanting to believe it.

"Natalia, it's very possible your father knew exactly

who was coming after him. We need to get a name before the rest of the family turns up dead too."

JULY 3 – 6:14 a.m. – Baltimore, MD

NATALIA'S FACE WAS PALE, her eyes glassy and her gaze unfocused. She was in shock. Not that he blamed her. He'd witnessed a lot of violent crime in his life, but seeing the way her father's throat had been slashed made him sick to his stomach.

The method of killing was favored by the Russian Mafia.

He pushed the speed limit as much as he dared, in a hurry to get back to the hotel room in Baltimore. He darted another glance at Natalia, concerned that this latest assault would be the one that shoved her over the edge.

Focus. He had to get her to focus.

"Where would your father go if he was in trouble? Who would he turn to?" Sloan figured the only thing that might help pull her back from jumping off the ledge was helping to find her father's family. Especially the twin boys.

"I don't know." She sat with her head down, her blonde hair covering her face. "I haven't seen him in a long time. I just don't know."

"What about the friends he had back then?" Sloan pressed. Passing a billboard sign advertising their hotel made him realize they should be there in less than ten minutes.

"There was a man, James Lorbeck, who was a friend of my father's. My mother didn't care for him much, but he was the best man at their wedding."

James Lorbeck. Probably a dead end, but at this point he was willing to grab at straws. "Okay, good. James Lorbeck. That's good, Natalia. Keep thinking." Sloan pulled up to the hotel parking lot and drove around to the back, where their room was located out of sight from prying eyes.

He untwisted the wires beneath the broken steering column and shut off the car. Natalia sat, staring blindly at her hands twisted in her lap.

There was no way he could ignore her pain. Helpless, he shoved a hand through his hair. What did he know about offering comfort? Reaching over, he pulled her awkwardly against him, across the gap between the bucket seats. "I'm sorry." Platitudes were useless, but he offered them anyway as he stroked a hand down her back. "I'm sorry. I'm sorry you had to see that."

"Do you think my stepbrothers are dead?" The question was muffled against his shirt.

"I don't know." He couldn't lie to her. He thought there was a good chance her father had been murdered for a reason, maybe because he'd double-crossed someone. At the very least, her father had stumbled into something he shouldn't have. Was the crime linked to the Solntsevskaya? His gut was telling him it was, but he had no idea how.

"I—can't do this anymore." Natalia's voice was low, broken. "I just can't. Too much death. Too much blood. I can't do this—I can't . . ."

He didn't know what to do to snap her out of it. Words didn't seem to work, so he did the next best thing—tipped her chin up and covered her mouth in a simple kiss.

His intent was to offer comfort, to draw her safely away from the precipice she teetered on. It took a moment for her to return the embrace, curling her fingers into the fabric of his T-shirt and pulling him closer.

He kissed her again and again, soft, gentle kisses that felt new to him. Somewhere in the back of his mind, he realized he longed to drag her away from the coldness of death to the warmth of life.

She kissed him back, lightly at first, then with a sense of desperation.

"Natalia." He whispered her name. "I'm sorry. So sorry." He had no idea what he was apologizing for, but ached to do something, say something that would make her feel better.

"It's not your fault." She kissed him again, and as much as he reveled in her embrace, he knew this was a result of her grief.

Not because she cared specifically about him.

He had to force himself to break off the kiss, to tuck her head beneath his chin and simply hold her.

Humbling and terrifying to realize no woman had gotten past his defenses the way Natalia had.

CHAPTER NINETEEN

July 3 – 6:55 a.m. – Baltimore, MD

SLOAN'S HEART sounded like galloping horses in her ear, and his musky scent filled her senses. Natalia's lips tingled from his kiss, and the way he held her with such tenderness made her want to cry.

For a few brief moments she'd forgotten the horror, but now suddenly everything came tumbling back. Her dead father. Her missing stepmother and the twins.

Too much death. Ivan. Her father. Why? Because of her?

"Hey. Don't dwell on this." Sloan either acquired the sensitivity of a bat or possessed supernatural powers the way he picked up on her thoughts. "We'll find your stepbrothers."

She lifted her head and looked up at him, longing to kiss him again. "I wish I could believe that."

Unlike last time they'd kissed, Sloan didn't interject a mile of distance between them but reached up and cupped her face in his hands. His gaze held hers as one thumb gently stroked her cheek in a tender caress. "We will. Trust me."

Tears pricked her eyelids, and she nodded. The fact was she did trust him. More than she'd ever trusted her fiancé, Dirk. More than she'd trusted anyone. She trusted Sloan Dreyer with her life.

With her heart.

Not that he'd appreciate the gift. As much as she longed to stay sheltered in his arms, ignoring the rest of the outside world, they had to find her brothers. Besides, their awkward position in the car was pretty uncomfortable, so she moved away, running her fingers through her tangled hair.

"You're beautiful." His words made her glance up at him sharply.

"You don't have to say that." She was knocked off balance by his compliment.

"Yes, I do. You need to understand I haven't kissed a woman in two years," he said in a gruff tone. "But I know that these aren't normal circumstances."

What was he trying to say? "They're not but thank you. I needed these moments with you."

He stared at her for several long minutes, then gave a terse nod. "Me too." He cleared his throat and pulled out some papers that were wrinkled from being shoved down between the seats. "Come on, I want to see if we can find anything about your father or James Lorbeck on Jordan's computer."

Memories of her father crowded her mind as she climbed out of the car and followed Sloan inside. When he opened the hotel room door, she experienced a moment of déjà vu and closed her eyes, afraid to look. Afraid to see—

Blood. Too much blood.

"What are you doing out of bed?" Sloan asked in an incredulous tone. "Aren't you supposed to be recuperating?"

Opening her eyes, she saw there wasn't any blood. No dead body. No horror. Only Jordan seated at the makeshift desk in front of the satellite computer. She drew a shaky breath and focused on the room. From the looks of the empty coffee cup beside him, Jordan had been there for a while.

"What took you so long?" Jordan asked in a sharp tone.

Natalia glanced at Sloan who surprised her with a quick wink.

"We have a lot to cover. Natalia's father owns a place called The Antique Shoppe in Old Town Alexandria that specializes in Russian antiques." Sloan crossed to Jordan and dropped the crumpled papers on the table. "I found these invoices, several by one specific Russian dealer, Viktor Azimov. It's possible he's our link to the mob."

"Why? Because the guy deals antiques?" Jordan frowned at the invoices. "This doesn't prove anything."

"No. Because we went to Natalia's father's house and found him dead with his throat slit. His wife and twin boys are missing."

"What a disaster." Jordan stared at him, then shot a guilty glance at Natalia. "I'm sorry."

"Thank you." The words were a mere whisper. A mixture of regret and guilt clogged her throat. Maybe if she hadn't called her father from her cell phone that first night. Maybe if she'd kept in touch with him after her mother had died. Maybe if she hadn't agreed to take care of Josef that day. Maybe—

"Michael Cummings is dead—he's the prime suspect in the Kazakhstan pipeline bombing." Jordan gestured to the computer screen where he had the CNN top story displayed on the website. "The Feds are going to claim he was the mole, leaking information to the Solntsevskaya."

"Yeah, they'd be quick to disown him." Sloan stared at Jordan. "Alek Nevsky was working with Cummings on something that involved several trips back to Russia. We found communication between Nevsky and Korolev, which proved they knew each other. Korolev's trip here was planned so he could get in touch with Nevsky. Do you think it's possible Cummings really was the leak?"

"No way," Jordan said in disgust. "This whole situation stinks. If Cummings had choreographed the attempt on Korolev from Moscow, why would he kill himself? And be stupid enough to leave traces of explosives in his hotel room? No, I'm not buying this. Someone else is involved, someone who set up Cummings to take the fall. The real question is, just how high up the chain of command does the leak in the FBI go? To one of the regional assistant directors? Or to the director himself?"

"I don't know." Sloan rubbed his chin. "Why does it matter?"

"Because sooner or later we need to trust someone." Jordan glanced between them, a hint of compassion in his gaze. "Preferably before any more potential witnesses end up dead."

JULY 3 – 7:27 a.m. – Washington, DC

ALEK TRIED to keep his expression impassive as they poked at him.

"This cut is deep, managed to nick his liver. No wonder

we can't get his wound to stop bleeding." The city jail doctor examined the depth of his wound while the nurse, a woman about Natalia's age, kept a reassuring hand on his arm. Alek clenched his jaw and stared at the ceiling. "I don't want to take any chances with a liver laceration. I think we'd better transfer him to the hospital for treatment."

The hospital? A flare of hope brightened his heart. Which one?

"If you write the order, Dr. Quill, I'll call and arrange for the Marshals to transfer him." The nurse handed the doctor—who didn't look old enough to have finished medical school—a computer tablet. Alek watched as he entered the order.

"I'll pack this wound, give him a hefty antibiotic to ward off any chance of infection until we can get him there."

Alek tensed, then relaxed. Antibiotics were okay. He'd refused the pain medication they'd offered because he preferred to be awake and uncomfortable rather than groggy and unaware of what was going on around him.

There were very few he could trust.

"Which hospital?" he asked when the doctor had finished packing his wound.

"Washington University is closest." The nurse picked up the tablet. "I'll be back in a minute. I have to make a couple of phone calls to make all the arrangements."

He wanted to tell her to hurry but bit his tongue so he wouldn't give anything away.

Washington University Hospital was where he'd been treated for his recent bouts of angina. He'd been medically cleared at last, but over the past year he'd undergone several cardiac tests and procedures, and during his frequent visits he'd grown to know many of the staff members on a personal basis.

For the first time in hours, Alek felt as if things were finally taking a turn for the better. God hadn't abandoned him at all, and he should never have given up hope. Anticipation swelled in his chest even as a deep sense of urgency wouldn't leave him alone. Hours ago someone had tried to kill him. To silence him forever. He couldn't fight the true enemy from behind prison walls.

He needed a break. One tiny moment to slip away.

His chances for accomplishing that small feat were better at Washington University Hospital than here in the jail infirmary.

How ironic that the man who'd tried to kill him had provided a huge favor instead.

JULY 3 – 7:49 a.m. – Brookmont, MD

HE WAS LUCKY. Lara Nevsky was still sleeping.

For a moment he stared down at his middle-aged target, contemplating how pale the skin around her neck looked, and found he was thankful he didn't have to slit her throat.

At least, not yet.

He didn't particularly care for the bloody mess left as a result of dragging a knife across pulsating carotid arteries, but since he needed to keep the aura of suspicion pointing at the Solntsevskaya, he didn't have an option. Compared to the more brutal methods those creepy Russians deployed, the switchblade across the throat was the method he preferred.

But it was still disgustingly messy.

Drawing his gun from its holster, he knelt on the edge of the bed and leaned his forearm across Lara's pasty-white throat. She awoke instantly and struggled in alarm, until he pointed the gun at the center of her forehead.

"Stay quiet and get up. One wrong move and I'll kill you."

Her eyes bulged with fright, but she stopped her useless and ridiculous attempts to evade him. He felt a surge of satisfaction at the power he wielded. He removed his weight from her throat and stood before her, his gun level with her chest. "Are you listening?" When she gave a frightened nod, he smiled. "Good. Get up. You're going to call Natalia and tell her to meet you here."

Lara's face crumpled. "I can't. I don't have a way to contact her."

"Don't lie to me." He fought the urge to slap her. "I've listened to your conversations with your jailbird husband. I know you've been in contact with Natalia."

"Because she called me." The woman was weeping now, curled up against the headboard of the bed as if afraid for her virtue. He didn't bother to hide his disgust. As if he'd force himself on this woman.

But Natalia, now she was another matter. She deserved everything he could dish out, and more, for the way she tap-danced just out of his reach for so long.

Too long. He had to get his hands on her. Today. The deadline was today.

"Who are you?" The woman on the bed was almost babbling. "I promise I don't have a number to contact her. I don't!"

This was not what he wanted to hear. Could she be lying to him? Nah, the woman was too scared to mess with him. He considered slitting her throat now, but he needed her alive in order to lure Natalia out of hiding. He gestured with the gun. "Get out of bed. If you want to live, you'll do exactly as I say."

Lara's weeping faded, and she gathered herself together, staring at him as if realizing her life hung by a very thin thread. One he wouldn't hesitate to clip. Slowly, with a strange sort of dignity, she sat up, pulled a robe over her nightgown, and climbed out of bed.

He followed her to the kitchen, relieved she'd stopped blubbering. "You'd better hope Natalia gets in touch with you soon. I'm not in the mood to be patient."

JULY 3 – 9:34 a.m. – Baltimore, MD

"FOUND HIM." Sloan glanced up from the computer and tapped the screen. "James Lorbeck is still in the area, not far from here."

"Do you have a picture?" Natalia peered over Sloan's shoulder, afraid to hope it would be this easy to find her stepmother and half brothers. "There could be more than one James Lorbeck."

"A couple of them actually, but only one in the correct age range." Sloan moved the remnants of their takeout breakfast so she could see the grainy DMV photo on the computer screen. "Is this the guy?"

She nodded. The picture wasn't flattering. James Lorbeck hadn't aged well, but it was definitely the same man.

"Good." Sloan drained his coffee cup and stood. "Will you please stay here with Jordan?"

"No." Her refusal was automatic, because she honestly

didn't think she could stand to see Darlene, Daryl, and Daniel lying in a pool of blood like her father. The blueberry muffin she'd nibbled for breakfast lurched sideways in her stomach. She put a hand over her belly, praying she wouldn't throw up. Hardening her resolve, she met Sloan's gaze defiantly. "Lorbeck isn't going to trust a stranger. I'm coming with you."

Sloan muttered something she couldn't catch in Ukrainian.

"It's a good thing I've acquired another car, since you're planning to drive around DC in broad daylight." Jordan walked out of the bathroom door, his battered face slightly less swollen after his shower. "I picked up another couple of cell phones for us too."

"You've been busy," Sloan drawled. She knew it bothered him the way Jordan refused to rest. Jordan had been the one who'd stolen another car and decided to ditch the convertible, much to Sloan's chagrin. "Maybe you should take over on the computer, take it easy for a while."

Jordan raised a brow, the one over his uninjured eye. "No. We're running out of time. I think we need to probe the FBI, find out who we can trust."

With a dark scowl, Sloan asked, "How do you plan to do that?"

Jordan shrugged. "I don't know. I'll figure it out."

"Yeah, and get yourself killed in the process," Sloan snapped. He dragged in a harsh breath. "Don't go there. Not yet. If you want to do something constructive, work on the antique dealer angle."

Jordan picked up the invoices Sloan had taken from her father's antique shop. "All right, I'll start here. But we're not going to be able to stay hidden forever. Our former employer has far more resources than we do. You know as well as I do we can't win the game by only playing defense. Eventually we'll have to switch to offense."

Natalia held her breath while Sloan and Jordan stared each other down. Sloan had the unfair advantage, considering Jordan's injuries, but Jordan wasn't about to give in.

Finally, Sloan turned away. "We won't be long. When we get back, we'll talk strategy."

Natalia followed Sloan out the door, glancing back to where Jordan stood, watching them go. With an uneasy feeling, she took note of the fiercely determined expression on his face.

And prayed he'd be there when they returned.

JULY 3 – 10:07 a.m. – Washington, DC

SLOAN PULLED over a block or so from James Lorbeck's house and killed the engine. The truck Jordan had stolen for them rattled worse than the cargo van.

He missed the convertible. Memories of Natalia's passionate kisses were blazed into his mind.

"Are you ready?" Natalia asked.

He scrubbed the lingering fatigue from his eyes and nodded. There was no way to know for sure if the Feds were staking out Lorbeck's house, but he didn't think so. His fears over her father's house had been unfounded; they couldn't have been watching the place with a dead body rotting away in there. He hadn't said anything to Natalia, but he'd seen signs that told him her father been dead for a while, maybe even a few days.

More than twenty-four hours, that's for sure.

He glanced at her, wishing she'd stay put in the truck

but knowing she wouldn't. Even after the horror she'd been through, she'd follow him to that house to meet James Lorbeck. He didn't want to think about what they might find.

"Let's go." He shoved open the truck door. Natalia didn't move, and he hesitated just for a moment before going around and opening her passenger door. "Are you all right?"

"Fine." Funny, she didn't look fine. She looked awful—her eyes sunken into her cheeks and her skin pasty white. But she angled her stubborn chin, so he stepped back, giving her room to jump down from the truck.

He took her hand, setting the pace for a casual stroll up the residential street as if they didn't have a care in the world. After walking up to Lorbeck's house, they knocked at the door.

The main door was open, and Lorbeck peered at them through the screen door. "Yeah?"

"This is Natalia, she's Gordon Polaski's daughter. She's worried sick about his family. Can we come in?"

"No. I haven't seen him." James Lorbeck reached for the door handle, no doubt to lock it, but Sloan was quicker and yanked the aluminum door open before Lorbeck could get it latched.

Lorbeck bolted. Man, he hated when they made him run. Lorbeck headed through the kitchen, shoving a kitchen chair in Sloan's path as he made for the door. Sloan hurdled the chair like a track star, hot on Lorbeck's heels, when the guy darted outside into the backyard.

Sloan had youth on his side, and he easily gained ground. He tackled Lorbeck just as he was about to make a break for it. They hit the ground hard, rolling over and over, but Sloan used the momentum to his advantage, coming out on top. He leaned his forearm over Lorbeck's windpipe and pressed hard while Lorbeck bucked and tried to wiggle free. Within seconds, his face turned a mottled shade of red.

"Where is Polaski's family?" Sloan asked, breathing hard. Lorbeck gave his head a frantic shake, so he pressed harder. "Tell me! Where are they?"

"Sloan, stop it. You're hurting him."

He ignored Natalia's outrage, and soon Lorbeck went lax. Sloan eased up and pulled out his gun.

"No!" Natalia ran up and grabbed his arm. "You can't shoot him!"

Really? Despite everything they'd been through together, she obviously didn't have a high opinion about him. He let out a loud sigh. "I'm not going to shoot him. Find me some rope or twine so I can tie him up. When he comes to, we'll get our answers."

She glared at him for a moment, then stomped back into the kitchen, returning a few minutes later with some duct tape. He took the roll from her hands and then quickly wrapped the versatile stuff around Lorbeck's wrists before hauling him upright.

Lorbeck was already starting to come to, struggling weakly against him. He pushed the guy into the house and shoved him into the nearest chair.

"Okay, let's try this again." Sloan propped his foot on the base of Lorbeck's chair, pinning him in. "Where is Gordon Polaski's family? His wife and boys are missing."

"I don't know." Lorbeck leaned back, raised his bound hands to massage his sore throat.

"Do you know he's dead?" Sloan persisted. "Murdered in his bed?"

A flicker in Lorbeck's beady eyes betrayed him, and he dropped his hands. "Gordy was here a couple of days ago, said he needed to find someone to protect him and his family."

"Who did he need protection from, the Solntsevskaya? Does the name Viktor Azimov ring any bells?"

Again, the flash of recognition gave Lorbeck away. The older man's shoulders slumped in defeat. "Yes, Viktor has connections to the Solntsevskaya. Gordy knew that. But Viktor didn't kill Gordy or threaten to harm his family. They've been working together for years. Gordy would never double-cross Viktor."

Years? "If Azimov didn't kill him, who did?"

Lorbeck shook his head. "I don't know. Someone from the FBI was in the shop on Saturday, asking questions. Darlene called Gordy to tell him about it, said the guy threatened her. Gordy insisted Darlene and the boys leave town so he could handle it." Lorbeck shrugged, his tone turning bitter. "You ask me? I think that FBI agent killed him."

CHAPTER TWENTY

July 3 – 11:35 a.m. – Washington, DC

ALEK SAT in the emergency room cubicle for what seemed like forever while they discussed his case. The US Marshal sat right outside his room on guard duty.

After going back and forth, the doctor finally decided to take him to surgery to clean out and repair his wound. Even then, he waited another fifteen minutes before they came to take him away. The US Marshal walked as far as the double doors leading into the surgical suites but didn't follow him inside the sterile area.

The anesthesiologist asked him questions as the orderly wheeled him down the hall. Did he ever have surgery before? Did he ever have problems with anesthesia? Did he have any allergies?

A nurse poked her head from a nearby OR suite, a mask covering most of her face. "Dr. Pitcher? The PACU is looking for you. The patient you dropped off earlier is in respiratory distress."

The anesthesiologist sighed and glanced at the orderly. "Just take him into OR suite five. I'll be right back."

With a shrug, the orderly did as he was told. "Don't worry," the guy assured him. "The team will be here in a minute. They're finishing up another case next door."

Alek nodded. He'd figured he'd have to wait until after surgery to make his move, but this was his chance. When the orderly turned to leave, Alek abruptly sat up and reached over his shoulders to grab him around the throat. He yanked him backward and pressed against his carotid arteries until he passed out. Alek felt bad for having to hurt the young man, but there wasn't a moment to spare. He quickly stripped off the useless hospital gown and pulled on the orderly's scrubs instead.

He wasn't as familiar with the operating room area, but he found a hat, face mask, and booties to hide his bare feet in the boxes stacked along a shelf near the doorway. Putting everything on, he tried his best to blend in.

God helps those who help themselves.

Wearing the orderly's hospital ID around his neck, he walked through the doorway, past a team of staff members who were wheeling another patient toward what he assumed was the recovery room.

A sign for the men's locker room caught his eye, and he slipped inside, almost running into some guy on his way out. The doctor gave him a nod as he went past. He returned the gesture, and when the door shut behind him, he let out a sigh of relief. So far, so good. Alek glanced around the room, seeing several pairs of discarded shoes. He found a pair of sneakers large enough to fit him and donned a physician's white lab coat.

There was a shout and the sound of running feet from the operating room area. No! Not yet. Swiftly, he darted out the back door of the locker room, into a hallway behind the surgery area. He passed up the elevators in favor of the nearest stairwell, heading up instead of down.

He had to move fast. There wasn't much time before they shut down the whole hospital in an effort to find him.

JULY 3 – 12:08 p.m. – Washington, DC

"MY FATHER WASN'T WORKING with the Solntsevskaya." Natalia stared blindly through the windshield of the truck. She didn't care what James Lorbeck had said, she refused to believe it. "At least not knowingly."

Sloan sat beside her but didn't answer. Instead, he pulled out his cell phone and punched Jordan's number. "What do you have on Viktor Azimov?"

She listened to the one-sided conversation, but every word about Viktor intensified the sinking feeling in the pit of her stomach. Sloan had found the invoices at the shop, proof that her father had been doing business with the man. But what if James Lorbeck had lied about the rest? Maybe he was the one working with Viktor, turning against her father. For all they knew, James Lorbeck had made up a whopper of a story in an effort to save his own skin.

"All right, keep looking for him," Sloan said as he started the engine with the dangling wires. "We'll meet you back at the hotel in a little while."

"He wasn't involved with the mob," she repeated when Sloan shut his phone. Gordon was her adopted father, but considering how her search for her birth parents hadn't revealed much more than her mother's first name, she clung to the bond she once had with her father. "He's owned that antique shop for more than twenty years. He couldn't have been involved with the Solntsevskaya all this time." She turned to face Sloan. "You said yourself, they only just started to infiltrate DC."

"Natalia, you've got to face facts." Sloan reached for her hand, but she pulled away. "Your father was murdered, in a method preferred by the Solntsevskaya, and his family is missing. He wouldn't have sent his family out of town without a good reason."

"Weren't you listening? Supposedly, there was an FBI agent looking for him." She crossed her arms over her chest. "Your FBI is responsible for murdering my father."

"Yeah, there is that," Sloan agreed. "But don't forget, we suspect there's an FBI mole for the Solntsevskaya, which puts the deed right back on them. Your father's house was very nice, located in a plush part of town. What else did he do, besides running the antique store?"

She ground her teeth together in frustration. "He used to teach history when he was married to my mother, but after the divorce, his antique business took off, so he cut back. And I know what you're thinking"—she stopped him from speaking by putting up her hand—"but you're wrong. Don't you think I'd know if my father was involved with a group of heinous criminals?"

"No, I don't. You said yourself you haven't seen him in years." Sloan sighed and pulled into traffic. "But it doesn't matter. For your sake, I hope he was innocent and that Darlene and the boys are safe. For now, let's just worry about finding Azimov."

She hated the fact that he was right. What did she know about her father in these past few years? She shook off the terrible thought. "Jordan didn't have anything on him?"

"Not yet."

"Maybe we should call my Aunt Lara," Natalia murmured, rubbing her arms in an attempt to get warm. Despite the muggy air outside, she thought she'd never be warm again. Except for those moments with Sloan in the convertible. "She might know more about my father's relationship with James Lorbeck. Or maybe she's heard of Viktor Azimov."

Sloan shot her a surprised glance. "You're right. I was just thinking along those same lines myself." He pulled his phone off his belt loop and handed it to her.

She stared down at it for a minute, struck by a strange sense of apprehension. Everyone she had once been close to was dead.

No, not everyone, she amended swiftly. Her twin brothers were missing, but they could still be alive. She refused to believe the boys was dead. And she'd been in touch with her aunt earlier, met her outside the Washington Monument, talked to her about the case. Uncle Alek was alive, even though he was in jail.

Sloan and Jordan were here too.

God was watching over her. Over them.

She wasn't alone. As long as God watched over her, she was not alone.

Drawing a shaky breath, she punched in the numbers and raised the phone to her ear.

The phone rang once and was picked up almost instantly, as if her aunt was waiting for her call. "Hello?"

"*Tetya*? This is Natalia." The sound of her aunt's voice on the other end of the line filled her with relief. "I'm so glad you're home."

JULY 3 – 12:23 *p.m.* – *Brookmont, MD*

. . .

LARA GRASPED the phone with both hands, deathly aware of the man holding the gun to her temple directly behind her. She was so afraid she could barely speak.

"Don't come. A man is here, holding a gun at me," she said in Russian. When he growled and shoved the gun harder into her temple, she switched to English. "Natalia. I've been waiting for your call. We need to meet, as soon as possible. I have much to tell you."

There was a brief pause before Natalia responded in English, "Wonderful. I have much to tell you too. I can be there in thirty minutes. Is that all right?"

"Perfect. Thirty minutes is perfect." Tears pricked her eyelids as she realized she'd be dead long before Natalia arrived. She wasn't stupid. The man with the gun only needed her for this call. Now that Natalia had made contact, she was nothing more than a liability. How had everything gone so wrong? *"Ya lublu tebya, Natalia."* I love you.

"Ya tozhe tebya lublyu."

Lara's eyes glistened at Natalia's murmured, "I love you too," then she crossed herself, waiting for the blast. The man reached behind her and took the phone from her fingers and pushed the disconnect button. "Good. You did very well, except for using Russian. What did you tell her?"

Swallowing hard, she gathered her courage and turned to face her tormenter. She raised her chin. She was going to die anyway, and she refused to cower to this evil man. "I told her about you. I told her not to come."

"Tsk, tsk." He actually smiled. "I believe you did warn Natalia of the danger, in fact, I'm counting on it. For sure she'll come now, if only to try and save you."

Lara felt sick at how she played right into his hand. Because she very much feared he was right. Natalia wouldn't stay away, not now that she knew about the man with the gun. "So now what? Are you going to kill me?"

"Yes." He still wore the obscene smile on his face. "But not here. No, that wouldn't do at all."

Her knees were shaking so hard she had to lock them in place or fall down. Evil seeped from his pores, and she'd never, not even during the dark years, been so afraid.

While holding the gun on her, he reached into his pocket with his free hand and pulled out a large switchblade. He opened the knife with a faint hiss. Her stomach shot into her throat when he deliberately tested the blade with his thumb. "We're going back to your bedroom first."

Dear Lord, help me and Natalia! Spare our lives . . .

JULY 3 – 12:32 p.m. – Brookmont, MD

NATALIA HAD TOLD her aunt thirty minutes, but she had lied. They'd made it to her house in under ten.

"The door's locked," Sloan muttered, testing the doorknob with his hand. "Thankfully it's a flimsy lock, not anything like the security system at your father's house." He glanced up and down the rather deserted street behind him. "We'll need to break in."

Natalia gave a furtive glance over her shoulder, half expecting a neighbor to come out and ask them what they were doing. She prayed most of the neighbors were at work. "I hope no one sees us and calls the police."

"Yeah, I'm with you on that." He pulled out his picklock

tools and went to work. After a few minutes, the door clicked open. "I want you to stay here."

"No."

"Natalia." He swung around to face her, his gaze fierce. "You told me someone is holding a gun on her. He's armed, you're not. I'm begging you. Go back and wait in the car for Jordan."

She didn't want to go back or to wait. But what did she know about fighting a man with a gun? She swallowed hard. "I'd rather wait here."

"Fine. Just don't get in my way. After keeping you safe over the past two days, I'd rather not hurt you by mistake." Sending her a stern look, he held his gun in the ready position and then slipped inside.

The door shut behind him, and she reached out to grab the handle, instinctively ready to follow. Then hesitated. What if she messed up and caused her aunt to be hurt, or worse? What if she distracted Sloan and something happened to him? She wasn't stupid by nature. Stubborn maybe, but not stupid. Following him inside would only make things worse.

She forced herself to unclamp her fingers from the door handle. There were bushes lining the front of Lara's house, so she used them for cover from prying eyes and waited, Sloan's words echoing in her mind.

I'd rather not hurt you by mistake.

JULY 3 – 12:37 p.m. – Brookmont, MD

SLOAN STOOD statue still just inside the doorway, every

sense on hyperalert. He pushed thoughts of Natalia out of his head. He needed to stay focused.

He heard a muffled scream followed by a crash and a thud. No time to wait. He moved down the hall, in the direction of the bedrooms.

A male voice shouted a stream of curses.

Sloan rounded the corner, kicked in the bedroom door. Everything happened so fast it was a blur of motion. His brain barely had time to register the woman lying on the floor, surrounded in blood, when a shot rang out. Red hot pain blazed in his right shoulder, but he returned fire, praying his aim wasn't too far off.

A lamp came flying at his head. He ducked to avoid taking the blow but was caught off guard when the attacker charged him like a raging bull. Knocked off balance, Sloan hit the floor, buried under the guy's weight. He tried to bring his gun around to shoot him, but his attacker slammed a fist into his face. His vision went black for a moment, and Sloan lost his grip on the gun.

He blinked past the blurred vision, instinctively fighting for his life. His right arm hung useless, putting him at a distinct disadvantage. He took blow after blow from his attacker and realized it was only a matter of time before the guy finished him off.

He'd failed again. No! He couldn't fail. This guy would kill Natalia.

The sound of a car door slamming made the attacker freeze. Sloan used the moment to throw a left-handed jab, his knuckles meeting the hard jaw of his attacker with less force than he would have liked. Using his left hand had the impact of hitting like a girl.

The guy's head jerked back, then he surprised Sloan

again by surging to his feet. He managed to give Sloan one last kick in the ribs before taking off at a run.

Ears ringing and his vision blurry, Sloan dragged himself upright. He had to follow the attacker. Had to find out who was behind this.

He managed two steps, but then his knees buckled. He grabbed the doorframe with his good arm to keep from falling on his face.

"Sloan? What happened? Are you all right?"

He thought he saw Natalia, but he couldn't swear to it, all he could really make out was a blur of motion as someone moved toward him.

"Your aunt." Sloan forced the words past his aching jaw. "Check your aunt. He got her."

JULY 3 – 12:41 p.m. – Brookmont, MD

ALEK DIDN'T DARE GO MORE than five miles over the speed limit as he navigated the streets in the minivan sporting soccer decals on the back window that he'd borrowed from one of the nurses. He glanced at the clock, estimating he'd arrive at his wife's house in less than two minutes. Going straight to Lara's was risky, since it was no doubt the first place they would look for him. Yet, he had a good head start; they couldn't know he'd obtained a vehicle. If he could just get to Lara, they could use the minivan to escape and find a place to hide.

His hands tightened their grip on the steering wheel. His favorite cardiac nurse, Eloise, had believed his story and had willingly offered the use of her van. He didn't like to take advantage of kindness, especially from a nurse he liked and respected, but desperation forced a man to do many things he wouldn't normally do.

Like breaking out of jail and running from the law.

He put a hand over the throbbing wound in his side. The awkward angle prevented him from seeing it, but from the dampness of the gauze, he suspected it was still bleeding. Since he'd snuck out of surgery before they had time to suture him up, the cut was covered with a flimsy, temporary bandage. The doctors in the emergency department at Washington University Hospital hadn't bothered with a large dressing.

Lara would be appalled at what he'd done, but she'd still help him. He had to believe she'd still help him. Oddly enough, their relationship had taken a turn for the better since his arrest. Maybe once he fought his way out of this mess, he'd convince her to forget this notion of living apart. To give their marriage another try. He'd do whatever necessary to make her happy.

He parked in front of Lara's house, not caring who might see the car. They wouldn't recognize it anyway. Besides, they wouldn't be here long, they needed to keep moving. He got out and slammed the van door.

The front door to Lara's house was open.

Pungent fear congealed in his throat.

Lara! Alek raced inside the house, his heart hammering so loud he couldn't hear anything else. He stopped in his tracks when he saw a man sitting on the floor, his legs stretched out in front of him and his back propped against the wall. There was blood smeared on Lara's walls. It took him a moment to realize the man sitting on the floor was wounded.

"Are you a doctor?" The man on the floor gave him a dazed look and jerked a thumb toward the door. "I tried to save her but was too late. The woman in the bedroom is bleeding pretty badly."

"No, I'm not a doctor." Bleeding? Who was bleeding? Alek gave the wounded man a wide berth as he made his way to the bedroom. When he looked inside and saw his wife, his lovely gentle wife, stretched out on the floor surrounded in blood, his heart dropped to his feet. "Lara? What happened?"

"Uncle Alek!" Natalia knelt beside Lara, glancing at him in surprise. "Get me a ballpoint pen, hurry."

He stumbled back, ran to the kitchen, and returned with the pen. Natalia had a towel from the bathroom pressed against Lara's neck. The once yellow towel was stained dark red.

"Here." He handed over the ballpoint pen.

It was a cheap, old-fashioned pen, and she quickly unscrewed the two ends, dumping out the ink quill on the floor. He sucked in a harsh breath when she pulled the towel away, baring the wound.

"Who did this to her?" he whispered.

Natalia didn't answer as she inserted the widest half of the pen into an opening in Lara's throat. There was a gurgling noise, then Lara started to cough, spewing blood from the end of the pen. Natalia held the plastic tube in place, then reached over to rip away the operating room face mask dangling around his neck so she could use the strings to tie the makeshift tube in place.

"I'm afraid he may have nicked her carotid artery. We need to get her help, fast." Natalia glanced at him, her expression grim. "Call for an ambulance, Uncle Alek. Then get out of here, unless you want to be caught and thrown back in jail."

CHAPTER TWENTY-ONE

July 3 – 1:03 p.m. – Brookmont, MD

SLOAN ROSE TO HIS FEET, staggering like a drunk on a bender. He held a hand over his shoulder wound, the stupid thing hurt worse than a son of a gun. He propped himself against the doorframe, wishing he didn't see three overlapping figures that all looked like Natalia when he knew very well there was only one of her.

"No ambulance." He blinked, trying to focus. "We have to get out of here, before the cops arrive. I'm surprised they're not here already."

The guy dressed in scrubs who wasn't a doctor rounded on him. When the faces merged into one, he realized the features were familiar. Alek Nevsky. In some portion of his foggy mind, he realized this man might have some of the answers they needed.

Alek shouted, "Lara will not die. Do you hear me? She'll get an ambulance, she will not die!"

Sloan winced and nodded. "Fine. Call an ambulance. Natalia, we're out of here."

"You're injured too." Natalia didn't move, but her voice rose in panic. "I'm not equipped to handle serious injuries. I can't help you or Lara without the proper equipment, supplies. I need IV tubing, blood transfusions. Do you understand? He may have nicked her carotid artery!"

"Then call the ambulance for her, since her condition is more serious." Sloan glanced at Lara. "But we need to leave. I'll be fine. The bullet went through my shoulder. All I need is for you to sew it up, slap a dressing on it."

"I can't." Natalia looked pained. "I can't leave her, Sloan. I can't let her die."

He stared at her for a long, agonizing minute. Her eyes carried that stubborn glint he knew all too well.

"I can't leave you here either," Sloan said in a heavy tone. Another stalemate. It was his job to protect her. No way was he leaving without her. "So if you're staying, I'm staying. I guess we'll all go down together."

JULY 3 – 1:11 p.m. – Brookmont, MD

NATALIA COULDN'T TEAR her gaze from Sloan. He looked awful, his face ashen as he slumped against the door. He needed medical attention too, more than just her limited expertise, yet at the same time, she knew he wouldn't go to the hospital. If she stayed here and called an ambulance for Lara, she risked Sloan. If she left with Sloan, she risked something happening to her aunt.

Sloan or Lara? She couldn't choose. Her aunt, one of the few family members she had left in the world, or the man who'd risked his life for her? What sort of choice was that? She couldn't do this. He shouldn't ask her to.

"Go get Jordan," she pleaded, her eyes begging Sloan to listen. "Meet us at the nearest hospital. I'll get Lara to the ED, and then slip away to find you."

Sloan shook his head. "Too risky."

"You're risking her right now," Natalia shouted, losing patience. They couldn't stand here and argue. She'd have to make a decision and soon. Sloan or Lara?

Heaven help her, she was leaning toward Sloan.

Alek came forward, scooped his wife into his arms, staggering a bit under her weight. "We'll decide later. Right now we have to leave. We can take her to the hospital faster ourselves."

Sloan seemed relieved they were getting out of the house. Natalia sensed they didn't have a lot of time, and besides, this gave her the opportunity to postpone her decision a little longer. She followed her uncle outside as he headed straight toward a blue minivan parked in front of Lara's house. Just as she ran ahead to open the door, Jordan drove up.

"The cops are just a few blocks away," Jordan warned by way of greeting as he emerged from the car. Without being told, he seemed to assess the situation and come to the instant conclusion that the bad guy got away and that Alek was with them. The faint sound of sirens grew closer. "Is that soccer van stolen?"

"Of course not!" Alek looked affronted at the thought.

"Good. Give me the keys. All of you jump in."

Natalia was amazed at how quickly everyone followed Jordan's command, piling into the minivan and pulling the doors shut behind them. Jordan took control of the situation, climbing into the driver's seat and starting the engine. They pulled away from the curb, making it around the corner what sounded like mere seconds before the cops pulled up to the house.

After a few minutes, it was clear they'd gotten away clean.

Her brief sense of relief quickly evaporated. The sun was high in the sky, but the soccer van wasn't built with interior lighting like an ambulance. She could barely see her patients. Plural. Sloan and Lara both needed medical attention.

Which probably didn't matter much, since she didn't have anything that even resembled medical equipment.

They'd gotten away from Lara's house and the immediate threat from the police, but if they didn't make a decision about getting to a hospital soon, the choice would be taken out of their hands.

Sloan and Lara would bleed to death right here in the back of the stupid soccer van.

JULY 3 – 1:25 p.m. – Washington, DC

THE FLIGHT WAS AWFUL, far too many hours for anyone to be comfortable, but finally the wheels of the Lufthansa jumbo jet hit the ground. After what seemed like forever, the passengers, moving sluggishly, disembarked from the plane, taking their time as if they didn't have anything better to do.

Maintaining a calm demeanor wasn't easy. Peering out the window one could see the landscape, so different from Moscow. The streets were laden with cars and people in

Washington, DC. Home to the American president. Ha! At least for a while.

The surge of anticipation helped counteract the dragging effects of jet lag. Everything was in place. This plan could not be allowed to fail.

Where was the FBI contact? What was taking a man with immense resources at his disposal so long to find one woman?

There was a saying in America: if you want the job done right, take care of it yourself.

Skotina, it was time, far past time to take care of Natalia once and for all. Being forced to endure a horrible flight from Moscow was all her fault. Natalia needed to be found and silenced. There wasn't a moment to waste.

The return flight to Moscow was in twenty-four hours. Barely enough time to get back to the safety of Russian soil before the main event.

A grand plan which would effectively wipe out millions of American citizens, crippling the nation.

Allowing Russia to return to a position of power. Power it richly deserved.

JULY 3 – 1:57 p.m. – Brookmont, MD

NATALIA GLANCED up as Jordan pulled off to the side of the road. "What are you doing?"

He caught her gaze in the rearview mirror. "Hotel or hospital?"

"Hotel," Sloan said in a voice that was barely stronger than a whisper.

Indecision warred with logic. She didn't know what to

do. "If only I could get some supplies, some equipment. Like a stethoscope, hemostat, suture, pressure dressings, suction, a real trach tube." She closed her eyes, overwhelmed by the magnitude of the task in front of her. "Hospital," she said to Jordan. "Take them to Sibley Hospital."

"No." Sloan struggled to sit up. "Send Alek in. No one is likely to question him dressed in scrubs. He can get the equipment you need."

Natalia stared at him. "Are you crazy? Equipment is only part of the problem. I'm not a doctor. What if I'm wrong? Do you realize the longer we wait to seek treatment the more likely it is that you'll both die?"

"For me, the odds are better with you than in the hospital." Sloan's tone didn't allow room for arguing. "What do you think is going to happen the minute my name hits the hospital computer system?"

She fell silent, fearing she knew exactly what would happen. There was no doubt the FBI wanted to find her and Sloan very badly. Alek, too, for that matter. He'd escaped from federal prison for Pete's sake. Her gaze fell on Lara. The bleeding from her throat wound had slowed down a bit, but she couldn't be certain the artery wasn't damaged.

She was a critical care nurse, not a vascular surgeon.

Her aunt needed a proper trach tube. Surgery to repair the laceration. If she took Lara to the hospital herself, who would look after Sloan's wound? She couldn't make out the full extent of the damage except to know his exit wound was still bleeding.

Her gaze collided with Uncle Alek's, and she nearly choked on a wave of guilt. He must realize she'd made her choice. A choice that could cause Aunt Lara's demise.

"Hotel," she said, avoiding her uncle's gaze. "I can probably find many of the medical supplies I need at a drugstore."

"Give me a list for the rest. I'll get into the hospital for you." Alek winced and grabbed his side. "You may need to redress my injury first though. The blood has probably already seeped through my scrubs."

"Injury?" Natalia frowned but then realized it was strange that he was dressed in scrubs and a long white physician's lab coat. "You were at the hospital?"

"Yes, Washington University Hospital. This soccer van belongs to a friend of mine who works there." He shrugged. "I escaped before they could do surgery on the wound."

"Surgery?" Her voice rose in alarm.

"The cut is deep, may have injured my liver."

Three patients. Dear Lord, have mercy, she was responsible for the lives of three people.

And there was still a killer on the loose, someone who'd gone to great lengths to try and eliminate them.

All of them.

JULY 3 – 2:23 *p.m.* – *Washington, DC*

HIS PHONE RANG. Irritated at how he'd failed to kill Natalia, he growled, "Yeah?"

"Good afternoon." The familiar voice sent a warning chill trickling down the back of his neck. "Did you kill her yet?"

For a wild moment he considered lying, but then he realized he'd have to provide proof in order to get his money. Double the usual fee if he could get to Natalia by midnight. "No. She's not alone. She has help."

The hiss of Russian in his ear didn't make him feel any better. "Meet me at the Pelican Bay restaurant on Dover."

"Here? You're in DC?" He couldn't completely mask the panic in his voice.

"Yes."

Not good. He thought fast. "I'm in the middle of a meeting, and I can't leave without raising the director's suspicions. I'll get there when I can." He quickly disconnected the line.

He curled his fingers into fists. This wasn't good news at all. Things were skating downhill fast. First the Nevsky woman had sprayed perfume in his eyes when she tried to get away, then Sloan Dreyer had tried to shoot him. At least he'd managed to hit his mark; he noticed the way Dreyer's arm had hung uselessly at his side. When he heard the car door slam, he'd realized the odds had turned against him, even with Dreyer wounded. So he'd disappeared out the back door, without getting his hands on Natalia.

Now his Moscow contact was here in DC.

And his boss was really getting suspicious of his frequent disappearing acts.

This situation called for drastic measures. Because he wasn't about to let everything he'd worked for go swirling down the drain without a fight.

JULY 3 – 5:08 p.m. – Brookmont, MD

NATALIA FOUGHT A WAVE OF EXHAUSTION. This must be what it felt like to work in a military MASH unit, where one wound was just as grim as the next. Jordan had taken them to a small motel located not far from the hospital, and she'd examined each of the three injuries from a triage perspective, then had gotten to work.

Sloan's wound had bled the most, but Uncle Alek's wound wasn't far behind. Aunt Lara's neck wound was the most precarious, considering the damage to her airway, so Natalia started there first. Upon a closer examination of her aunt's throat, she realized the attacker's aim had been off, because the deepest part of the cut was actually right in the center over her trachea. From what she could tell, the rest of the wound was more superficial than she'd expected, and Lara's left carotid artery appeared intact.

She'd given Jordan a list of supplies and been impressed with the way he'd performed minor miracles getting almost everything she'd needed. Somehow, wearing Alek's scrubs, he'd gotten into the hospital to filch the size 7 trach tube, sutures, and a stethoscope.

Lara seemed remarkably better after Natalia inserted the trach tube. She'd placed a few sutures to keep the tube in place and closed the worst of the gap.

Then she looked at Alek's wound, irrigated the whole thing with sterile water, then sutured it up as well. He groaned loudly since she didn't have anything to use for anesthetic, and she felt every one of those sutures all the way down to her soul.

Guilt drove her to save Sloan's injury for last. She stared down at the messy exit wound in his shoulder. Dispassionately, she realized it was good the bullet had gone clean through. Jordan might have had trouble finding surgical instruments for her in order to remove it.

"This is going to hurt," she muttered, pouring a healthy dose of alcohol into the wound. The extra-strength dose of acetaminophen she'd given him probably didn't come close to touching the pain, but it was all she had.

Sloan didn't so much as utter a sound, although his brow broke out in a cold sweat. After irrigating the wound, much like she had Uncle Alek's, she was glad to see that the blood welling in the opening didn't seem to be bright red and pulsing, so she didn't think it was arterial.

She picked up the hemostat and the 3.0 silk on a curved needle. Her hands shook a little as she began to stitch the wound closed in an attempt to minimize the bleeding. She used antibiotic ointment on her handiwork for all three patients but suspected that without IV or, at the very least, oral antibiotics, everything she was doing was only a temporary measure at best. The biggest threat to each of them was massive infection.

"That's the best I can do," she muttered, standing and stretching her back, sore from bending over her patients at an awkward level.

Sloan opened his eyes. His voice was low, rough as he said, "Thanks."

She didn't know how to respond. Thanks for what? For listening to him against her better judgment? For following her heart? For making the choice to save Sloan, putting the lives of her uncle and aunt at risk?

Jordan had remained quiet during the time she was tending to the various injuries, but now he stood and came over to stand by Sloan. "Seeing as how everyone is patched up, we have to talk. I need to fill you in on what I know."

Sloan struggled to sit upright. "Go ahead."

Jordan hesitated. "I contacted Jerome Bentley from the bureau." When Sloan's eyes widened in alarm, he hastily added, "Hear me out before you go berserk. I told you we had to trust someone eventually. We can't fight this blind."

"Why Bentley?" Sloan asked. "He was our original

contact. Not only that, he's the least senior assistant director on the team."

Jordan snorted. "Do you think I should have gone straight to the top? To Clarence Yates himself?"

"Why not? If Yates himself is the leak, we're in really deep trouble."

"I don't have a way to contact Yates directly, you know that," Jordan responded patiently. "No one does. He's protected as tightly as the president. Trust me, the end result will, hopefully, be the same."

"Unless Bentley is the leak," Sloan said in a bitter tone.

Jordan gave an offhand shrug. "At least we'll soon know one way or the other. I told you it's time to start playing offense. And you'll be interested to hear Bentley confirmed the suspicion of an inside leak."

Sloan's brows shot up. "He did?"

Jordan nodded, a thoughtful expression on his face. "Apparently, Yates said as much at one of their last meetings."

"Good. That's good," Sloan muttered. "Maybe we have a chance to beat this thing after all."

Natalia didn't understand. "If you trust this Jerome Bentley, then why haven't we gotten in touch with him sooner?"

Sloan and Jordan exchanged a knowing glance. Jordan answered, "Because we don't trust him. Not really. He could mention us in some meeting where the mole is at. Or he could be the mole himself."

She tried to follow their twisted logic. "But for some reason, you don't think so?"

"Jordan took a gamble. Threw the dice, then stepped back to watch what happened," Sloan muttered in disgust. He turned to Jordan. "You'd better hope this doesn't blow up in our faces. We've managed to survive against pretty lousy odds up until now."

"I know. But the conversation went better than I'd hoped. I gave him enough information to convince him we're investigating this thing to the best of our ability."

"So do you think he'll let the upper brass know we made contact?" Sloan asked.

A ghost of a smile played along Jordan's mouth. "Yeah, I do. I bet we hear from him again, soon."

She wasn't sure she liked the sound of that. "He has a way to contact us?"

"Of course." Jordan looked confused. "How else would we take this to the next step?"

How would she know? She didn't understand the twisted rules in the game they were playing. Besides, they weren't anywhere near ready to take the next step, not when most of their team was seriously injured.

Alek stirred from the second bed, the one he shared with Lara. "Michael Cummings," he muttered, lifting his head to look directly at Sloan. "You need to get in touch with my FBI contact, Michael Cummings."

Sloan sighed and rubbed his aching shoulder. "I hate to tell you this, but Michael Cummings is dead."

Alek stared for a minute before hanging his head. "*Durachok*. I was afraid of that."

Jordan moved around Sloan's bed to hover over Alek. "Exactly what sort of work were you doing for Cummings?"

Her uncle shot a fugitive glance at his wife lying beside him. Natalia was relieved Lara appeared to be asleep from a combination of sheer exhaustion and the maximum allowed dose ibuprofen Natalia had given her. Alek kept his voice low. "I was trying to help him gather information."

"What sort of information?" Sloan asked in a sharp tone.

"I have connections within the Cheboksary chemical production plant, located outside Moscow." At their puzzled expressions, he continued, "Michael Cummings became suspicious when Russian President Vladimir Putin formally requested a five-year extension on the Chemical Weapons Convention, claiming they were unable to meet the deadline outlined in the original ratified agreement. Especially when he'd noticed an increase in activity around the Cheboksary production plant and at the Pochep storage facility shortly afterward. He found me, presumably through old employment records, and approached me for help one day here in Washington, DC. I agreed."

Jordan and Sloan exchanged a wry glance that didn't escape Alek's notice.

Her uncle squared his shoulders. "Russia may be the place of my birth, but my loyalty is to freedom, and I owe a debt to the United States of America."

"Connections? Old employment records?" Natalia didn't understand. "What sorts of connections could you possibly have at some chemical production plant?"

Alek's apologetic gaze met hers. "When I was a young man in Russia, I was trained to be a chemical engineer. My job," he hesitated and then continued, "I was trained to help create new and improved chemical weapons of mass destruction."

CHAPTER TWENTY-TWO

July 3 – 5:52 p.m. – Washington, DC

HE KEPT an impatient eye on the clock. He wanted this meeting over and done with already. His Moscow contact was no doubt getting antsy as well. Not his fault. He didn't encourage anyone, least of all his contact from Russia, to fly halfway across the world.

Before their boss could say anything, an assistant director named Jerome Bentley dropped his news. "Jordan Rashid made contact."

All members of the group swiveled to stare at Bentley.

"And?" Yates inquired sharply.

"He's working with Sloan Dreyer as we suspected. They have the Russian nurse, Natalia Sokolova, in protective custody."

His heart raced. He couldn't afford to let this chance go. He cleared his throat. "I think we need to convince them to come in. We can surround them with the highest level of security."

There was a moment of silence until Yates nodded. "I agree with you." The director turned toward Bentley. "Do you think either Rashid or Dreyer will trust you enough to agree to a face-to-face meeting?"

Bentley shrugged. "I don't know. I can try."

He stared at the newest member of their team. How much did he dare to push him? "I assume you have a number to contact Rashid."

"Yeah."

"Good. Set up the meeting, then. Convince them we'll grant immunity." He didn't dare ask for the number, but he could get the information off Bentley's phone soon enough. He had several people working for him who did as they were told without asking why.

He hid a smirk. This was exactly the break he'd been looking for.

He'd have no trouble meeting the deadline the Russian had demanded after all.

JULY 3 – 6:11 p.m. – Brookmont, MD

SLOAN FOUND it easy to ignore the throbbing pain in his shoulder when Natalia gasped and went pale. She looked like she'd be the next one needing medical care. Not good when she was the only nurse in the group. He turned to look at Alek, and suddenly, the pieces of the puzzle began to fall into place. "Cummings suspected there was a plan to actually use these chemical weapons of mass destruction?"

Alek nodded, his expression grim. "My job was to find out if there was, indeed, an increase in production of these weapons, and if so, which country might be the suspected target."

"Oh no," Natalia whispered.

"Sit down," Sloan ordered, tugging on her arm. It was a measure of how upset she was that she didn't argue with him but sank onto the bed beside him. Not that he blamed her. First they discovered her aunt was being held hostage, then she spent hours playing doctor to the three of them, and now this, discovering her beloved uncle had once created chemical weapons of mass destruction.

How much more could she take before she cracked? His protective streak emerged, and he suddenly didn't ever want to know. He wanted to protect her, not just now, but forever.

Jordan stepped forward. "What did you discover?"

"I had to go slow to reestablish my previous relationship with my source of information. But a few months ago, I was able to determine that a new chemical agent had been created in the Cheboksary plant, a deadly combination of a vesicant with a nerve agent."

Sloan scowled. "I understand nerve agents, but what's a vesicant?"

"Vesicant agents cause burns," Natalia whispered. Her eyes were dazed, and he reached forward to take one of her icy cold hands in his. "Blisters leading to severe burns."

Alek nodded in agreement. "She is right. There are different types of vesicants, but they used a type of sulfur mustard and combined it with VX to create a new, deadly toxin."

"So what did they plan to do with this deadly new agent they created?" Jordan asked impatiently.

"I don't know for sure, but they were creating large quantities of it. I also found a strange powdery substance outside the Pochep facility that I'd hoped to perform a full chemical analysis on, but my work was interrupted before I could finish."

"Interrupted how?" Sloan asked.

"My communication with Michael Cummings was severed." Alek stared down at his hands. "I tried several times to get in touch with him in our prearranged method, but with no use. He didn't return any of my calls. I needed more chemical resources to help identify the substance, but without Michael's help, I panicked. Fearing the worst, I took the next available flight out of Moscow to return home."

Sloan let out a deep breath, trying not to be too frustrated. He could sense they were getting close. "Okay, go back to the chemical substance you found in the storage facility. What did you find out about it?"

"I'd only just started my analysis, but I identified at least two of the chemicals present, potassium dichromate and stearic acid."

Alek could have been speaking French for all Sloan could tell. He reined in his impatience. "Great. What on earth are those chemicals used for?"

"Oh, there are many different uses," Alek assured him. "Stearic acid, in its purest form, is a simple saturated fatty acid which is often used as a hardening agent. But this sample wasn't pure stearic acid, it was combined with palmitic acid which is highly flammable. A form of palmitic acid was used by the Germans in World War Two to make napalm."

"Napalm? Isn't that like an explosive?" Jordan echoed.

"Exactly." Alek smiled as if he were a proud professor and Jordan the promising chemistry student.

Sloan glanced at Natalia, trying to gauge how she was

doing. She seemed to be listening, but her fingers were still cold, and not because of the temperature in the room. He rubbed her fingers between his hands and turned his attention to Alek. "Okay, we have an explosive agent, but what about the potassium dichromate?"

"That's what was so confusing," Alek admitted. "The most common use for potassium dichromate is in photography, to develop pictures. I'm sure there were other chemicals present that may have helped me to figure out what this powdery substance was used for, but I didn't have time to investigate further."

"We have a fatty acid, an explosive agent, and a photograph developing agent," Sloan murmured in frustration. "Unless we know what that means, we have nothing. At least, nothing we can take to the director of the FBI as proof."

"Surely once they hear Uncle Alek's story, they'll realize Michael Cummings isn't the leak?" Natalia lifted her gaze to Sloan's. "Couldn't they help us find the proof?"

Natalia's wide, haunted eyes tugged at his heart. For her sake, he wanted there to be an easy way out, but there wasn't. "Considering how your uncle escaped from the US Marshals transporting him to the hospital, I think it's best if we come up with something a little more concrete."

"Sloan, did you recognize the man who shot you?" Jordan asked. "Natalia? Did you see him too?"

"No." She shook her head. "I heard noises, as if he'd run out the back door."

Jordan nodded as if he'd expected as much.

Sloan took a deep breath and forced his mind to go back and replay the scene at Lara's house. There was an image, a brief impression, before the lamp came flying at his face.

"The guy was shorter than me by a good couple of inches and had brown hair. Both Ted Saunders and Jerome Bentley are shorter than me with brown hair." What was he thinking? Half the FBI agents had dark hair; both Harper and Wilcox did too. Although Wilcox could probably be scratched off the list since he couldn't have fought him with a bullet in his leg.

Sloan wished the image was clearer in his mind, but it wasn't. After he was shot and physically attacked, the events were a total blur. "I can't say with certainty who the guy was. It could be someone we don't even know."

"So now what?" Natalia looked to be on the verge of tears. "If there is really to be a terrorist attack, how do we know when and where it will take place? Where do we go from here?"

Sloan glanced at Jordan. "We can use the computer to cross-reference the chemicals Alek uncovered and see what pops up."

Jordan nodded. "Sounds good."

His cell phone rang.

"Who is it?" Sloan asked.

"Bentley. Guess it's time to play more offense."

JULY 3 – 6:48 p.m. – Washington, DC

THE PELICAN BAY restaurant was nice enough if one could stomach horribly bland American food.

He was late. The designated meeting time was six thirty. One would assume an important FBI agent could tell time.

Apparently not.

Keeping a polite smile while ordering dinner wasn't easy, but soon the waiter disappeared, order in hand. It was helpful to be fluent enough in English.

Another glance at the time confirmed it was even closer to 7:00 p.m. If he didn't show—

There he was, striding over to the table.

"It's about time."

He scowled. "Sorry, but I told you I've been tied up in meetings."

"So you said." Not that it mattered. This particular source of inside FBI information had just about outlived his usefulness.

"I know where she is," he hastened to reassure.

"Really?" Taking a sip of water helped keep the fury seething beneath the surface in check. "And where exactly might that be?"

His gaze skittered away. Interesting. He thought to keep the meeting place a secret.

"I'm on it. I told you, she's had help," he muttered defensively. "I've set it up so I'm on a small team designated to take them into custody. I'll make sure she dies quickly."

There was a long pause as options were considered—the worst ones discarded and the best one, the only one really—decided upon. "All right. When will this meeting take place?"

"Soon. Tonight." He glanced at his watch. "In roughly two hours."

"Excellent. Then you can join me for dinner." It wasn't an invitation, but a demand. He was smart enough to recognize the difference.

"Sure. Why not?" He leaned back in his chair and signaled for the waiter to come take his order. "I have time."

Poor choice of words. Because in truth his time left on this earth was very limited. He couldn't be allowed to survive the night.

All the more reason he deserved one last meal.

JULY 3 – 7:17 p.m. – Washington, DC

LARA STIRRED ON THE BED, called for Alek, then bolted upright in alarm when she realized she couldn't speak.

"Shh, my love, you must relax," Alek soothed, gathering her close in his strong arms. "There is a tube in your throat to help you breathe."

She clutched his shoulders as the horrible memories came flooding back, the evil man with the gun, how she'd stalled for time, praying Natalia would come earlier, spraying perfume in the man's eyes but then unable to get away.

The way he finally wrestled her to the floor, fearful of rape but just as horrified when the knife had sliced deep.

Lifting shaking fingers to her neck, she felt the tube Alek mentioned, trying to hide her panic. She supposed it could have been worse, but what if the damage was so severe she'd never speak again?

"*Lyubimaya moya*," he whispered. "You will be all right, I promise. Everything will be fine. Natalia has taken good care of you."

Natalia? She glanced around the room, noticing for the first time they were in a hotel. The man who'd accompanied Natalia to the meeting at the Washington Monument was working at the computer, with Natalia sitting beside him.

"They're working on a plan," he explained. "Their FBI contact has called a meeting for nine o'clock tonight. This will all be over soon, I promise."

Lara stared up at Alek, beseeching him to understand. Had he told Natalia the truth about the dark years? Did he explain about Josef Korolev? Did he tell her everything she needed to know?

She pulled out of Alek's grip, seeking something to write with. Maybe if they could make Natalia understand the depth of the danger, their lives would be spared.

How they'd survive, she wasn't sure.

"Lara, don't." Alek seemed upset. "Please, your breathing is becoming labored, you must rest."

Rest? How on earth could she rest?

Natalia glanced over, saw she was awake, and moved away from Sloan to come over. Thank heavens. Now, if only she could find something to write with. Didn't hotels have pens and paper anymore?

"*Tetya*, how are you feeling?" Natalia asked in a voice full of concern.

She gave a brief nod, indicating she was fine, but then traced on the palm of her hand, trying to make Natalia understand she wanted to write a note.

"She seems agitated, frightened about being unable to speak," Alek said.

Idiot, she shot her estranged husband a narrow glare. Of course, she was upset. He'd be upset too if he couldn't speak!

"Here, use this pen and paper." Natalia handed her the items from the bedside table.

Finally. She took a deep breath, picked up the pen and paper, and began to write. It took her a minute to realize she'd written everything in Russian, so she scribbled it out and started over, this time in English.

"Uncle Alek, I have a question to ask," Natalia said in a low tone as if she didn't want the men to overhear.

"Yes?"

"How well did you know my father? My adopted father, Gordon Polaski?"

Lara stopped writing and glanced at Alek who was looking at her too. He cleared his throat. "Why do you ask?"

"We found some paperwork at his antique shop that indicated he may be inadvertently working with the Solntsevskaya. A man named Viktor Azimov."

Lara knew this part of the truth must come out too. She nodded at Alek. *Tell her.*

"Yes, I'm afraid it's true," Alek said slowly. "Gordon Polaski was working with Azimov. Although I don't believe he understood the depth of Azimov's infiltration into the Solntsevskaya until the past few years."

"No," Natalia whispered, closing her eyes in despair. "I can't bear it."

"Natalia, it's not your fault. You couldn't have known." Alek put a comforting hand on her back.

Natalia looked at him. "My mother? Did she know?"

Again, Alek glanced at Lara as if getting permission to tell. She frowned and gave another firm nod. *Keep going, tell her the rest.*

"Yes, Katya suspected Gordon was making his money from less than legal means, so she divorced him and encouraged you to have very little to do with him," Alek admitted.

"Since the divorce? All those years ago?" Natalia went pale. "He's been working with the mob all this time?"

"I'm sure at first he didn't understand what he was getting into. That's how the Solntsevskaya works, you know.

They suck you in with easy money, and then once you're hooked, they reel you in deeper."

"He's dead, Uncle Alek. My father is dead, and his wife and boys are missing." Natalia looked at them through tormented eyes. "Do you think my adopted father's link to the Russian Mafia caused his death?"

Lara sucked in a quick breath and then coughed, forgetting she couldn't take such deep breaths so easily through the narrow tube in her throat. Alek wrapped his arm around her shoulders, holding a tissue at her throat.

"I'm afraid so, *ribka moya*," Alek murmured, dividing his attention between Lara and Natalia. "It's possible his family is in danger too."

"That's what Sloan said." Natalia reached up to hold the crucifix at her throat. "I hope that despite his sins God forgives him."

When her coughing spell was over, Lara went back to her note. They'd only scratched the surface of what needed to be discussed.

"Alek?" Sloan called out from across the room. "I think you should see this."

"What is it?" Natalia rose to her feet and crossed the room, no doubt anxious to change the subject from her father.

Sloan tapped the computer screen. "This is what came up when we cross-matched several possible chemical combinations with what your uncle found outside the chemical storage plant in Pochep." He paused dramatically. "Pyrotechnics."

"Pyrotechnics?" Natalia echoed in surprise.

"Yes!" Alek cried in agreement, abandoning her to cross the room. "Of course. I should have figured that out for myself. Pyrotechnics would also explain the strange combination of chemicals I found."

"Fireworks." Sloan's tone was grim as he glanced at Alek. "The Fourth of July is tomorrow. What if they've hidden chemical weapons of mass destruction in the guise of fireworks?"

CHAPTER TWENTY-THREE

July 3 – 8:03 p.m. – Washington, DC

"YOU CAN'T BE SERIOUS!" Natalia's voice took a hysterical edge. "It's not possible."

"I'm afraid it's very possible." Sloan glanced at Alek who confirmed his suspicions with a nod. "It's the perfect terrorist attack. Hiding chemical weapons in with the fireworks would literally contaminate thousands of people in one fell swoop while they're cheerfully celebrating the Fourth of July, Independence Day."

Jordan rubbed his temple. "That's really sick."

"Exactly," Sloan agreed. "Now how do we stop them?"

"We stop this by getting through to Bentley," Jordan spoke in a firm tone. "If we can convince him of the danger, he can get us in to see Yates."

"We have no real proof," Sloan pointed out. "All we have is theory and supposition."

"Once we have the Feds on board, we'll get proof."

Sloan sighed, not convinced Jordan's plan was the best

one. He had a bad feeling about this. "Unless Bentley is the mole, then we're done."

A rare flash of anger darkened Jordan's eyes. "Knock off the negative attitude. If you don't stop working against me, this plan really will fail."

"Okay, you're right." Sloan tried to back off, although the nagging itch along the back of his neck wasn't easy to ignore. "Let's walk through this one last time before we get going. The meeting has been set up in Rock Creek Park. You and Natalia are going to be hidden nearby. Alek and Lara are going to wait here. I'll meet with Bentley."

"Once we're convinced that Bentley isn't the mole, we'll insist he get us directly in front of the director, Clarence Yates," Jordan agreed. "But Natalia will need to be with you at the initial meeting."

"No." There was no way he was conceding on this. "She needs to be safe."

"With you and me covering her, she'll be safe," Jordan pointed out in a reasonable tone. "But the reason I was able to get through to Bentley was because we had Natalia. She's the one they want to talk to."

"I don't care." Sloan rubbed his injured shoulder, knowing the odds were already stacked against them. He wasn't very accurate shooting a gun with his left hand. "We're not using Natalia as bait."

"We're not setting her up as bait," Jordan snapped. "It's a meeting with the FBI."

"The same FBI who has killed one of their own, Michael Cummings."

"The entire bureau isn't at fault here—we just have to find the bad apple."

Sloan wasn't buying Jordan's rationalization. "For all we know, the whole bushel is rotten."

"Oh sure, the whole agency is in cahoots with the Solntsevskaya." Jordan gave a loud snort. "Right."

"I'll do it," Natalia spoke up from beside him. "If it means stopping this horrible attack, I'll meet with Bentley."

"No." A red haze of fury blurred his vision. He couldn't bear the idea of Natalia being in danger. He swung toward his partner. "I mean it, Jordan, I'll call the whole thing off."

Alek and Lara exchanged a horrified look. He knew what they were all thinking. The clock was ticking, in just a few short hours the country would celebrate the birth of their nation.

A celebration that would result in mass murder.

"Sloan." Natalia put a hand on his arm. He stared at her tapered, dainty fingers. Capable, strong fingers that had stitched each of the wounded back together again. "We don't have time to argue. We must do this. There's too much at stake."

They weren't ready. They didn't have all the pieces of the puzzle fit into place yet. They didn't have proof. They needed time.

They didn't have time.

He lifted his gaze to Natalia. She was so strong, had proved herself to be much more than the haughty princess he'd first thought. He couldn't imagine losing her. He'd protect her with his life but feared he wasn't strong enough. Wasn't capable enough, especially now that he was injured. The ache in his shoulder wasn't just a result of the damaged muscles. He could tell infection was setting in. Even with Jordan hidden nearby, without proper surveillance equipment the odds were stacked against them.

He'd have to count on Jordan's expertise. Depending on others to do his job wasn't easy. But he couldn't see an alternative.

"All right," he agreed on a sigh of defeat. "Natalia and I will meet with Bentley."

JULY 3 – 8:45 p.m. – Washington, DC

DESPITE LIVING her entire life in DC, Natalia had only been inside Rock Creek Park a handful of times and never at night. It was a lovely nature retreat spread across dozens of acres hidden in the affluent part of the city. Technically, the park closed at dusk, but no one stood guard against them as they slipped inside.

Beside her, Sloan vibrated with tension. Yet he'd also kept a warm, firm hand on hers, almost as if he needed the contact as much as she did.

He'd been so different toward her the past few hours. Kind, caring. Sweet and comforting. She wasn't quite sure what to make of it.

Other than admitting how much she liked it. Liked him.

She drew in a deep calming breath and peered through the dim light as they negotiated the path toward the designated meeting place at the stone bridge. In the silence, she could very faintly hear the sound of water rippling through Rock Creek. Under different circumstances, the sound would soothe her ragged nerves.

But not tonight. She wanted to ask how they'd know when Jordan was safely hidden but suspected she wouldn't like the answer. According to Sloan, they were hampered by a lack of technical equipment such as microphones and tracking devices. They wouldn't use the cell phones except in the case of a dire emergency.

They had to trust Jordan would be there.

A chill rippled over her skin, and she suppressed a shiver. She'd be glad when this was over. In spite of her brave words earlier and volunteering to do this, she was scared out of her mind.

"Are you all right?" Sloan asked in a low tone as they followed the curving path.

She wasn't, but she swallowed the urge to vocalize her thoughts. Would any of them be all right if they didn't stop the potential terrorist attack threatening their nation? She'd been to the Fourth of July celebration in DC several times, always in awe of how the brilliant fireworks exploded in the sky, beautifully framing the Washington Monument. Imagining droplets of chemical poison, vesicant, and nerve gas infiltrating the masses of people watching the display made her sick to her stomach.

"How much farther?" she asked instead. Sloan was far more familiar with the layout of the park than she was.

"Less than a mile." He tightened his grip on her hand as if to reassure her.

They hadn't taken more than a dozen steps when they heard the noise, a rustling in the trees to the right of the curve.

Sloan reacted instantly, releasing her hand and grabbing his weapon. He gave her an awkward shove with his injured right hand, urging her to take shelter behind his body.

Natalia clung to Sloan, holding her breath and praying the noise was nothing more than a deer or a fat raccoon.

A high-pitched moan quickly dispelled that hope.

Sloan moved backward into the thicket that lined the path, still holding his weapon with his left hand, dragging her along with his right hand. Natalia frowned. The moan had come from a human. Shouldn't they investigate? What if the injured person was Jordan?

"*Pomogite, pozhaluysta, pomogite mne.*" Help me, please, help me. The whispered words of Russian could barely be heard.

A woman. She sounded hurt. Thoughts of how the body of Chandra Levy was found here years ago invaded her mind. Rock Creek Park wasn't a place rife with crime, but this was DC. Anything could happen.

"She needs help," Natalia hissed near Sloan's ear. He had her sandwiched between his body and a tree.

He shook his head and lifted a finger for silence. Hiding in the brush while someone moaned for help was almost more than she could take.

The brush across the path moved, and slowly the pale frame of a woman, clothes ripped and hanging from her shoulders, emerged from the growth. Head down, she crawled on her hands and knees, pulling herself onto the path, her alabaster skin marred with streaks of blood.

She sucked in a harsh breath. The poor woman had been attacked, possibly sexually assaulted. Natalia broke free of Sloan's grip, bolting to the woman's side, ignoring his harsh protest. They couldn't blithely attend their meeting with Bentley without promising help to this poor woman who was so obviously a victim of a horrendous crime.

"Shh," Natalia whispered as she dropped to her knees beside the woman. "You're safe now."

"No!" The battered woman cringed from her touch, rolling into a fetal position. Appalled, Natalia stared, imagining what unspeakable horrors she must have experienced.

"Natalia, don't. Please, step away from her," Sloan urged in Ukrainian. "This could be a trap."

She ignored him, her gaze absorbing the woman's deep scratches covered in dried blood. "I won't hurt you, I promise," she whispered in Russian. Natalia did her best to remain calm, to keep her touch nonthreatening and soothing.

Natalia reared backward, caught completely off guard when the woman surged to her feet.

"Too bad I can't promise the same." The woman's fingers dug into her skin, and she pressed a gun against the vulnerable skin of Natalia's temple. Then the woman pulled Natalia in front of her. "Mr. Dreyer, drop your weapon and come out or I'll shoot her right now."

JULY 3 – 8:58 p.m. – Washington, DC

SLOAN WATCHED the events unfold in excruciating slow motion. Natalia's frightened gaze squeezed his heart. He couldn't see the woman's facial features clearly in the dim light, but he knew with sickening certainty this woman holding a gun to Natalia's head was responsible for all the death and destruction they'd witnessed since the beginning.

Come on, Jordan, give me a sign you're on this. I need to know you're behind her and ready to help take this woman down.

Sloan took a deep breath and stepped from the foliage. He didn't immediately toss his gun aside, trying to buy time. "So, I take it Jerome Bentley isn't going to make our meeting."

The woman didn't bite. "Throw your gun down." She tightened her grip on Natalia, pushing the muzzle of the gun so firmly into Natalia's temple he could see the indentation from where he stood. "Now."

He threw his gun into the trees behind the woman,

hoping like mad that if Jordan couldn't find it, none of the bad guys could either. "There. You happy?"

"No, I am not happy." The woman's face remained shadowed, illuminated only by the light of the moon. "You have caused me a great deal of time and trouble. I will not be happy until you're both dead."

Natalia gasped, and the woman holding her smiled. The evil semblance of humor chilled him to the bone. There was something vaguely familiar about her. Searching the woman's facial features he tried to find any hint of vulnerability, a weakness or edge he could use to their advantage.

But there was nothing. The woman holding Natalia was a very experienced cold-blooded killer.

"What did you do with Bentley?" he asked, desperate for a sign from Jordan. Anything. He couldn't believe this woman had somehow gotten to Jordan the way she must have gotten to Bentley.

"I killed him along with a few others," the woman said in a conversational tone. "But you already knew that, didn't you?"

Did that mean Bentley was the mole? He wished he knew for sure. He wanted to hear her say it out loud so Jordan would follow the sound of their voices. What was taking him so long? They weren't that far from the stone bridge. "Yes. And I'm sure you enjoyed every minute of it."

"Of course." She didn't bother denying the truth.

"*Tvayu mat*. You're a vile, despicable human being," Natalia sputtered in a harsh tone. "You must know you'll never get away with this."

The woman threw back her head and laughed. "My dear Natalia," she said in a mocking tone. "Such language. I'm impressed at how well you speak Russian. But your manners are appalling. Didn't my sister teach you it's not polite to insult your mother?"

JULY 3 – 9:07 p.m. – Washington, DC

HER MOTHER? Natalia couldn't breathe, couldn't speak. The charoite pendant at her throat burned against her skin. Her mind reeled from the truth, couldn't wrap itself around the idea that the woman about to kill her was her own flesh and blood mother.

She'd searched so long for her mother, imagining a woman who'd loved her, who'd been reluctant to give her up. But apparently her dream was little more than a horrible nightmare. Closing her eyes, she whispered a prayer of apology to her adopted mother, the woman she'd loved with her whole heart.

And prayed for God to save them all.

She never should have tried to find her roots. All she'd found was a cold-blooded killer.

"What do you want?" Sloan asked abruptly. "Name your price."

"I want nothing from you," Anya said in a venomous tone. "This is something I should have done a long time ago. It's past time to end it."

"Why?" Natalia forced herself to ask. "I haven't done anything to you. I didn't even know you!"

"But that didn't stop you from trying to find me, did it?" Anya hissed in a low tone directly into her ear. "No, you had to keep looking, searching. Somehow your amateur attempts to find me paid off. I was shocked when Josef told me he'd found our daughter here in Washington, DC. How it was time our sweet, innocent daughter knew her parents. Oh, he was so anxious to meet you, to reunite with you. And you're still wearing the necklace he bought when you were born. Isn't that sweet?" The bitterness radiated off her in waves. "He didn't care that my husband, Boris, didn't know about you. Didn't care that finding you threatened my position of power. I'm the wife of the minister of defense, and very soon Boris will become president. Then we will rule all of Russia."

Natalia's thoughts swirled as the truth formed a clear picture in her mind. The letter between Alek and Josef suddenly made sense. He'd recognized the pendant. Because he'd purchased it for her. "Josef Korolev was my biological father."

"And if my sister hadn't betrayed me by whisking you out of the country, you'd already be dead. However, better late than never, yes? Hmm. Who should go first? The daughter or the daughter's boyfriend?" Anya pretended to think. Then smiled. "Say goodbye, Natalia," Anya murmured in a singsong voice.

She swallowed hard, bracing herself as she stared at Sloan, trying to tell him without words how much she loved him.

Would always love him.

When the pressure of the gun eased off her temple, Natalia understood her mother intended to shoot Sloan first. "No!" she shouted and threw herself at Anya.

A sharp report echoed through the night.

Pain, hot and blistering, registered a millisecond before the ground came rushing up to meet her.

CHAPTER TWENTY-FOUR

July 3 – 9:19 p.m. – Washington, DC

"NATALIA!" Sloan shouted her name as he jumped over Anya's dead body in his haste to reach her. "Natalia!"

Some distant part of his mind registered the fact that Jordan was calling for an ambulance. He owed his partner a debt of thanks for coming through at the last minute and shooting Anya at the same moment Natalia leaped into the line of fire. He saw a wound in the hollow of Natalia's right shoulder. The oozing blood made him dizzy. Gritting his teeth, he shook off the sensation. As much as he wanted medical help for Natalia, he couldn't really believe the danger was over.

"We can't leave her alone in the hospital, not for a second," he told Jordan as he balled up her shirt on the exit wound and then leaned his weight over the site in an effort to hold pressure. "Not until we know for sure the mole is dead."

"I stumbled across Bentley's body as I was trying to get

behind the woman," Jordan told him. "If he was the leak, he's not a threat any longer."

"But we don't really know for sure he was the leak," Sloan protested. "Where is the stupid ambulance?"

"They're not going to be able to drive this deep into the park, Sloan." Jordan's tone was maddeningly reasonable. "We'll carry her out to the clearing."

"We need to keep pressure on her wound," he muttered, mostly to himself. Without hesitation, Sloan ripped off his shirt and, using his teeth, tore it in half so he could cover both the exit and entry wounds the best he could. Awkwardly holding the pressure pad against the bleeding area, he lifted Natalia's limp body into his arms, barely noticing the strain against his own injury.

"Let me carry her," Jordan offered, stepping forward as if to take the burden.

"No." His fingers tightened on her body. "Lead the way." Sloan couldn't bear the thought of letting her go. He strode quickly along the path, trying to hurry. In his mind's eye, he relived the moment Natalia moved into the path of the bullet, protecting him from harm.

He was supposed to protect her. Instead, she'd taken the bullet meant for him.

Following Jordan wasn't easy. He couldn't see the ground at his feet, and twice he tripped, almost falling on his face. Finally, they reached the clearing. He gently set Natalia down, reapplying pressure to the gunshot wound in her upper chest. Her breathing was shallow, choppy, and he prayed for the first time since losing his sister that God would have mercy on him and spare Natalia's life.

Please, Lord, save her!

It seemed like forever before the ambulance arrived, and even then, he was loath to let her go. Once the paramedics had inserted an IV for fluids and stabilized her, they lifted her into the back of the ambulance. Sloan insisted on riding along, and after taking one look at his crazed expression, the paramedics had given in.

"After I pick up Lara and Alek, I'll meet you at the hospital," Jordan assured him.

He nodded. They also had to figure out a way to get in contact with the director of the FBI and convince him to stop the fireworks.

And he would. As soon as he was sure Natalia would survive.

JULY 3 – 9:22 p.m. – Brookmont, MD

ALEK SHIVERED, his body shaking so hard Lara glanced up at him in concern. While she couldn't speak, her stern gaze spoke volumes.

You're sick. You need antibiotics, you stubborn oaf.

She was right. He closed his eyes to avoid her accusing stare. Alek knew he was growing weaker, sicker, as the minutes ticked past. Their job was to stay here, wait for Sloan or Jordan to return. But what if something happened? What if their meeting with Bentley didn't go as planned?

He could die waiting here for them. And he had too much to live for to give up that easily.

"Wait a li-little bit lo-longer," he stuttered between shaking spells. He'd taken some acetaminophen a couple of hours ago, but the over-the-counter medication hadn't touched his fever.

His side ached with a burning pain, and he imagined he could feel the infection infiltrating his body, one red blood cell at a time. He pulled his wife close, reassured by her presence beside him.

"I lo-love you, Lara," he murmured. He kissed the top of her head and leaned against her. He didn't want to think about the future and the possibility of failure. If he died right now, he'd die a happy man. "Gi-give me another ch-chance to prove how much I lo-love you."

She held him for a moment and then yanked out of his arms. Dazed, he peered at her. What had he said to make her angry? Was she still set against giving their marriage another try?

She pulled on his arm, hard, until he realized she wanted him to stand. Then she dragged him toward the door. Belatedly, he realized what she was doing.

Forcing him to get help.

The fierce determination in her eyes made him smile.

There was still hope. She wasn't giving up on him. On their marriage.

She wasn't giving up on them.

He stumbled as she tugged him toward the tiny hotel office. One look at him and the woman behind the desk would no doubt call for an ambulance.

Praying he wasn't making a giant mistake, he followed his wife inside.

JULY 3 – 10:15 p.m. – Washington, DC

THE RUSSIAN WOMAN had tried to kill him.

He stared down at the dead rat lying in the alley and realized how close he'd come to dying himself.

Good thing he'd listened to his instincts, forcing himself

to throw up minutes after he'd ditched the woman, bringing up the remains of the celebratory shot of Russian vodka they'd shared. The rat lying beside his vomit proved the drink had been poisoned. As it was, some of whatever substance she'd used had gotten into his system, causing him to pass out shortly after he'd puked his guts out.

Had he told her what she wanted to know?

He blinked away the fog and squinted at his watch, realizing he'd lost a lot of time. Past ten. The timeframe for the meeting with Natalia had passed. No doubt Anya had gone in his place. Had she already killed them all? Natalia? Dreyer? Rashid?

He had no way of knowing for sure.

Swearing under his breath, he stumbled to his feet, using the brick wall beside the dumpster for support, swiping his hand along the back of his mouth. Pulling his cell phone from his pocket, he searched for missed calls.

There was one message.

"You told me to let you know if any of our suspects surfaced and they have. Two of them. Both Natalia Sokolova and Alek Nevsky were admitted to Sibley Hospital on the border of DC and Maryland. Wasn't that nice of them to end up at the same place? Let me know if you want me to follow up."

The hospital?

Seriously? She wasn't dead? He wanted to slam his fist against the building in frustration. How hard could it be to kill one woman? Since Anya had tried to kill him, he pretty much figured out he wasn't going to see his money.

Which meant he didn't really need to kill Natalia. Unless she knew the truth. The thought brought him upright. Witnesses. The last thing he needed was witnesses.

If he moved fast, he could still salvage what was left of

his career. There was just enough time to eliminate the witnesses and get out of the country before the big bang.

Afterward, he could return and be the hero who pulled the country from the depths of despair.

Fueled with determination, he pushed away from the wall and stumbled toward the car.

Yes. There was still time.

JULY 4 – 12:05 a.m. – Washington, DC

SLOAN STUCK CLOSE to Natalia throughout her stay in the ED, up until the time they whisked her off to surgery. Even then he paced outside the operating room area until the doctor came to tell him Natalia had pulled through just fine. They'd been forced to remove the upper lobe of her lung, which had sustained the worst of the damage, but she was stable enough to go to a regular room.

He'd have felt better if she'd gone straight to the ICU where there was more security, but then again, he couldn't deny he was grateful she was alive. It wasn't long before they transferred her to a private room. He pulled up a chair to sit at her bedside.

Sloan stared at her. She was achingly beautiful. He'd almost lost his mind, thinking she might die. Not just because he didn't want another death on his conscience but because he couldn't imagine his life without her. Strange considering he'd only met her a few days ago. He reached out to touch her hand. She continued to sleep peacefully, no doubt still under the effects of anesthesia.

He dropped his head into his hands, swallowing a groan. His entire body ached, and he was running a fever, but he wasn't ready for a hospital bed of his own. Not until someone was standing guard over Natalia. He couldn't believe it was over.

What was taking Jordan so long anyway? He should have been here by now.

Sloan pulled his cell phone from his pocket to see if Jordan had left him a message. Nope.

He lifted his head when a nurse walked into the room carrying a Styrofoam cup filled with ice and soda. "Here, this is from your partner. He told me to let you know he's here and working on getting in touch with the boss?" She lifted a shoulder to indicate she didn't completely understand the message. Her gaze turned to Natalia. "How's our patient?"

He took a sip of the soft drink and then set the cup aside. "You tell me, you're the nurse." He gazed down at Natalia. "She's a nurse too."

"Really?" The nurse, whose name tag read Christy, glanced over in surprise. "Where does she work?"

"Washington University Hospital."

"Wow, small world." Christy put her stethoscope in her ears and proceeded to examine Natalia, listening to her heart and lungs, then her blood pressure. After taking inventory of her vital signs, she checked the surgical dressing.

Sloan scrubbed a hand over his face, feeling woozy. He stood, fighting the urge to lay his head down next to Natalia's. The events of the past few days were obviously catching up to him. He tried to concentrate. "Where is my partner? I need to talk to him for a minute."

"In the hall, making phone calls." Christy took her time hanging a minibag of antibiotic on Natalia's IV tubing before she turned away. "I'll let him know you're looking for him."

"Thanks." The room blurred, and Sloan gave his head a hard shake. He needed to hang on for a little while longer. His body couldn't fail him now.

Christy left the room, and in less than a minute, the door opened again.

"Well, if it isn't the infamous Sloan Dreyer. You never did like to follow orders, did you?"

The dry sarcastic tone was familiar, but it didn't belong to Jordan. Sloan turned to look at the man who'd walked into Natalia's room, tensing when he realized the guy had closed the door behind him. Sloan's vision remained blurred, but he blinked, struggling to bring the man's face into focus.

Ted Saunders. One of the trusted assistant directors of the FBI.

Saunders lips were moving, but Sloan couldn't make out what he was saying. But when Saunders lifted a syringe and smiled, Sloan finally figured out his dizziness wasn't just the effects of a fever.

He'd been drugged.

His gaze fell on the Styrofoam cup. The soft drink he'd barely tasted. *This is from your partner.* But it hadn't been from his partner at all.

Saunders was the mole.

"No!" Gathering every ounce of strength he possessed, he threw himself at Saunders, catching the guy off balance.

They fell against the wall with a thud. For a moment they wrestled for the syringe, but Saunders was stronger than he looked, and in his weakened condition, Sloan couldn't pry the weapon from his fingers. Saunders threw a punch, and Sloan's head snapped back from the force of the blow, giving him a strange sense of déjà vu. This was almost an exact replay of the tussle in Lara Nevsky's house.

Saunders had bested him that time. Sloan knew he couldn't allow him to get away again.

He hung on to Saunders by sheer force of will. How long did he have before someone came to investigate? Where was Jordan?

Pain exploded in his jaw as Saunders's fist connected for the second time. The metallic taste of blood filled his mouth, and Sloan dimly realized it was possible Saunders had already taken care of Jordan.

If so, he was on his own.

Saunders hit him again, and stars danced in his eyes. He slumped against the wall, struggling to remain conscious. After a long moment, he lifted his head and caught a glimpse of the syringe in Saunders's hand as he leaned over Natalia's bed and lifted her IV tubing. He blinked, and Saunders slid the tip of the needle into the IV port.

No! With one Herculean effort, he rushed Saunders, caught the man's wrist, and yanked the needle from her IV. They struggled for the syringe. Sloan didn't try to get the syringe away, but he used all his energy to turn Saunders's wrist so he could jam the needle into his chest.

"Noooo!" Saunders yelled, trying to pull the syringe out. But Sloan leaned all his weight on the plunger, injecting whatever drugs Saunders had prepared directly into his system.

Saunders's body gave a series of violent spasms before falling limp. Dragging himself to his feet, Sloan got up and pulled Saunders off Natalia, not caring when his body hit the floor with a loud thunk.

"Natalia? Are you all right?" He gathered her close, reassuring himself that she was okay.

"Hurts," she murmured, blinking up at him. Obviously the fight had roused her from the heavy sedation.

"I know, sweetheart. But it's over." He stroked a hand down her back. "We found the mole, Ted Saunders. It's finally over."

She frowned. "The fireworks?"

Huh? Rats. He'd almost forgotten. He needed to get in touch with someone at the FBI who would get him in front of the director himself. And where was Jordan? A warning chill settled at the base of his spine. Gently, he set her back against the pillows. "You're right, it's not over. Not yet. I'll be right back."

He didn't like leaving her. Not one bit. He double-checked the body of Ted Saunders and verified the guy was, indeed, dead.

Hoping the nurse didn't stumble across Saunders's body, yet needing to find out if Jordan was alive, Sloan walked out of Natalia's room and down the hall. He flipped open his cell phone and dialed his partner. When he heard a phone ringing in the room down the hall, his gut clenched as he went over to investigate.

The name outside the room was Alek Nevsky. Inside, he found Jordan slumped in a chair, barely breathing. A quick glance at Lara Nevsky confirmed she, too, was unconscious, half lying on Alek's bed.

Saunders had gotten to them. They must have ingested more of the drugged soft drinks than he had.

He yanked the cord from the wall to summon emergency help. When the response wasn't quick enough, he poked his head outside of the room and yelled.

A couple of nurses ran into the room. Sloan propped himself against the wall and gestured to the victims. "I have reason to suspect these people have all been drugged, even the patient. Get your emergency team here, now!"

Soon the room was filled with medical personnel, three groups clustered around each of the victims. Sloan couldn't do much but prop himself against the wall, standing back to watch helplessly.

He tried to estimate how much time had passed before Saunders had found him in Natalia's room, but he couldn't honestly say for sure. Nor did he know what drug Saunders had used on them.

When more people arrived with carts and additional medical equipment, his heart sank. There were so many people he couldn't see exactly what was going on. Soon, Jordan, Alek, and Lara were put on carts and all three of them were whisked away, he hoped to the ICU rather than to the morgue.

No, if they were dead, they wouldn't have hurried. *Please, Lord, don't let them all die!*

Sloan slowly sank to the floor, his legs refusing to support his weight any longer. When the dizziness returned, he put his head down on his knees. His last conscious thought was that while he may have bested Saunders in the end, the price had been steep.

Far too steep.

CHAPTER TWENTY-FIVE

July 4 – 7:17 a.m. – Washington, DC

SLOAN GRADUALLY BECAME aware of his surroundings, hearing beeping noises that were familiar and yet foreign. Why couldn't he remember? Pain throbbed throughout his entire body, but especially his shoulder and his throat. He tried to lift a hand to his throat, but he couldn't move. Something held him captive.

Adrenaline spiked and he forced himself to open his eyes, to see where they were holding him hostage.

The IV tubing and the beeping monitor seemed wrong somehow, until he realized he was the one lying in bed. He must be a patient. He stared at the straps encircling his wrists. What in the hell? He gave another tug, but they remained fast. Why had they tied him down?

He saw a nurse across the room and called out to her, but he couldn't speak. The pain in his throat grew worse, much worse when he continued to try.

Fighting panic, he yanked the restraints, rattling the

side rails of the hospital bed to get the nurse's attention. What time was it? How long had he been out? What if it was too late and he'd slept right through the Fourth of July fireworks?

A nurse hurried over. "Relax now, Mr. Dreyer. You're in the ICU. Are you in pain? Do you need me to give you more pain medication?"

Realizing he was at this nurse's mercy, he forced himself to calm down. If she thought he was psychotic, she'd pump him full of drugs faster than he could blink. He shook his head to answer her question and tried to indicate he wanted to write.

After what seemed like forever, he learned he had surgery on his shoulder because the stitches had been pulled open and the wound was infected. They'd irrigated the wound and left it open. There was also a breathing tube in his throat. Thanks to the ventilator he'd needed after surgery, he'd bought himself an ICU bed. He'd begged the nurse to take the tube out, but she only promised to get in touch with the doctor soon.

He was tempted to rip the stupid thing out himself, but after he'd written his notes, she'd tied his wrist back down. Helpless, he couldn't do anything except wait.

His thoughts were still fuzzy, but he remembered Jordan, Alek, and Lara had all been taken away for treatment. He wanted to know how they were doing.

And Natalia. Had the nurse found Saunders's body? What had happened? He was somewhat surprised there wasn't a Fed already sitting beside him. With everyone hospitalized, he figured it was only a matter of time until the FBI arrived, seeking answers.

He squinted at the clock hanging on the wall of his room. Almost eight o'clock in the morning. For the first time since this mess started, he was actually looking forward to the arrival of the FBI. He had plenty he needed to talk to them about.

And top on his list? A formal request to speak to the director himself.

JULY 4 – 9:38 a.m. – Washington, DC

NATALIA PULLED herself upright in order to sit at the side of her bed, wincing at the pain slicing through her chest. She couldn't believe how much she hurt. As a nurse, she'd always forced her patients to get up after surgery, but never had she realized just how stupid that rule was. At the moment she couldn't have cared less if she suffered a blood clot or pneumonia from lying in bed too long. Getting up this quickly after surgery was insane.

Knowing there were more important problems to worry about than her physical discomfort, she set her feet flat on the floor. She hadn't seen Sloan in hours. There had been a big hullabaloo when a body had been found under her bed. The details were fuzzy, but she vaguely remembered Sloan fighting with someone and falling on top of her bed. After they'd moved her to another room, the nurse had notified security and they'd asked her for a statement, which she'd given as best she could. Then she'd also told her story to the police. Her old room was no doubt a crime scene.

She assumed the body they found belonged to the guy Sloan had fought. But what had happened to Sloan? Where was everyone else? Jordan? Alek and Lara?

Gathering her strength, she tried to stand. The pain was more intense than she'd imagined, partially because she'd refused the last dose of pain medication. But while she was able to support her weight briefly, she couldn't walk far, not with the chest tube draining from the right side of her chest. Knowing she'd do more damage than good if she pulled it out, she plopped back down on the bed and pressed the call light.

When the nurse arrived, she didn't look at all pleased when Natalia demanded a wheelchair. After a brief argument, the nurse gave in and brought her one.

With the IV pole and the chest tube affixed to the wheelchair, she was mobile at last. Ignoring the pain along the right side of her chest—her incision mirrored that of the one Josef Korolev had suffered—she wheeled herself to the nurse's station. Ironic how both she and her father had undergone the same surgery.

Maybe not so ironic, considering her birth mother had ultimately been the one responsible for both wounds.

Those moments when she realized her mother intended to kill her and Sloan flashed in her mind. She tried to shake off the painful memories and focus on the present. "Is there a patient by the name of Sloan Dreyer here?" She wanted to believe he had a good reason for leaving her with a dead body in her room, like needing medical attention himself.

"Yes, but he's in the Surgical ICU on the third floor," the secretary behind the desk informed her.

The Surgical ICU? Why? What had happened? "I'd like to see him."

The woman frowned. "I'm sorry, he's a prisoner patient. I'm afraid they're not allowed visitors."

Prisoner patient? Because of the man found in her room? She wheeled around and made her way over to the policemen gathered around her old room.

"The man you found dead in my room tried to kill me."

Sounding authoritative while wearing a hospital gown that flashed open in the back wasn't easy, but she gave it her best shot. She subtly put a hand over her incision to splint the wound. "Why are you holding Sloan Dreyer as a prisoner?"

The detective exchanged a knowing glance with the officer on duty. "I'm sorry, but you'll need to return to your room."

"No!" She held on to her temper with an effort. *Skotina*, were these men stupid? Didn't they realize what was at stake? "You don't understand, I must see Sloan Dreyer. It's a matter of national security."

The detective had the nerve to smirk. "Sure. When the Feds are finished here, we'll let them know your request." He dismissed her with a wave of his hand. "Officer Nicholson will escort you back to your room."

She wanted to refuse, wanted to fight, demand to see someone in charge, but really, what could she do from a wheelchair? Fuming, she sat back and allowed the police officer to push her back to her room.

Back in her bed, she stared at the clock over her doorframe and watched the minutes tick by slowly. The holiday was here, but it was still early in the morning. They still had time. The fireworks displays weren't scheduled to go off for hours yet. She'd read somewhere how fireworks companies usually took up to twelve hours to set up a display, and she could easily imagine a team of men handling fireworks containers that were really chemical weapons of mass destruction.

What would happen if the FBI didn't come and talk to her? Didn't believe her story? What if Sloan was so sick he didn't make it? And what had happened to Jordan? Alek and Lara?

Helplessly, she watched the second hand go around the clock, the sound echoing loudly in the room.

Tick. Tick. Tick.

JULY 4 – 11:09 a.m. – Washington, DC

"I UNDERSTAND you've requested to meet with Sloan Dreyer." Two men she didn't recognize stood beside her bed. They looked like twins, dressed in similar dark blue suits and red ties.

Finally. The twins had to be FBI. "Yes. Who are you?"

"Special Agent Neil Hammond, ma'am." The one standing to her left didn't try to shake her hand but gave her a brief nod. "And this is Special Agent Mark Jefferson. Can you tell us what happened to Assistant Director Ted Saunders?"

Her mind had been in a drug-filled haze at the time, but she remembered two men fighting, remembered watching while the man had pierced her IV tubing with the needle. Then Sloan gathering her close. *It's over, sweetheart. We found the mole, Ted Saunders. You're safe, now.*

She cleared her throat. "Ted Saunders tried to kill me. Sloan Dreyer stopped him and used the syringe he'd tried to inject into my IV tubing against him instead."

The special agents exchanged a skeptical glance. "I see," Neil Hammond said with a frown. "Why would Assistant Director Ted Saunders try to kill you?"

She battled a wave of panic. They had to believe her. They were on a tight timeline, and there wasn't a second to waste. She took a deep breath but then winced as pain shot through her chest. "He tried to kill me because I knew the truth. Ted Saunders was leaking information to the Solntsevskaya branch of the Russian Mafia. We discovered my birth mother, Anya Tereshkova, planned a terrorist attack so horrible it will cripple the United States and likely cause another world war." Her dramatic statement caused Neil Hammond to give her a placating smile.

"Do you have proof Ted Saunders was leaking inside information?" Mark Jefferson asked.

"You'll find the dead body of my mother, Anya Tereshkova, in Rock Creek Park." Was the body really proof? She doubted it. She stared at the two men. "I saw Sloan and Saunders fighting in my room. Have you spoken to Sloan Dreyer? He'll corroborate my story."

Neil Hammond shook his head. "We tried, but Dreyer won't talk to us. Claims he'll only speak directly to the director himself."

The closed expressions on their faces was not reassuring. Her chest tightened, and she struggled to remain calm. These two were idiots, but she needed the FBI to understand the danger. "Sloan absolutely needs to talk to the director. It's a matter of national security."

"Can't." Mark Jefferson gave a negligent shrug. "The director is out of reach until after the holiday."

JULY 4 – 2:20 *p.m.* – *Washington, DC*

SLOAN WAS RELIEVED when they finally transferred him out of the ICU to a regular room. The cop sitting outside his door accompanied them, which didn't make him happy, but slipping out of the hospital would be easier now that he was out of critical care. His throat was sore.

He was very glad to be rid of the breathing tube and restraints. The pain in his shoulder was still there, but strangely enough, it felt a little better now than it had before. Maybe the antibiotics were successfully fighting his infection.

Progress if you were an optimist. Lately, he wasn't.

He'd hoped the Feds would want answers badly enough that they'd let him talk to Clarence Yates. But so far it was a no go. He needed to get out and track down Yates at his home if necessary.

Exactly how he'd manage to accomplish that feat, he wasn't sure. It wasn't as if Yates's address was common knowledge or listed anywhere online. He battled a wave of helpless frustration. There wasn't time to mess around.

"You have a couple of visitors," the floor nurse, by the name of Steffie, said as she entered his room.

Sloan wasn't surprised when the two agents, Neil Hammond and Mark Jefferson, came strolling back in. He was, however, stunned to see Jefferson pushing Natalia in a wheelchair.

He raked his gaze over every inch of her, hardly daring to believe she was really all right. At the moment she was in a wheelchair, which was one step ahead of him.

"Sloan," she murmured, reaching over to take his hand. "How are you?"

"Good." He was embarrassed to admit his heart felt lighter just from seeing her and holding her hand. Man, he was a mess. This wasn't the time to focus on his personal life. Until meeting Natalia, he'd never really had a personal life. Dragging his gaze from Natalia, he faced the Feds. "Have you gotten in touch with your boss?" he challenged.

"They told me the director is out of touch until after the holiday," Natalia said in Ukrainian.

"Knock it off," Mark Jefferson growled. "If you don't speak in English, I'm hauling your butt out of here."

His gut tensed. If what Natalia said is true, he didn't have a choice but to trust these two. Sloan hastened to explain. "She only told me that you both informed her how the director is out of touch until after the holiday."

The two exchanged a glance. "Yeah, he is."

Sloan knew very well that no one at that level was ever really out of touch, but basically these clowns weren't going to budge unless they had proof. He sighed. "Okay, I need you to compare the substance in the syringe I stuck in the center of Saunders's chest to the soft drink I left on the table in Natalia's room and to blood samples in Jordan Rashid, and Alek and Lara Nevsky. I'm sure you'll find a match. Saunders is the one who tried to kill us all."

"So we've heard," Neil Hammond said in a bored tone. "What we haven't heard is why."

"Because he's been working with the Russian Mafia. We have reason to believe there are chemical weapons of mass destruction disguised as fireworks." Sloan stared at the Feds, willing them to believe him. "Alek Nevsky was working undercover for Special Agent Michael Cummings. Alek was once a chemical engineer whose job it was to create those chemical weapons. He's identified an increase in activity at the Russian chemical production plant. I'm telling you, Cummings didn't kill himself. Almost everyone involved in this mess has been killed. You have to believe me when I tell you the entire country's future is at stake."

"And you have proof chemical warfare will be used against the US?" Mark Jefferson asked.

"I know Alek Nevsky identified the substance found outside of the chemical plant as the same components found in fireworks," Sloan admitted. "I don't know why

Saunders was working with the Mafia, but the real threat is the fireworks. We can't afford to ignore this information."

"There are dozens of huge fireworks manufacturers here in the States. How would Russian fireworks get transported in?" Neil Hammond asked with a frown.

"Good question." Sloan sighed and rubbed his sore shoulder. "I don't know for sure. Maybe those companies get components from overseas? If I had a computer, I could investigate a little further."

"Leave the investigating to us," Jefferson spoke up.

Sloan resisted the urge to smack him. "We don't have time. I was working on this transport angle before things went downhill in Rock Creek Park." He grimaced. "By the way, you'll find a dead body of a woman in there, Anya Tereshokova. She's the wife of the Russian minister of defense."

"What?" Neil Hammond swung an accusing gaze toward Natalia. "You didn't mention that fact."

"Sorry. Must have slipped my mind when she tried to kill me." Natalia's dry sarcasm made Sloan smile. That was his girl, holding her own with the Feds.

"There's also another body, our FBI contact, a man by the name of Jerome Bentley," Sloan added. "The best we can figure is that Anya killed Bentley in order to make the meeting with Natalia."

"Bentley's dead?" Natalia echoed.

He captured her gaze with his. "I'm afraid so. Have you heard any news on Jordan, Lara, or Alek?"

"All I know is they're listed in serious but stable condition in the intensive care unit," Natalia told him.

He nodded, not bothering to hide his overwhelming relief. They weren't dead. He hadn't been too late.

He hadn't failed. Yet.

"I really need that computer access." Sloan kept his tone even. "I know I can find the proof you need."

There was a long pregnant pause as the agents glanced at each other.

"I'll get it for him," Jefferson muttered. He turned and left the room.

Alone with just one Fed and a guard outside his door, Sloan would have once tried to take them both out and make a run for it. There was nothing worse than bureaucracy, especially within the FBI. But seeing Natalia laden with equipment forced him to realize the time for running was over. This was too important. He'd play by the rules if it killed him. Who knows? Cooperating could win him brownie points.

Maybe.

"Sloan?" Natalia squeezed his hand, her gaze earnest. "What about the China connection? The bombing of the Kazakhstan-China oil pipeline? We never did figure out how that factored into all of this."

"You're right," he said slowly. It clicked into place. "China must export tons of fireworks to the US." Sloan's fingers itched to work the computer keys. He turned to Hammond. "If we can prove there's at least a chance of these dirty fireworks making their way here to the US without being detected, will you contact Director Yates?"

Mark Jefferson entered the room carrying a laptop computer. The rooms were equipped with wireless internet access. As Jefferson plugged in the computer, Neil Hammond gave a reluctant nod. "If you can give me something more to go on."

Sloan quickly accessed the internet and began searching. First he located the largest fireworks companies along the East Coast. Then he began a media search on those companies. He didn't exactly know what he was looking for until the article popped up on his screen.

"The Zabollini Fireworks Company, the largest family-owned company in Larkspur, Pennsylvania, suffered an explosion two months ago." Sloan raised his gaze to Hammond's. "How much do you want to bet this company supplies fireworks to all the big cities on the East Coast? New York, Boston, even Washington, DC?"

Natalia gasped. "Of course. Would they risk losing the business especially this close to the holiday? Or would they forgo their own privately made fireworks and export what they could get their hands on from other sources?"

"Like China," Sloan finished her unspoken thought. They were on the right track, he knew it. "We found our link. This is too much to ignore."

Neil Hammond glanced at his partner. "I'm really starting to believe them."

"You should." Sloan couldn't hide a surge of satisfaction as he waved a hand at the clock. "And we don't have any more time to wait. You need to get in touch with Yates. Now. Before it's too late."

Hammond sighed and reached for his phone. "I'll try, but I can't promise anything. I wasn't kidding about him being out of touch until after the holiday."

CHAPTER TWENTY-SIX

July 4 – 5:02 p.m. – Washington, DC

SLOAN COULDN'T BELIEVE how much time they were wasting. Almost three hours had gone by since Hammond had started going through the chain of command, one level at a time, in his quest to reach the director of the FBI. At this rate, they'd be too late. He was all for security, but it shouldn't be this hard to reach one man.

He was half tempted to go straight to the president. Not that he had any chance of succeeding. But at this point, it was worth a try.

Anything was worth a try.

Hammond entered his room. "We found both bodies you mentioned earlier in Rock Creek Park. The woman, Anya, and the other one is definitely Jerome Bentley."

"I'm trying to figure out how Saunders managed to get all the information from Bentley. Was he part of the task force?" Sloan asked.

"Yeah, unfortunately he was. Yates was worried about

an inside leak, especially after Cummings's name was blasted out by the media." Hammond shook his head. "I guess Yates's plan backfired."

Sloan scowled. "It's going to backfire in a disaster worse than 9/11 if he doesn't get back to us and soon. What's taking so long?"

Hammond actually looked embarrassed. "I'm doing my best. With Saunders and Bentley out of the picture, I had to find upper brass that would actually listen to your side of the story. I finally got through. Yates is willing to meet with us down at headquarters."

They'd gotten through to Yates. Then Hammond's words registered. He frowned. "Meet with us?"

The agent nodded. "Yeah. We're lucky he agreed to that much."

Sloan couldn't believe it. What was wrong with everyone? "Didn't you explain what was going to happen? The risk of the fireworks?"

"I started to explain, but he cut me off," Hammond's tone was defensive. "Yates only wants to talk to you."

"Fine." Sloan threw back the covers on the bed. "Then call my doctor and get me medically released so I can get out of here."

JULY 4 – 6:30 p.m. – Washington, DC

"NATALIA?"

She opened her eyes, surprised to find Jordan in a wheelchair next to her bed. "Jordan. What are you doing up? Are you all right?"

"I'm fine, but I've come to see you because I have some news."

"Sloan?" She struggled upright, panic gripping her throat. "Is he okay? What happened?"

"Not Sloan," he quickly reassured her. "And nothing bad. Your stepmother and her sons are safe in Canada."

She stared at Jordan for a long moment, relief hitting like a tsunami. "They're alive? Daryl and Daniel are alive?"

"Yes." Jordan offered a lopsided smile. "She's been notified about your father's death and may need some help planning the funeral."

She nodded. "Hopefully, she'll allow me to help."

"I hope so too."

She forced a smile. "I've learned it's better to let go of the past hurts to focus on the future. I only wish I could have mended my relationship with my father before . . ."

He died.

Now it was too late.

"Have you heard from Sloan?" he asked, changing the subject.

Her smile faded. "Not yet. But he'll get through to the director, I'm sure of it."

"I hope you're right," Jordan muttered.

She watched him wheel away, hoping she was right too.

JULY 4 – 7:02 p.m. – Washington, DC

IT TOOK them an inexcusably long time to negotiate the traffic through the holiday crowd in DC. Sloan stared at the throngs of people milling about the city, imagining what might happen if Yates didn't believe him. He didn't want to even think about the hideous fate that awaited if they didn't get to the shore of the Potomac River in time before the crews set off the fireworks.

He felt sick to his stomach from the disaster about to strike or from being released from the hospital too early, he didn't know. When they finally reached the building, he followed agents Hammond and Jefferson upstairs to the top office where Clarence Yates was waiting. He steeled himself against puking and faced the director across the massive desk.

"Mr. Sloan Dreyer." Yates glared at him. "I understand you used to be one of ours."

By ours, he meant a member of the bureau. Sloan slowly nodded. "Yes, sir."

Yates stared for a long moment, before sitting back in his chair. "Start at the beginning and don't leave one pertinent detail out."

Sloan let out a breath he hadn't realized he was holding.

He started at the beginning, when he and Jordan's company, Security Specialists, Inc., had been hired by Bentley to assist in providing protection for Deputy Prime Minister Korolev. He didn't try to gloss over the details, but he kept a wary eye on the clock.

Somehow, he had to convince Yates to call a halt to all fireworks across the country. The only thing working in their favor was that DC happened to be located in the eastern time zone. If they could stop the fireworks here, they could save the entire country.

He couldn't afford to fail. Not this time.

JULY 4 – 8:32 p.m. – Washington, DC

. . .

NATALIA HATED nothing more than to be stuck on the wrong side of a hospital bed. Especially now, when there was so much at stake. Patience had never been one of her strengths, and as she stared at the clock, she couldn't help wondering what was taking so long. Hadn't the director believed Sloan's story? There should have already been an announcement canceling the fireworks.

She clicked on the TV remote, turning up the volume so she could hear the NBC broadcast of the local fireworks display.

"There's a great crowd gathered here tonight, isn't there, Ed?" Tonya Jacobs, the female newscaster turned to her co-host, Edward Colton.

"Absolutely," Ed readily agreed. "And to think, the president himself is here to watch the main event."

"Yes, he's truly showing his support and commitment to a great American tradition," Tonya added.

The cameraman panned to the restricted area where the president and his wife were seated to watch the event. Natalia stared as the president leaned forward to catch something his wife said.

"How many people do you think are here for the great fireworks display?" Ed asked, changing the subject. The camera angle moved back to the show's co-hosts.

"I don't know." Tonya gave an exaggerated glance over her shoulder to the crowd milling about in front of the Washington Monument. "But I'm guessing at least a few thousand or so."

"Give or take a hundred," Ed agreed with a laugh. "Dusk is beginning to fall. We hope you'll stay with us to watch the fireworks display after we take a quick break to hear from our local sponsors."

Natalia stared at the television commercials flashing across the screen without seeing them.

Come on, Sloan. Where are you? What's taking so long?

JULY 4 – 8:45 *p.m.* – *Washington, DC*

SLOAN FOLLOWED Clarence Yates as they pushed through the mob of people, gaining access to the protected area cordoned off for the president of the United States to watch the firework show.

The sky was growing darker by the minute. Sloan stared at the area behind the monument, almost expecting the fireworks to start ahead of schedule.

He couldn't believe it when the Secret Service stopped Yates at the entrance.

The director flashed his badge and his Federal ID. "I need to speak with the president personally. Now."

Sloan clenched his hands into fists as the Secret Service agents took their time clearing the way for them to get up to the president.

The orchestra playing before the president and his wife ended their song on a loud crescendo. As he and Yates approached the stage, the president and his wife stood, anticipating the first of the fireworks to be going off momentarily.

"Mr. President?" Clarence Yates called, lengthening his stride. "Sir? We need to talk to you about a matter regarding national security."

JULY 4 – 8:56 *p.m.* – *Washington, DC*

. . .

NATALIA COULDN'T TEAR her eyes from the TV screen.

"The sky is getting dark," Ed claimed as the commercial break ended. "And the orchestra has just completed its final song. I'd say the fireworks display will be starting in a few minutes."

"Isn't it exciting?" Tonya asked as both announcers turned to gaze expectantly at the sky above the monument. "I just love the Fourth of July holiday."

"Me too. Wait a minute, the president is standing up, waving his hand for silence," Ed exclaimed. "Someone is handing him a microphone."

"I didn't know he was giving a speech tonight," Tonya said with a frown.

"Let's listen to what the president of the United States has to say." Ed turned, and the camera honed in on the president.

Natalia held her breath.

"My fellow Americans. It is with regret that I must declare a moratorium against all fireworks displays taking place tonight, intended to celebrate the birth of our fine nation." The president and his wife both wore grave expressions on their faces as he made the announcement. "Thanks to the hard work and diligence of the FBI, we have learned of a potential terrorist attack through the use of fireworks. As of this moment, all fireworks displays are banned until further notice. I repeat, all fireworks are banned until further notice."

Natalia let out a sigh of relief. Sloan did it. He stopped the fireworks and the terrorist attack.

Thank you, God. Thank you!

Natalia closed her eyes, allowing the tears to fall.

Sloan had saved the entire country.

JULY 4 – 9:25 p.m. – Washington, DC

SLOAN SANK down and dropped his head into his hands. It was over. The Secret Service had radioed into the area beside the Potomac River where the fireworks were going to be set off. A team of chemical experts had been sent in to make sure none of the staff setting up the display had been contaminated by the tampered fireworks.

They'd managed to convince the president of the danger, who then made the announcement on national television. As he was giving his brief speech, Sloan knew FBI agents were being notified throughout the country to confiscate any and all evidence. The rippling effect of this would go through the nation for a long time. There would be dozens of questions, the media would be in a feeding frenzy.

But for now, the threat was truly over.

With God's support, he hadn't failed in the biggest mission of his life.

JULY 4 – 10:54 p.m. – Washington, DC

NATALIA GLANCED up when Sloan walked into her room. His eyes widened when he saw she was awake and waiting for him.

"Hey. I thought you'd be asleep by now." Deep furrows

of exhaustion lined his face. Obviously, he'd been discharged from the hospital too soon.

"No." She didn't like the awkwardness that hovered between them. She knew he must not be feeling well, but why wasn't he happy? Relieved? They'd done it.

Unless there was more going on than the thwarted terrorist attack. Was their relationship over now that the danger had passed? Her heart squeezed painfully, and she forced a smile. "Of course not. I've been waiting for you, hoping you'd come here. I'm so glad you got through to him, Sloan."

"Yeah, I had my doubts for a few minutes there," he admitted dryly. He dragged a hand over his face. "I just wanted to come by to let you know, in case you hadn't heard the news."

"In case I hadn't heard the news?" she echoed incredulously. "Are you serious? Don't you realize I've been glued to the television the whole time?"

He glanced back at the muted television set. "I guess you didn't need me to stop by then."

What was wrong with him? Why was he acting like such a goofball? She frowned, trying to read his mood. "Sloan, I do need you. Far more than you realize."

He stared at her for a long minute. Then cleared his throat. "Ah, have you seen Jordan, Alek, or Lara?"

She stifled a sigh. Gathering every ounce of patience, she allowed him to change the subject. "Yes. They're fine. I owe you a sincere debt of gratitude. Without you, the rest of my family would have died."

"You almost died."

His stark statement caught her off guard. "But I didn't."

"What were you thinking to jump in front of the gun

like that?" Sloan scowled at her from his position at the foot of her bed. "You lost half your lung with that stunt."

"Don't remind me." Natalia couldn't bear to think about that split second when she knew her mother was going to shoot Sloan. "I saw my life pass before my eyes when my mother turned her gun toward you."

"Don't call her that," Sloan protested, stepping closer. She took it as an encouraging sign. "She wasn't your mother. She didn't raise you, and you're nothing like her. You're beautiful, Natalia. Inside and out."

Hope bloomed in her chest. Maybe there was something between them after all. "She almost killed us both." Natalia swallowed hard. "At least I know my adopted mother was really my aunt. Katya was a wonderful woman."

"So are you."

She wanted to throw herself at him, but he was still too far away. Reaching out, she snagged his hand. "Come here. I need a hug."

As if against his will, Sloan sat on the edge of her bed. "I don't want to hurt you," he protested.

"You won't hurt me." She wrapped her arms around him and breathed in his musky male scent. She relaxed even more when he cuddled her close. This was what she'd wanted. What she needed. "Sloan?"

"Hmm?" He buried his face in her hair.

"I love you."

His chest beneath her cheek went still as if he'd stopped breathing. "What?"

A smile tugged at the corner of her mouth as she lifted her head to look at him. "I love you," she repeated calmly. Then she repeated the words in Ukrainian.

His expression couldn't have looked more surprised.

"You're on pain meds, I understand you might be a little confused. You've been through a lot."

Her smile dimmed. "I'm not confused. Not anymore. For years I've obsessed over the past without really thinking about the future. But now I realize I was only running away, rather than moving forward. God has provided me this chance for a future. I'm not about to let you go."

He was quiet for a long moment. "I've been obsessed with the past too," he finally admitted. Sloan lifted a hand to stroke her cheek. "I lost my sister to the Solntsevskaya. I failed to protect her. I'm not sure if I can put that aside long enough to have a future."

No wonder he was so preoccupied with protecting her. Guilt was a powerful emotion. But he needed to learn the power of forgiveness. "Did you know they were going to attack your sister?" she asked.

"No. But she was my responsibility. The FBI sent Jordan on a trip overseas, and he asked me to watch over her."

"I don't get the feeling that Jordan holds you responsible," she pointed out.

Sloan frowned. "No, but he should. I failed them both."

"Is that what I am to you, Sloan? A responsibility?"

"Yes. No. Wait." She wanted to laugh at how he agonized over his answer. "Natalia, I don't know what to say. I wasn't looking to get involved. But the moment I met you, I couldn't seem to let you go. Please don't ask me to walk away from you, because I can't."

"I don't want you to walk away." Couldn't he try to accept her feelings for what they were? "I love you, but I don't expect you to feel the same way." Although that was what she'd hoped for.

Prayed for.

"Ah, *Natashen'ka*. I love you too." He leaned down and captured her mouth in a sweet kiss.

She smiled, then frowned. "Are you sure? You just kissed me like a friend, not as someone you love."

"Hey, I'm trying to restrain myself here." The teasing glint was back in his eye. "The woman I love is lying in a hospital bed because she'd lost a portion of her lung."

"I'm not going to break, Sloan. Kiss me like you mean it."

He obliged her, kissing her with an urgency that belied his earlier restraint. His mouth possessed hers, exactly the way she wanted.

"Natalia," he whispered, resting his forehead against hers and struggling to breathe. "I really do love you. I can't live without you."

Much better. "I love you too."

"Oh, for Pete's sake," a male voice interrupted them. "I get it, you love her, she loves you. Enough already."

Natalia blushed and then glanced over to see Jordan sitting in a wheelchair next to her bed. "Hi, Jordan."

Sloan sat back and stared at his partner. "Glad to see you managed to convince your nurse to get you out of bed. How are you?"

Jordan shrugged. "I'll live. I heard the news on television. CNN is going nuts with their coverage of the historic event of canceling the fireworks, and there's already a leak about the potential biochemical attack."

"I guess Security Specialists, Incorporated will survive another year after all," Sloan said.

"I wasn't worried." Jordan tilted his head quizzically. "How did you figure it out?"

"With Natalia's help, we realized the fireworks were transported from China. At this point, we don't know exactly what Anya planned. Clearly she was into some sort of power game."

Jordan whistled through his teeth and gave Natalia an admiring look. "You made the connection? Guess I'll have to offer you a job."

"Me?" She didn't understand.

"Of course. We could use your Russian expertise. Sloan here is pretty useless; he can only speak Ukrainian."

"I don't think so," Sloan spoke up before Natalia could say a word. "There's a company policy against married couples working together."

"Married?" Jordan echoed in surprise.

"Married?" Her voice came out a high squeak.

"Yeah." Sloan glared at him as if daring his partner to argue. "Married. So back off."

Jordan didn't look upset. In fact, he flashed a weak grin. "Glad to hear it. About time you let go of the past."

Sloan nodded. "I have, with Natalia's help. And maybe a little guidance from God."

Natalia smiled and rested her head on Sloan's shoulder feeling content. At least for now. Somehow, she didn't think this newfound peace would last for long. Living with Sloan would be anything but dull and boring.

But she wasn't afraid. No more looking back. Instead, she was ready to live the life God had provided for them to the fullest.

Starting right now.

DEAR READER,

I hope you've enjoyed the first book in my Security Specialists, Inc. Series. Sloan and Natalia's book was so much fun to write and very different from what I've written before, having more of an international focus while maintaining a Christian theme. My goal was to make this story packed with action, and I hope I've succeeded in doing so.

I'm blessed to have such wonderful readers like you! As you know, reviews are very important to authors, and I would very much appreciate you taking the time to leave a review from the vendor where you purchased the book.

If you're wondering about Jordan's story, I'm hard at work on his book now. I have included the first chapter of *Target for Ransom* here.

Lastly, I adore hearing from my readers! I can be contacted through my website at https://laurascottbooks.com. Also on Facebook at https://www.facebook.com/laurascottbooks/ and Twitter at https://twitter.com/laurascottbooks. Lastly, please take a moment to sign up for my newsletter, I offer a free novella exclusive to all subscribers. This book is not available for purchase on any platform.

Until next time,
Laura Scott

TARGET FOR RANSOM

September 9 – 1:25 p.m. – Washington, DC

"LET ME GO!" The young dark-haired girl squirmed in her seat, fighting the ropes holding her arms ruthlessly behind her back, her eyes covered by a black blindfold. "Let me go!"

Jordan's gut clenched and bile rose in his throat as the girl repeatedly sobbed, begging to be released. Unable to tear his gaze from the live webcam, he forced himself to think like an agent, concentrating on the pertinent details. The room was dark, windowless, and anonymously bare. It could have been any city in any country across the world. The rope was basic twine, and the chair the girl was sitting in was a cheap card-table type of chair readily available in any store.

"Can't you understand English? Let me go!" Panic mingled with defiance in her tone.

Jordan curled his fingers into helpless fists. What sort of people tormented a child? What did they want? He leaned closer, straining to analyze the situation despite the child's heartrending cries. The girl's young voice sounded American, but he couldn't be certain of her ethnic background without seeing her eyes. What little he could see of her face revealed tan skin. Even though the girl appeared to be alone, he knew she wasn't.

It was a macabre scene, staged solely for his benefit.

"Jordan Rashid, if you want to see your daughter alive, you must follow our instructions exactly." A deep male voice, altered by some sort of mechanical device, came from somewhere beyond the view of the camera. "If you don't obey our instructions, or if you go to the authorities, we will kill her."

"Help me!" the girl shouted, struggling again in earnest. "Please help me. They're going to hurt me!"

A hooded man stepped in front of the camera and slapped the girl sharply, causing her to cry out in pain as her head snapped sideways from the blow. What the—Jordan leaped from his seat, grabbing the computer screen as if he could prevent the next attack.

"Silence, infidel," the man shouted. He let out a stream of instructions in low, rapid Arabic that Jordan tried to understand, then quickly stepped back out of the camera's view and switched to English. "Jordan Rashid, you will receive further instructions within an hour of accessing this website."

The screen went blank. Jordan stood there, his heart hammering in his chest. He couldn't breathe. His vision momentarily blurred. He struggled to focus.

What in the world was going on?

He tunneled his fingers through his hair, pacing the span of his office, trying to block the echo of the young girl's pleading voice. Was this part of the most recent case the

FBI had dropped in his lap a few weeks ago? The fact that the guy spoke Arabic and the FBI case had ties to ISIS made it likely. He stopped, jotted down the few phrases he'd been able to pick up from his rusty Arabic.

Teach her to obey. Respect authority.

Jordan swallowed hard, trying not to imagine what might be happening in that room off-camera. He stared at the blank computer screen, wishing he could watch the video again. Who was that poor girl? He didn't doubt she was nothing more than an innocent pawn in a deadly game. Whoever she was, those guys had gotten defunct information. She couldn't be his daughter. He didn't have a daughter.

He didn't have any children at all.

SEPTEMBER 9 – 1:42 p.m. – Washington, DC

Diana Phillips sat on the edge of her hotel room bed and stared at the number written on the note. The image swam and she blinked, peering through the exhausted haze blanketing her eyes.

She was to contact Jordan Rashid the moment she arrived in DC. Her daughter's life depended on it.

How had this happened? In one moment her peaceful, ordinary life in Jacksonville, North Carolina, had been shattered. Her daughter had vanished, kidnapped sometime after leaving school and before Diana had come home from work. A hysterical sob welled up in her throat. Bryn. Dear, sweet Bryn. Her daughter had to be alive.

She just had to be.

Diana swallowed a cry, struggling to remain calm. She couldn't fall apart. Bryn was counting on her. Bryn needed her to be strong.

Think. She had to think. If she followed the kidnapper's demands, there was a good chance she'd get Bryn back alive.

She needed to call Jordan. It couldn't be a coincidence the kidnappers had sent her to him. Especially since she hadn't seen Jordan in twelve years. Had, in fact, never told him about his daughter.

He'd be shocked to know Diana was alive, and even more stunned to learn about Bryn. So much had happened back then, their brief yet passionate love affair and then the cold hard betrayal he'd accused her of mere hours before the explosion that nearly killed them both.

A wave of helplessness rose in her throat. After everything that had happened, he'd never believe her. How in the world could she make him believe now when he hadn't before?

She wasn't sure, but she had to figure out something.

Bryn's life depended on it.

With trembling fingers, she punched the numbers into her mobile phone. When Jordan answered, his deep, husky voice caused a riptide of memories. Images she hastily blocked.

She swallowed hard, willing herself to be strong. "Jordan? It's me, Diana Phillips. Don't hang up! I know you think I'm dead, but I'm not. I need to talk to you. I need your help. My daughter needs your help."

"Who is this?" he asked in a sharp tone.

"Diana Phillips," she repeated. What could she say to convince him? Panic lanced her heart, and she gripped the phone tighter. "Jordan, listen to me. I swear I'm telling you the truth. Remember the night we spent together in Paris? We ate dinner at *Les Deux Magots*. It's really me. And my daughter needs your help."

"Are you connected to the kidnapping?" His tone was blunt. "Is that how you got this number?"

He knew about the kidnapping? For some reason that bit of information struck her as odd. How could he know prior to her call? Confused, she stood and stared out the window of the hotel room. "The kidnappers gave me this number. Please, Jordan. I need to talk to you. In person."

"Fine. I'll be waiting." He disconnected from the line.

Sucking in a harsh breath, she stared at the phone. After everything they'd gone through together twelve years ago, after she mentioned their evening in Paris, the first night they'd been intimate, he still didn't believe her. But somehow he knew about the kidnapping.

Whoever had masterminded snatching Bryn had figured out Jordan Rashid was her daughter's biological father.

A cold shiver lifted the hairs on the back of her neck. How could anyone know the truth? She'd never told Jordan. Hadn't dared to break the rules surrounding her placement in Witness Protection, especially after Bryn was born.

The FBI might have figured it out though. Oh sure, she'd been told that only the US Marshal assigned to her case knew her location, but she didn't doubt the FBI had a way to find out the truth. Had they assumed once she'd given birth to Bryn that Jordan was the father?

Bitter guilt coated her tongue. Ever since Bryn had disappeared, twenty-one hours and seventeen minutes—no, eighteen minutes—ago she'd been trying to figure out what was going on. Twelve years had passed since the explosion had nearly cost her her life, and Jordan's too. Twelve years in Witness Protection. If this was related to hers and Jordan's tangled past, why go after Bryn now, after all this time?

Or was this kidnapping the result of something more recent? A fist of fear knotted in her belly. She couldn't deny having a few secrets—taking Bryn may be an attempt to get back at her. But if that was the case, why send Diana to Jordan? How would anyone discovering her secret mission even know about her and Jordan?

No, this might not be her fault. She'd been beating herself up enough, knowing if she hadn't stopped for groceries on the way home from work, Bryn might still be safe and sound.

Was it possible Bryn's kidnapping was related to her mother's brother, Omar Haram Shekau? She didn't see how since Omar was dead. She'd watched Jordan kill him twelve years ago, shortly before the crash. She hadn't been in contact with anyone from her mother's family since going into Witness Protection.

Not that she'd wanted to. Her family was dead to her.

Except for Bryn.

None of this made any sense. Bryn's kidnapping had to be connected to Jordan. To one of his FBI cases.

It had to be his fault her precious daughter was taken.

Spurred into action by a sudden flash of anger, she swept her purse off the bed and flew toward the door. The note directed her to call Jordan Rashid at his office number. It also gave her the location of his office in the Washington, DC Piermont Office Building.

She'd find him and demand his help in rescuing Bryn. Bypassing the elevator, she ran down the stairs, tripping and falling heavily against the wall in her exhausted haze.

Muffling a startled cry, she yanked herself upright and pulled herself together. Ignoring the pain of her twisted ankle was easier than losing her mind over Bryn. In the lobby, she found the bellman and requested a cab.

Glancing at the crumpled paper in her hand, he noted her destination. "The Piermont Office Building?" He tipped his hat back and raked a skeptical glance over her. "You don't need a cab, lady. It's right there, across the street."

It was? She stared. No wonder she'd been directed to this hotel. The coincidence was too much. The extent of their well-organized and carefully planned approach gave the kidnapping a deep sinister tone.

Bryn. She had to find Bryn. Fresh tears sprung to her eyes, and she dashed them away with an impatient hand. Where was her anger? Being mad was better than weeping. She strode outside and across the street, running on pure adrenaline.

Bryn was in danger. That's all that mattered. She ripped open the door to the office building and glared at the directory, searching for Jordan. Through a process of elimination, she figured out that Security Specialists, Inc. had to be where she'd find Jordan's office.

Twelve years ago Jordan used to be with the FBI, but it seemed that had changed. She paused outside the doorway to his office, assailed by a towering inferno of doubt. Should she have gone to the authorities? Had she made things worse for Bryn by not going straight to the police? Or to the FBI? What sort of mother was she?

Jordan needed to understand she was telling the truth. And if he didn't believe her, surely he had enough compassion to care about the life of an innocent girl. If he told her to go to the authorities, she would.

At least so far, she was doing exactly as directed by the kidnappers. She was meeting their demands, hence assuring Bryn's safety. Or so she hoped.

She couldn't afford to consider the alternative.

Yet aside from how Bryn had been dragged into this mess, despite the belief it was all Jordan's fault, she knew he'd also protected her with his life twelve years ago. Surely that meant something.

Deep down, she firmly believed that Jordan offered the best chance at finding her daughter.

He had to believe her.

He had to help her get Bryn back.

Made in the USA
Monee, IL
05 October 2021